NIGHT MONSTER

A NOVEL

MELISSA S MEYER

First Published by Melissa S Meyer in 2021.

Designations used by companies to distinguish their products are often claimed as trademarks. All brand names and product names used in this book and on its cover are trade names, service marks, trademarks and registered trademarks of their respective owners. The publishers and the book are not associated with any product or vendor mentioned in this book. None of the companies referenced within the book have endorsed the book.

First Edition

ISBN 978-1-7368269-0-4 (Paperback)
ISBN 978-1-7368269-1-1 (Hardback)
ISBN 978-1-7368269-2-8 (Digital)

Typeset by Aaron Meyer
Cover Art by Aaron Meyer

Find out more at melissasmeyer.com.

For eight-year-old me:
You did it.

PREFACE

Please be aware that this book contains scenes of violence and sexual assault. Remember to take breaks and practice self-care when reading material of this nature.

Also be aware that this book deals with being a closeted gay high school student and bullying as a result. Please remember to take breaks and practice self-care when reading material of this nature.

The following is a list of organizations you can reach out to if you need help.

National Suicide Prevention Lifeline
1-800-273-TALK (8255)
Suicidepreventionlifeline.org

RAINN (Rape, Abuse, and Incest National Network)
National Sexual Assault Telephone Hotline
1-800-656-HOPE (4673) Confidential Hotline
RAINN.org

The Trevor Project
The TrevorLifeline
1-866-488-7386
thetrevorproject.com

ACKNOWLEDGEMENTS

Contrary to popular belief, a book does not happen with one person in a dark room typing away at a keyboard. Sure, the story does, but the book can often, like a child, take a village. This can include things such as cheering for you on social media so that you don't give up, telling their friends and family about your book, donating to your GoFundMe so that you can get your ISBNs to make this happen, listening to you develop your plot line over date nights (sorry, Aaron), and so much more. So, to my village, thank you.

For your endless support, and for your financial contributions toward this book: Aaron Meyer, Rebecca Creech, Rosa Creech, Kayla Meyer, Jennifer Dee, Chelsea Kelly, Renita Kelly, Ashley Pelletier, Kristen Wilson, Desiree Horton, Jena Sand, Jenny Jones, Brent Schebler, and Sean Jones.

To everyone who ever said I was too loud, too assertive, too bossy, and too honest: thank you.

To Rita Jacoby and Elizabeth Thole, two teachers who not only encouraged me to write, but made space for me to produce bodies of work that not only challenged myself, but challenged traditional ways of thinking. To Ms. Thole specifically, thank you for never complaining too much when you had to alter your lesson plans when I'd already read the material, and for understanding that I hated outlines and paper grids. You have no idea how much you have inspired me. And thank you for sharing some incredible pieces of literature with me.

To Ava, I hope that I am helping to light a small path for you. I hope that you never lose your wild, and that you remain fiercely committed to battling for things that you believe in. Even at nine-years-old, your courage inspires me. I cannot imagine the beautiful, bold, and utterly untamed version of you that is being unleashed on the world. Please do not let others try to tie you down. Just "shake it off." I love you, beautiful girl.

To Hudson, Jackson, and Elliott, you three bring so much joy to the world. Your mamas are not the only ones lucky enough to know you. You are surrounded by strong, brave women, and I have no doubt that it will impact the kind of humans you grow up to be. Never, ever lose your wild, even if it drives your parents bonkers. The world needs more people who aren't afraid to get messy. I love you, Hank, Tank, and Buggy.

To my wild and wonderful family, y'all are awesome. From videos of Jackson to the Marco Polo Breakfast Club to just texting and asking how the book is going, thank you. I love you.

To Dad, I love and miss you. So much.

To Halsey and Taylor Swift, your music got me through so many drafts. Thank you.

To Elizabeth Wurtzel, Glennon Doyle, Stephen King, Joyce Carol Oates, Shirley Jackson, and countless other writers, thank you for the inspiration.

To Anne Shirley, I swore I'd be just like you someday, and I think I'm getting closer.

Finally, to Aaron. There are not enough pages or ink in all of the world to thank you. You are the most incredible human being that I have ever had the honor of knowing. I am so very grateful for the twists and turns of my life that brought you to me. I cannot imagine a world without you in it. Thank you for reminding me that coffee is not a food group. Thank you for making endless cups of tea, making sure the house is always stocked with Kleenex, for reading countless drafts of this novel, often just for fun, and for helping me to build our beautiful, messy life. I am sorry that you've had to sit through plot-induced breakdowns. You are my person, my butter half, and I am so glad I will always get to binge true crime documentaries and cooking shows with you. I love you from here to the moon and back.

CHAPTER
ONE
EVIE

IN THE BEGINNGING THERE WAS ONLY A HUM.
It was faint at first, just a barely noticeable vibration as my feet crunched over the gravel parking lot toward Henry's Diner. When I opened the glass door, the hum intensified. It wasn't an unpleasant feeling. It was more like the feeling that I was finally waking up, like I'd been asleep for so long and something was finally jolting me out of it, or when my hand falls asleep, numb and lifeless, and then the blood finally rushes through it. With each step I took toward a worn, tattered booth near the back, the feeling intensified. It was almost impossible to remain calm. Everything inside the diner seemed to be business as usual, so it was clear that I was the only

person feeling it. I think that made it even weirder.

To distract myself, I began eavesdropping on a conversation between Mae Hesser and her best friend, Ruth Jacobson. They were finishing their daily lunch at their usual table at the center of the diner. Ruth was the wife of the only preacher in town. He also happened to be the mayor. Mae, on the other hand, wasn't so bad. I'm not sure why they were even friends. Mae was quieter, usually kept to herself, and seemed to be a little less inclined to pass along gossip, while Ruth was happy to spread around anything she heard.

They were picking at slices of cherry pie and drinking cups of criminally weak coffee with too much cream while talking about the weather. Normally, the weather wouldn't have been a topic of conversation for them, but in their defense, it was weird. Summer seemed to only last a month before autumn came roaring in.

The change in weather started at the beginning of July when the thick green canopies of leaves along Main Street turned to fiery shades of orange and red. The scent of dying foliage began to replace the scents of chlorine and coconut sunblock, forcing the public pool to close by the end of the month. Fortunately, it didn't end the month-long break from school.

I'd always had a love-hate relationship with year-round schooling. Sure, there was a month off every three months, but how was I supposed to track the start of my senior year when I was always in school?

"I'm telling you, this is not normal," I heard Ruth tell Mae.

I signaled to Alice, the waitress behind the counter, that I was ready for a cup of coffee. It might be bad, but we didn't have any other place in town to get a cup of coffee. Alice pretended not to see me, and I couldn't really blame her. She'd have to pass Ruth and Mae's table to get to mine, and Ruth would stop her every single time with complaints about water spots on the glasses, a bent tine on a fork, crumbs left from the previous customer. Alice should be nominated for sainthood, she'd get to me eventually.

"I know it isn't normal, Ruthie," I overheard Mae say as she lazily scooped up the last cherry on her plate. "But I don't think it has anything to do with terrorists. The weather is more God's department."

I tried to stifle my laughter as I watched Ruth's mouth open and her eyes widen at Mae's audacity.

"Don't you talk to me about God, Mae Hesser. I will have you know that just yesterday, that lady reporter in Portland said that terrorists are finding ways to manipulate all kinds of things." She ran a hand down the front of her pearl-colored blouse, carefully dusting away any stray crumbs from her own meal. "Besides, I didn't say it was the work of terrorists. I said it's something terrorists might do."

People in this town were ridiculous.

That's when I met her, the girl who would, in less than a month, change the entire direction of my life's trajectory.

I heard her quiet chuckle from the booth behind me. I hesitantly turned my head to see who it belonged to and was met with a shock of red hair that rivaled everything red in existence – rubies, maple trees in the fall, pomegranate seeds, and Red Hot candies. The hair's owner turned her head at the same time, putting us almost cheek to cheek. She was both incredibly ordinary and completely otherworldly. To say that she was beautiful was an understatement, but there was no other way to describe her. The hum in my veins reached a level of intensity that made me suck in a breath. Somehow, she seemed familiar. How did I miss her when I walked in?

I saw her eyes widen for a second, as if she recognized me too, which was impossible. I'd remember someone like her. She tried to look away, and so did I, but neither of us did. Finally, she raised an eyebrow and a smile tugged at the corner of her mouth. And then she laughed at me.

"Are you okay?" she asked me, smiling.

I opened my mouth to answer when I realized that we were being watched. A group of kids from my school were looking at us, laughing and whispering. Ruth and Mae were also staring, and the waitress was pretending not to. My face flooded with heat.

"Uh, yeah, I'm fine." My throat went completely dry.

The girl stared at me like she was trying to figure something out. Admittedly, I was doing the same thing to her. She narrowed her amber eyes, cocking her head to the side quizzically.

"What?" I asked her, reflexively reaching up to touch my face. She smiled again, and my stomach flipped.

"My name's Lilith, by the way," she said. "Since you're not going to ask."

"You're not from here," I stupidly blurted out. "I didn't see you when I walked in."

"I was in the bathroom. And no, I'm not."

My interest was piqued. Not by the bathroom thing, but by someone willingly coming to Benson, Oregon. I'd never met anyone who wasn't already from here, unless you counted the rare trips to Salem or Portland. I didn't count those trips.

"I'm Evelyn." I winced and immediately wanted to crawl underneath the table. No one called me by my real name. "I mean, I'm Evie."

She just stared at me.

"No one calls me Evelyn," I tried again. "Just Evie."

"Evie, huh?" Lilith asked, leaning in toward me. I stopped breathing.

After a moment, Lilith picked up a napkin, blotted her maroon lips with it, and then turned around to set the napkin on her plate. She slid out of her booth and I couldn't take my eyes off of her. She stood in front of me, hands on her hips.

"I had no idea this town was going to be so interesting. I'll be seeing you around, yeah?"

She didn't wait for me to answer. Instead, she turned and sauntered out of Henry's Diner, the eyes of all its patrons following her right out of the door.

And, just like that, the hum in my body stopped and I went back to feeling numb.

CHAPTER TWO

LILITH

I WALKED INTO MY HOUSE AND LET THE HEAVY door slam behind me, still smiling from my encounter with the brunette in the diner. I dropped my keys on the black walnut table in the hall where at least a week's worth of mail was stacked, which I was still pretending would just go away. I walked into the living room and flipped the light switch on the wall to my right.

"Hi, Samael," I said, my voice a little more jovial than normal. "Did you miss me?"

My six-foot Motley Goldenchild python rippled along the length of its substantial body. His black scales were iridescent under the soft light of his overhead lamp. Samael was a gift when I was younger, and the only thing I'd managed to keep while moving from place to place, and from person to person. I unlocked the lid to his habitat, which stretched the length of the largest wall and stood about three feet high. I reached inside without hesitation, running my hand along his body.

"So, I met a girl today," I told him. "Not unusual for me, I know, but there's something different about her. I can't put my finger on it, but I'm not sure I was given complete information about her." Samael coiled tightly around himself, a signal that he wasn't interested in what I was saying. I sighed, rubbing the spot between his eyes with my purple-tipped index finger. I put the lid back on his habitat, careful to lock it tightly. I had no desire for him to get out again. The last time ended with a missing cat and an angry neighbor.

I sat down on the sofa, wondering what Jax would think when I told him about my encounter this afternoon. Unfortunately, my bag was in the car with my cell phone inside it, so that was going to have to wait until later to find out.

Jax was easily my oldest non-reptilian acquaintance, though he was just as cold-blooded. He was much older than me, and while I wouldn't call him a friend, he was certainly a mentor. He taught me so much over the years. He gave me a great deal of freedom if I agreed to do certain things on his behalf, and that was more than a lot of people could say about him. I wasn't looking for any advice, but I was wondering what he hadn't told me about this girl. But, something made me a little reluctant to tell him right now.

Before I even locked eyes with the girl named Evie, I felt her. I felt her when she walked through the door of that diner. I felt a buzzing deep in the center of me when she sat down, her back against mine with only a booth between us. I knew girls that had a desperate need to escape, who were never satisfied with where they were in a given moment. They always wanted more - more experiences, more adventures, more knowledge. While I knew instinctively that Evie wanted these things as well, I also knew that there was more to it than that. I leaned my head against the back of the sofa, remembering the tightness in my chest when I saw her, the way my blood sung, vibrating like two tuning forks striking against one another. The thought of being able to get closer to Evie sent sparks down the length of my spine. Something was making me doubt that I would be able to complete the task Jax sent me to do.

I sighed and closed my eyes for a few moments. When I reopened them and sat upright, my eyes immediately fell on the elegant antique desk across the room. I stood up, taking long strides through the length of the room. I opened a small velvet box that sat on top of the desk and retrieved an old skeleton key from it. I unlocked the drawer that held an old book. It was bound in worn black leather, and there was no title on the front of it. There was only a symbol. The book was ancient-looking, and Jax had given it to me right before I came to Benson. I lightly ran my fingers over the intricate embellishments, the delicate swirls in the leather, the symbol in the center that Jax had told me belonged to his family.

The book hummed with energy in my hands. I'd felt this happen before, a very long time ago.

The last time, the world barely survived it.

CHAPTER THREE

LIAM

I WAS STANDING NEAR THE FRONT DOUBLE doors of the high school, staring up at a sign that read, "Abigail Scott Duniway High School, Home of the Fighting Badgers." I heard Evie step up beside me.

"The badger really is a stupid mascot," I said, not taking my eyes off of the sign.

"Tell that to Hufflepuff," she countered. "Besides, I heard that those things can rip your face off if it feels surprised or threatened."

I looked over at her, rolling my eyes and shaking my hair out of my eyes. "You have to stop reading *Harry Potter* so much. You sound like a freakin' nerd."

"First, I haven't even been able to read those books

after that Twitter rant. Second, I *am* a nerd. Why does everyone think that's offensive?"

I nodded. "You're right. I stand corrected."

"Anyway, you're one to talk. How many times have you seen *Lord of the Rings? Star Trek? Game of Thrones?*"

I rolled my eyes at her again. "Hold up. You love *Game of Thrones* as much as I do, maybe more, so settle down."

Evie shrugged. "What's not to love? Dragons? Awesome. White Walkers? Terrifying. Olenna Tyrell? Hero status. Lannisters? So gross."

"Except Tyrion," I said, pointing a finger at her. Paint was caked around my nails.

As Evie was opening her mouth to respond, Matt Kromer and a few of his friends were heading our way. I hated that guy. He made life a living hell for everyone, but Evie was his special project.

"Dyke," I heard him say as he passed us.

"Fuck off," I groaned. Matt's girlfriend, Amy, thrust a middle finger in the air.

"Such class," I said.

I saw Evie freeze up. It wasn't the first time he'd said it, and it definitely wasn't the worst thing he'd called her. It made me want to punch him in the throat.

"That guy is such an asshole," I said out loud. Evie was chewing the fingernails on her right hand.

"How is there already paint on your hands?" she

asked, her voice shaking a little as she tried to change the subject. "It's not even eight in the morning. Or is that just years of build-up?"

I wasn't going to force her to talk about her feelings, or why people were saying this shit about her, so I looked at my hands and shrugged, turning them over. They were covered in splotches of yellow and red paint.

"I was up late working on something. Very late. Like, I quit about four hours ago," I told her.

Art was my escape from everything. I would hide away in my attic for hours, painting landscapes that evolved into angry splotches across the canvas. I was always pretending I didn't hear my dad's belligerent yelling from the living room, or the refrigerator door slamming shut as he grabbed a ninth, tenth, or eleventh can of beer. The year before, Evie got me a really great pair of headphones. When my dad realized that I was using them to drown him out, he cut the cord into little pieces and left them on my bed.

"You've got to start sleeping," Evie said, looking worried.

"I'll sleep when I'm dead," I proclaimed loudly, throwing my arm loosely around her shoulders and dragging her inside the school.

The school's main hallway was packed with the sounds of screeching girls pretending they hadn't seen each other every day over the break, people banging on lockers, and football players yelling to the people right next to them about football tryouts. Evie attempted to squeeze through without bumping into anyone, but she accidentally knocked into Maddie Turner. Maddie called her a freak and gave her a shove. Maddie thought anyone without a cheerleader uniform was a freak. It's a mystery why we all weren't friends. As usual, Evie just kept walking.

"Choke on a pompom," I spat as we walked past Maddie. I hated that girl.

Evie picked up speed, her head down, trying to get out of the hallway as quickly as possible. I grabbed the top strap on her backpack in an effort to keep up. The first few weeks after a break were always the worst. No one seemed to know where they were going, even though the school wasn't big enough for anyone to get lost. A shrill bell sounded overhead and I winced at the sound. I definitely didn't miss that bell. Everyone scattered in a panic, like roaches reacting to the flip of a light switch.

The alphabet being what it is, Evie and I have always shared a homeroom, and it was always with Mrs. Wilson. Evie must have spotted Mrs. Wilson's frizzy dirt-colored hair because she was steering us in that direction.

"Welcome back, Ms. Franklin, Mr. Donovan," she said, motioning us to step inside. Her voice lacked any enthusiasm, which I expect from someone who'd been teaching for as long as she has. Evie gave her a short nod, and I gave her a salute for some reason before we found our seats in the back of the room. As I was setting my backpack on the floor next to me, I caught a fruity scent nearby. I sniffed the air, looking up and searching for the source of the scent. Standing in front of Evie was a girl with flaming red hair. I heard Evie's sharp intake of breath.

"Well, well, we meet again," the girl said, looking down at Evie. She had one hand on her left hip and the other on the back of the chair in front of Evie. I couldn't stop staring at the girl. Neither could Evie. I watched as Evie's eyes slowly scanned the entirety of the girl. The girl's eyes were trained on Evie, her eyebrow cocked slightly and the corner of her mouth tugging upward. I saw Evie's face flush. I wasn't sure what was going on or who this girl was, but apparently Evie did.

"It would appear so," Evie finally answered, her voice thick. She cleared her throat before she continued. "You certainly seem dressed to impress today."

I looked at the girl, noticing what she was wearing for the first time. Her dark skinny jeans and black button down shirt that hugged her curvy frame. She wore several necklaces, including one with a red stone in it.

"Aw, you noticed," the girl said playfully.

They stayed silent for a moment, just staring at one another. I didn't like it. I didn't like the way she looked at Evie. Their eyes never left each other, and something about their expressions…

Evie looked at her in a way she didn't look at me, or anyone else in this town.

The thought caused me to clench my fists. Annoyed, I cleared my throat, looking at the two of them.

"Liam, this is Lilith. Lilith, Liam," Evie finally said. She seemed reluctant to introduce us, though I didn't know why. Lilith didn't look at me, but she smiled at Evie.

"Are you introducing me to your friends already?" she asked, her voice low. She sounded like the girls at school when they talked to a guy they liked, but much more confident. But when she looked over at me, her expression changed. Her smile, which was so friendly with Evie, had entirely disappeared when she looked at me. It was almost a scowl.

"Hello," she said, a slight icy edge to her voice. We stared at one another for a moment, like some kind of standoff. It was weird. Then she abruptly turned and sat down in front of Evie.

"Nice to meet you too," I said, just loud enough for Lilith and Evie to hear. I didn't know what Lilith's problem was. Evie shot me a look that told me to shut up and stop being a jerk. Mrs. Wilson then stepped into the room and the final bell rang, saving me from having to defend myself.

It took a solid ten minutes for Mrs. Wilson to call

everyone's name for attendance. The entire class seemed to be talking about Lilith in quiet hisses, not paying attention to the teacher at all. For some reason, this irritated me too. Other than this girl being new, I didn't understand what they were freaking out about.

"Lilith Gatlin?" Mrs. Wilson called out loudly, her voice booming over the chatter. A hush immediately fell over the room. It was suddenly like everyone in the room was holding their breath, waiting for her head to spin or something.

"Right here," Lilith sang, wriggling the fingers on her right hand, the light glittering off her silver ring. She was leaning back in her chair, and I could see Evie lean in just a little bit and take a deep breath.

My eyes darted back and forth between Evie and Lilith. Something was definitely going on. After a few seconds, it hit me. The way they looked at each other, the way they talked to each other, the way Evie leaned in toward her, I'd seen that behavior before. It was the same way that every girl acted around every guy in every romance movie I'd ever had to sit through.

Evie looked like she was into this girl.

I clenched my jaw and stared at the back of Lilith's head. Evie never showed any real interest in anyone, and now this girl? I was probably wrong, but if I wasn't...

My thoughts were interrupted by Mrs. Wilson's voice yelling that she was getting ready to hand out locker assignments. She had to keep stopping to get the room under control. One by one, we all started spilling out into the hallway, struggling with locks and slamming locker doors when we finally did get them open. It took me three tries to get my locker open, and when I finally did, I closed the door to see Lilith and Evie together. Their lockers looked like they were right next to each other. Great.

Every time I saw Evie in the hallway that day, Lilith wasn't far from her. They seemed to be following each other everywhere. Either they were in a lot of classes together, or Lilith was a stalker. Meanwhile, I had no classes with Evie, but I had one at the end of the day with Lilith.

When I walked to AP English, my final class for the day, I saw Lilith sitting near the window. I spent the entire class staring over at her. I was only slightly aware of why I hated Lilith without knowing her at all, and I knew I'd have to deal with my feelings about Evie sooner rather than later, but I didn't know how Evie would react. Did she only see me as a friend? Were the rumors about her true? And if they were, did she even want anyone to know yet? Why wouldn't she tell me?

Or did she feel like I did and was waiting on me to make the first move?

I have no idea what happened in that class, but I was thankful for the bell at the end of it. Students burst into the hallways with such force that a freshman ended up on the floor. It was like they all forgot we'd be back the next day, and the day after that one. I maneuvered the sea of students carefully, steering myself toward my locker. Normally, I'd wait for Evie at her locker, but I had a shift at the bookstore Evie's parents owned, so I quickly threw my books in my locker and hurried outside.

CHAPTER FOUR

EVIE

FOR SOME REASON, HAVING LILITH AND I IN the same room with Liam and everyone else was unbelievably uncomfortable for me. The energy between the two of them felt almost combative, and I didn't understand it. It was the exact opposite of the energy whenever Lilith and I were together. She seemed almost flirtatious with me, and the pull to her was overwhelming. Being near her left me almost breathless, and it didn't help that our lockers were right next to one another, or that we had all but one class together.

In each class, Lilith sat as close to me as she could. I found myself going from one class to another, hoping she'd walk in right behind me. When she did, my stomach fluttered. Lilith seemed to find it amusing that we kept ending up together, smiling at me and winking. I wasn't sure if I could keep being distracted by her all year. My GPA would definitely tank.

When I walked into my final class for the day, I expected Lilith to go there too. But she walked right past the door. The disappointment I felt surprised me, and I didn't understand it. She was just a new girl, but every time she was near me, I felt this…pull. It was like an invisible vibrating bungee cord and we were holding opposite ends.

As soon as the dismissal bell rang, I practically sprinted toward my locker. I wasn't sure why I needed to see her, but I did. I spotted Lilith at her locker, and I watched as two boys stopped, trying to make conversation with her. I watched Lilith smile, seeming to be amused by them, but not so much that she stopped what she was doing. The two guys, Max Brady and Philip Simpkins, weren't the brightest, but they were the most popular. Max was popular because his parents had money, he was attractive, and he was on every sports team in school. Philip was popular because he latched onto Max in preschool and never let go. To the girls at school, dating one of these guys was a big deal. It meant invites to the best parties and instant friends. I wasn't into any of that stuff, so I didn't get it. I got along with them well enough, but I wasn't part of their social group. Still, they didn't treat me the way everyone else did. Well, Philip did on occasion, but Max usually squashed it.

Max and Philip were each trying their hardest to get Lilith's undivided attention, that much was obvious. It looked like Max might be succeeding, which made me feel weirdly jealous of him. I approached my locker, pulling Lilith's eyes away from Max.

"Evie," Max started, sounding relieved that I was there. "Will you please tell her she needs to hang out with us this weekend?"

"Ooh, I'd love to, but you hang out at Philip's dad's farm, and no one wants to spend the day smelling manure," I said, trying to make my voice sound more playfully sorry and less acidic. Lilith laughed. Philip did not. Max just rolled his eyes.

"You suck, Franklin, you know that?" Philip asked, narrowing his eyes at me. He never liked me, and it drove him crazy that I didn't seem to care. He was a jerk to most people. Max, on the other hand, was very easy to like, and I didn't mind him so much. He was nice to everybody. He seemed to fit in with any group. He even tried out for drama club productions from time to time. Philip followed Max like a puppy begging for attention. Liam thought Philip was in love with Max, but I didn't think that was it. I thought it was more likely that Philip wanted to be Max. I don't know, maybe it was both.

Lilith scrunched her nose at the boys. "Evie's right.

Besides, these shoes just aren't suitable for a farm," she said, pointing down at the one-inch heel on her boots.

I laughed, throwing my trigonometry book into the back of my locker. "Yikes, now you really can't go. There's a dress code."

"Sorry, fellas," Lilith said, sticking her bottom lip out in a pout. "Maybe another time."

Max laughed like she was genuinely being funny, his blue eyes sparkling. "We'll see you around."

"I'm here Monday through Friday," Lilith joked. Max shook his head and turned to leave, Philip hot on his trail.

"Don't worry about them," I told Lilith. "They're harmless. Max is a good guy. Philip's a little weird though."

Lilith's amber eyes widened. "A little?"

I shrugged. "Well, hopefully he won't go out of his way to bother you. He bothered one girl for six months before she finally had to have her father intervene. It was a bad scene."

Lilith's eyes followed Max and Philip down the hall. "He'll be sorry if he tries," she muttered under her breath. For some reason, this comment took me by surprise. It seemed vaguely threatening, and I wasn't even sure I was supposed to hear it.

Lilith swung around to face me, a smile on her face. "Hey, how about we go get fries or something somewhere?"

My stomach flipped at the thought of it, and I wasn't sure I was ready to deal with getting anything with her just yet. "Um, I should probably get home. I have homework, and I don't want to get behind on the first day." If I was being honest, I wanted to go with her, but I felt a little worried about what that might mean.

"Aw, come on," Lilith said, reaching out and tugging at the hem of my shirt, twisting it in her fingers. "Just for an hour? I'll buy."

Something about the way Lilith grabbed the edge of my shirt and tugged felt so personal and so intimate. I struggled to find a better excuse than homework, but I was coming up blank. Lilith's constant eye contact didn't make it any easier.

I closed my locker door and slung my backpack over my shoulder. "Yeah, okay. An hour can't really make a difference, can it?"

CHAPTER FIVE

EVIE

THE DINER WAS QUIET WHEN WE WALKED in. I expected it to be a little busier given it was the first day of school, but there were only a handful of people: three older men at the counter, a booth of four kids from school near the front, and a table of two more near the center. Mae Hesser was sitting alone near the back. It was strange to see her without the preacher's wife, and her eyes seemed to be following us.

I led Lilith to my favorite booth in the very back. I always chose this one because it was quieter, and it was closest to the bathroom. For some reason, I always felt weird walking to and from the bathroom with people watching me. We slid into the booth with me taking the spot against the wall so that I could see the entire diner. By this point, almost everyone stopped staring at us. The exception was a table of kids from school who kept sneaking glances and snickering.

Lilith sat down across from me and grabbed a slightly sticky black and white menu, looking it over carefully, her brow furrowed. "So, what's good here anyway?"

"In all honesty, that depends on your definition of 'good,' and whether or not you like greasy diner food. I usually stick with the chili cheese fries. Henry's chili recipe is the only thing they don't shortcut or buy frozen. Plus, they're super gooey." I felt like a food critic for terrible diners in America. I was starting to feel like I couldn't shut up around Lilith. It was uncontrollable word vomit. I was annoying myself.

Lilith smiled warmly, catching me a little off-guard. "That sounds so good. Chili cheese fries it is."

Patti, a waitress I usually only saw on Friday nights, came over and took our order, smacking neon green gum the entire time. A few minutes later, she brought our sodas and fries, walking away without a single word. Lilith and I were silent for a few minutes. I didn't know what to say, so I picked up my fork and began poking at my fries, struggling to find something to talk about.

"Where are you from anyway?" I finally blurted out. I immediately felt like an idiot. I was literally asking Lilith for a topographical map of her birth location.

"Far away from here," Lilith answered, popping a chili-smothered fry into her mouth. I waited for an explanation, but nothing came.

"So, like, outer space? Michigan? The Czech Republic?"

Lilith looked up at me through her eyelashes. "You're a curious one."

"Yeah, well, I'm an amateur detective."

"I see that."

Lilith took a deep breath and then sat back against her seat. "I'm sorry, I'm not trying to brush you off. That's just a very long and complicated story for another time. Tell me more about you," she finally said.

I just stared at her, waiting for her to change her mind, but it didn't happen. Something in me wanted to tell her everything. I didn't even know where that feeling was coming from, but there it was, and I had no idea where to start. So I turned it back to her.

"No way. You didn't tell me anything. Quid pro quo."

A smile slowly crept across Lilith's burgundy mouth. "I'm boring. You're not."

I scoffed, wrinkling my nose at her. "I'm not boring? Please. I'm the reason that word even exists. I've actually put people to sleep just by talking."

Lilith picked up a forkful of fries and lifted them to her mouth. "Tell me about your favorite memory growing up," she said before wrapping her mouth around her fork.

I was a little surprised at what she wanted to know. I searched my memory for something worth mentioning. And then I remembered the red bike.

"You're smiling," she said. "What are you thinking?"

I smiled a little bigger, looking down at the table. "I was just remembering Christmas when I was six years old. For three months before, all I did was talk about this bike I felt like I just had to have. It was red, and had these really cool streamers on the handlebars. There were no training wheels, which felt like such a big deal to me. Anyway, I begged and begged for it, but my parents kept telling me we couldn't afford it, maybe next year. So I wrote a letter to Santa and told him all about it. My dad said he mailed it on his way to work. Sure enough, on Christmas morning, I was up at, like, five. I ran down the stairs so fast, so sure that bike would be there. I searched the living room, the dining room, the kitchen. No bike."

Lilith just stared at me. "That's your favorite memory?"

I laughed. "I'm not finished yet. Anyway, I was obviously disappointed. I cried, telling my mom and dad that Santa must not have gotten my letter in time, or that I hadn't been good enough all year. I cried so hard. I was just sure that bike would be under the tree. But my dad, he hugged me and said maybe we should check one more place. He and my mom took me out to the garage, and there it was, the red bike with the streamers. And on either side of my new bike were matching bikes, one for Mom and one for Dad. There was at least a foot of snow on the ground, but my dad cleared the driveway, and we spent the next hour riding them in a circle."

I shrugged, trying to downplay the memory, but it was one of my favorites. I took a bite of my fries, unable to look up, worried Lilith would be laughing at me. Or worse, disgusted or something. But when I finally got up the nerve to look at her, she was staring at me, smiling.

"That's really nice, Evie. It sounds like you have great parents."

I nodded. "I do. They're good people."

"Any siblings?"

I nodded again, trying to swallow the fries I'd just shoved in my mouth.

"Yeah," I answered, swallowing hard. "I have a little sister, Bea. Well, Beatrice, but we all call her Bea. She's pretty great. What about you? Parents? Siblings?"

"No one worth mentioning. I don't have any siblings, and my parents aren't really involved."

"I'm sorry," I said, staring at her. She didn't look sad or anything. She seemed fine with it.

"So that guy you always hang out with, Liam. Is he your boyfriend?" Lilith asked. I almost choked on a glob of cheese.

"Oh my God, no. Gross. I mean, we're best friends, but that's it."

Lilith laughed at me. "Well, tell me how you really feel."

I laughed a little, but it disappeared quickly. "He's the only person in this town I can even talk to, the only person that doesn't treat me like a pariah. He makes Benson a little more bearable. He's been acting really weirdly for a while now though. I'm not really sure why."

Lilith nodded. "And he won't tell you why?"

"I just kind of assumed it's because I want to go away to school next year. Like, far away."

"You don't like it here." It was more of a statement than a question.

"No, I don't. I mean, it's okay, but I can't stay here. My family has been here for so many generations that I'm pretty sure they helped found the town. The kids at school...they make it unbearable. If I don't get a scholarship, I'm screwed. I'll end up working at the library or the school cafeteria and have to marry someone boring who works at the farm. And then we'll have kids who do the same thing. I don't want any of that, at all."

I had her rapt attention, and it was a little embarrassing after everything I'd just said. That's when Lilith reached across the table and lightly touched my hand. It felt like a burst of sparks shooting across my skin. We both reacted to it, one set of eyes immediately looking into the other's. My eyes then darted around to see if anyone was watching. I thought I saw Mae Hesser looking, but I wasn't sure. The last thing that I needed was Mae running back to Ruth and telling her that a strange girl was trying to hold my hand in the diner. The kids from school, on the other hand, were whispering and laughing while they watched us. I was definitely going to hear about this at school. Reluctantly, I slowly pulled my hand away from Lilith. I felt a stab in my chest at the subtle disappointment on Lilith's face. She recovered quickly and I felt relieved to see it.

Lilith leaned in. "Let's get out of here."

Lilith's house had the scent of Autumn air, like cinnamon and cloves with a hint of dead leaves after the rain. It was warm and well-lit, especially considering all of the dark wood in the entryway. She led me into the living room, flipping a light switch on the wall. Yellow light poured over everything in the room. I scanned the room. Seeing the inside of Lilith's house felt personal, voyeuristic somehow, but also a little strange. There were no family photos, no shoes kicked off in the corner, no evidence that a family lived there at all.

"Do you know that every kid in this town has wanted to see the inside of this place for years?" I asked, sitting my backpack down near the entryway. "Every Halloween, kids dare each other to sneak inside. No one's ever did though." Normally, vacant houses were overgrown, dilapidated. This house was always pristine. The lawn was kept up on, the flowers around the house, the garden in the back, they were all very well taken care of. It was part of the reason that kids were so creeped out by this house.

"How long have your parents owned this place?" I asked.

Lilith didn't look at me. "It's been in my family for a long time," she answered.

I didn't know why, but her answer made me a little uneasy. Still, I didn't want to leave. I continued surveying the room until I saw it. There, against one wall, was a huge glass enclosure holding the largest snake I'd ever seen outside of a zoo or a nature special.

My face must've shown my intense panic, because I heard Lilith laughing. "That's Samael. He's harmless, so long as you're not a big rat," she joked.

I was not amused. I didn't have a phobia exactly, but I wasn't eager to test it out, especially with one the size of my sister. I swallowed hard. Was I sweating?

"Um, Samuel is a weird name for a snake."

Lilith looked at me, raising her eyebrows. "Wow, you just butchered that, didn't you? It isn't 'Sam-you-ul,'" she said. "It's like 'Sam-eye-el.' It means 'venom of God'," Lilith explained, walking over to the tan over sized sofa and sitting down. I watched her tuck her left leg underneath her, making a motion with her left arm as she propped it on the back of the sofa. She wanted me to join her. I took a shaky breath and made my way slowly over to the sofa, my heart pounding harder inside my chest with each step. We sat mirroring one another for a moment, our eyes locked. It made me want to throw up, but it also felt safe.

Why was being around Lilith simultaneously the best and the worst feeling in the world?

I was suddenly aware of our proximity to each other. I'd never been alone with someone like her, someone that made my stomach feel like it was going to explode into a million wildly-flapping butterflies. I'm not sure what I expected by being here, but anxiety and excitement coiled around each other in my stomach. I tried to take a deep breath, but I couldn't steady myself. Just then, Lilith placed a solid and steady hand on my left knee. I thought I might stop breathing altogether.

"You're fine, Evie. There's really no need to be nervous, I promise. No one's going to hurt you. We're just talking, getting to know one another."

Her words caught me by surprise. Hurt me? The thought hadn't even crossed my mind, not until she said it. I thought maybe she wanted to trade secrets or just get to know each other, not that I was in any danger.

"You're not," Lilith said.

"I'm not what?" I asked in a measured tone.

"You're not in danger."

"How did you…?" Was she reading my thoughts?

Lilith smiled, withdrawing her hand and leaning against it. "You're easy to read, and I'm very good at reading people."

"Why am I here?" The question was out of my mouth before I could stop it. I didn't mean to ask, and I wasn't sure why I did. I didn't know what answer I was hoping for. Being around Lilith made me feel wound up, confused, and like my body was constantly buzzing with a weird energy. I didn't want her to ask me to leave, but I was scared of what might happen if I stayed.

"Do you not want to be here?" Lilith asked, her eyebrows drawing together.

I didn't know what to say, so I stared at her for a moment. "I don't know."

Lilith shrugged and smiled, a vague look of sadness on her face. "That's okay," she said. "If you want to leave, that's okay. If you want to stay, that's okay too."

"Do you want me here?" My voice came out so quiet that I wasn't sure she even heard me. I also immediately regretted asking because I didn't want her to say no.

"I do."

I stared at her for a minute. I was always staring at her. I didn't know what to do. Something about this choice felt important, more important than any other. I couldn't make sense of the feeling in my body either. I'd never felt this way around anyone, ever. I didn't know if it was a warning to leave, or the desperate need to stay near her, but either felt like a risk.

"Tell me what you're thinking," Lilith said, her voice low, even. If she was worried about my decision, she didn't let on.

I took a deep breath and let it out slowly, trying not to let my nervousness be so obvious.

"I don't know what I'm doing here. I don't know what's happening." I searched her face for any kind of sign.

"We're just talking," she repeated. "Tell me why you want to leave."

"Your house?"

"No, Benson."

I didn't know where to start. There were a million reasons, and there was one reason. How could I convey all of that in one conversation?

"Just start at the beginning," Lilith said.

"I don't even know where that is." I could feel the tears welling up, and I fought hard to keep them from falling. I blinked rapidly, hoping it would help.

"Tell me more about your family."

And I did tell her. I told her about how my family had been here for so many generations that I wasn't sure the Franklin genetic line existed any place else. I told Lilith about my father's job on the hay farm and how he looked so much older than his thirty-seven years. I told Lilith about how I was born when both of my parents were only nineteen, and how my mother had never thought college was a worthwhile option for herself. I told her more about Bea, my ten-year-old sister, who was so good at singing and acting in school productions, but who only ever talked about being a mother and marrying a man like my dad when she was older, never about pursuing anything but that. I talked about Liam, who had been my best friend for so long, but that I was starting to feel a little suffocated by him and his talk about us moving away together. I told Lilith about how all I wanted was to get into a school clear across the country, to travel to places like Japan, Norway, France. Before I knew it, I was going on and on about wanting to see the sunset wash across the Great Plains Conservation in Zimbabwe.

Lilith listened to me, focused on my every word. She never interrupted, she never laughed at me, and she never seemed uninterested.

"So, what's keeping you from doing all of those things?" Lilith asked me, leaning in. She had a habit of leaning in toward me.

I rolled my eyes at her question. "Money. The expectation of my parents, of Liam. Money."

Lilith smiled a little. "You said 'money' twice."

"Yeah, well, my family isn't exactly made of it."

"The lack of money is an excuse, Evie. You can do whatever you want to do, if you want to do it badly enough."

I shook my head. "No, I really can't."

"You seem to be letting a lot of things force you to stay."

I stayed quiet. This conversation, the turn of it, was not something that I'd expected. I wasn't sure if I wanted to stay any longer. Something about the way she was looking at me was unsettling. She seemed almost manic, her eyes widening, her breath a little quicker. It made me uncomfortable.

I watched her blink rapidly and sit back. "I'm sorry, I don't mean to push or make you feel uncomfortable. But I can help you."

Against my better judgment, I asked her how.

"The need to do what is best for others, that societal. It's indoctrination. They led you to believe that putting yourself first is the mark of a terrible person, that to be good, you have to sacrifice yourself to make others comfortable. They made you believe that suffering is an act of charity."

"Are you talking about…God?" I asked. This was definitely going in a weird direction.

"Sort of. God, religion. The whole thing kind of seems to work together, doesn't it?"

I bit my bottom lip to keep from laughing. The idea of religion was a weird concept for me. A giant man in the sky telling everyone down here what to do, ready to punish evil-doers. My family went to church every Sunday, but I never bought into it. I never felt comfortable there.

"Am I about to get saved?" I asked, making an ill-timed joke, hoping to lighten the atmosphere a little. But Lilith didn't laugh. I wanted her to go on, to somehow make this make sense, but we were also sitting in a room with a snake filled with God's poison or something. I involuntarily found myself scooting backward on the sofa, needing a little distance, some breathing room, between me and Lilith.

"I think that I should probably get home," I said, more to myself than to Lilith.

Her expression fell, looking almost sad. "Look, I didn't mean to scare you. I'm sorry, I can take you home." She started to stand up but I raised a hand to stop her.

"It's okay. I can walk."

Lilith looked disappointed. "Are we okay?" she asked, sitting back down.

I didn't know how to answer her. Were we even a "we?" I wasn't even sure if we were friends yet. The idea of being near Lilith that felt so exciting a moment before was now a little scary. I forced a smile anyway.

"Yeah, we're cool. I'll see you later, okay?" Without waiting for a response, I grabbed my backpack from the entryway of the living room and headed for the door.

CHAPTER SIX

LILITH

I PACED BACK AND FORTH, TRYING TO KEEP MY frustration in check, and very close to failing. I finally plopped down onto the sofa, hoping that sitting still would calm me down.

Jax was calling for an update, and he wasn't liking what I had to say. He was now questioning every decision I'd made so far. I hated that I was having to deal with this at the same time I was having to try and figure out what to do about Evie on a personal level, but I also hated that he was questioning my ability to secure his target in the first place.

"Jax, it's fine. We both know that she'll go home, give it some thought, and she'll be on my doorstep in a day or two. That's what you wanted, right?"

"You have no idea what's at stake if she tells anyone what you've told her. At minimum, you'll be run out of that disgusting little town," Jax said, his disdain for Benson obvious. "I should have sent someone else."

"You have got to be kidding me," I said, rolling my eyes. "I'm the best you've got, and you know it. Don't worry about Evie. She won't tell anyone anything. Right now, she thinks I might be crazy, and she's probably questioning her own decision-making skills. She doesn't want anyone knowing any of it."

"We made a deal, Lilith. If you can't keep your end of the bargain..."

I threw a pillow from the sofa across the room in frustration. Obviously, sitting wasn't helping at all. I always kept my end of the bargain. I was allowed to do my own thing, as long as I agreed to take on these "special projects," as he liked to call them. They were usually girls around Evie's age who had some special skill or talent that Jax found useful, but I had no idea what he wanted with Evie. Granted, he'd only sent me one other time. That one went pretty off-the-rails, but I got her.

"You know I can do this. She's already on the hook. I'm just waiting to reel her in." I hated the way that sounded.

"While I do enjoy a good fishing metaphor, I need this to be by-the-book," he said. "If it isn't, you'll be the one cleaning it up, because the last time —"

"The last time was different," I told him. "Something was wrong with her before I ever got to her."

"Regardless, try to remember that if this one gets away, it will be on you. I'll check in with you in a few days. Let me know if anything happens in the meantime." With that, the line went dead.

"Ugh!" I yelled, throwing my phone next to me on the sofa. If there was one thing I hated, it was being second-guessed. I especially hated it when Jax was the one doing it. Up until tonight, everything with Evie was fine. It may have gotten a little weird at the end, but I planted a seed. This wasn't even the most difficult person I'd ever dealt with. Erica in Salt Lake City went back and forth for months about whether she wanted my help, but ultimately it worked in my favor. Phyllis in Cleveland wanted my help immediately and then abruptly changed her mind. She ended up dead in Cuyahoga Falls a few months after I left. But Jax didn't care about any of them. They were my special projects.

True, those two were tough, much more frustrating than Evie, but they didn't affect me the way that Evie did. The trouble was that I didn't know why. The way she looked at me, the way she acted around me, the way I that I was looking at her... Over the years, women had certainly had crushes on me from time to time, and I wasn't above indulging them for a night or two from time to time, but this was different. This time, it wasn't just about how she reacted to me - it was how I was reacting to her, and that was new territory for me. I felt different around her. I wanted to know her. I wanted her to know me. I wanted to tell her things about myself that I never told anyone, ever. There was a deeply rooted knot in the pit of my stomach when I thought about her, a pull in the center of me, especially when she wasn't around.

But I had a job to do, and I was going to do it. That was the deal.

Evie was practical, driven. She loved her family, but there was something she kept hidden from everyone, and I sensed a bit of resentment in her about it. She was frustrated, angry, and scared. The only thing keeping her afloat at all was the hope of a scholarship big enough to take her far away from Benson.

I needed to rethink my strategy though. Evie was too smart to just jump in without weighing the risks.

CHAPTER SEVEN

EVIE

I KICKED A ROCK ON THE PATH AHEAD OF ME AS I approached the cove, a place Liam found by accident when we were twelve. Shortly after his birthday that year, he was riding his bike through the woods, took a wrong turn, and ended up at a small spot downriver. No one else ever seemed to visit it. As soon as Liam and I were old enough to do things on our own, we hung out there all the time. Thick trees kept it cooler in the summer, and there was a rock formation that looked like a cave. It had a small beach, which was nice in the summer when the trees couldn't keep the heat from beating down on everything.

Before Liam brought me here for the first time, he

spent time cleaning it up. He got rid of all the broken branches and the trash that washed up on shore. He pulled a log over for us to sit on. Eventually, the two of us learned to build a fire pit.

When I left Lilith's house, I was feeling restless, my brain turning over everything she said. How was putting others first a bad thing? Was she right, was I just indoctrinated to think that putting others first was the more noble thing?

I took a deep breath as I got closer to the cove, deeply inhaling the familiar and comforting scents of pine, crisp air, and the light breeze coming off of the water. In the sky to my right, the light blue shade that had been present all day was interrupted with a burst of orange so intense that it looked like the sky could actually be on fire. Soon, it would just be a sky full of lava before becoming black as obsidian. I was going to miss that sky once I was out of Benson.

I knew Liam hoped we would room together in an off-campus apartment in Portland next year, but I had other plans, plans I'd been building for a few years. I exhausted myself every single year to make perfect grades, and it wasn't so I could get stuck two hours away from home. No, thank you. My parents couldn't afford a big college, so my only hope was a scholarship, preferably to a school on the east coast, although I'd prefer halfway around the world. While Liam and my parents knew

I wanted out, I hadn't told them exactly how far out I meant. Liam was being weird enough lately anyway.

I spotted Liam sitting on a log with his back to me, staring out at the water.

"I thought you'd be here," I called out to him. He started, standing up and spinning around. He visibly relaxed once he realized it was me.

"Oh, hey," he said, sitting back down. I tried not to be offended by the lack of fanfare and walked over to sit next to him.

"I tried calling you. When you didn't answer, I figured you'd be here."

"I could've been at home, painting," he said without looking over at me.

I nudged him with my right arm. "Unlikely. You answer the phone when you're at home."

He nodded. Something was wrong. He wasn't usually someone who sat and brooded, but here he was, sitting and brooding.

"Are you okay?" I asked tentatively.

He stayed quiet for a minute or two, like he was either ignoring me, or trying to figure out how to answer my question. His left knee was bouncing, so I knew something was wrong. He just stared out at the water. It was freaking me out.

"Dude, seriously. What's going on?"

He took a deep breath. "I don't know. Something

feels weird."

"Would you like to vague that up for me?"

He finally looked over at me, studying my face. "What's the deal with that Lilith girl?"

His question caught me off-guard. "What are you talking about?"

Liam shrugged. "I don't know. I just got a weird vibe between the two of you."

I had no desire to answer that question. I had no idea what was going on with Lilith, with me and Lilith, so I definitely couldn't explain it to him. So, I made a joke.

"'Vibe?' How 'new age' of you," I said.

He let out a quiet laugh and shook his head. "You're so lame. Anyway, what are you doing here?"

"Like I said, you didn't answer, so I came looking."

He nodded and looked back at the water. Something between us felt off, and I didn't know why. I didn't know if I'd somehow pissed him off, and I really wasn't sure if I wanted an answer. I thought that maybe something happened with his dad, but something told me not to push him on that today. Instead, neither of us said anything for a while, both of us just staring out at the water.

My mind drifted pretty quickly. It was doing that a lot today. I couldn't focus on anything. As I stared out at the rippling water, I went from worrying about Liam to thinking about which colleges I still needed to apply to, and then to Lilith. Liam said he felt like something was going on between us. It was true, something was happening, and if I was being honest with myself, I knew I was attracted to her, but I wasn't sure if I was ready to do anything about it.

"Did you hear me?"

Liam's voice pulled me back to the reality in front of me. "Huh? What?" I asked dumbly.

He smiled. His green eyes lit up a little whenever he smiled, which was nice. He might've been like a brother to me, but it was easy to see why some of the girls at school hung around my parents' bookstore a little too long when he was working. He was a good-looking guy, with his dimples and perfect teeth and weirdly chiseled cheekbones. His hair fell in thick, dark curls around his face, which he attempted to keep back by wearing a knit beanie. But he ignored every single one of those girls. I was the only one he ever hung out with.

"Where are you?" he asked me.

I shrugged. "I'm good, I'm here."

He laughed a little and shook his head, gazing off in the direction of the sunset. I couldn't help but feel like I was abandoning him, and I felt awful for it. Since his mom left ten years ago, it was just Liam and his dad. Liam's dad wasn't the nicest guy before his wife bailed, and he's only gotten worse over the years. When he was sober, he barely spoke a word to anyone. When he was drinking, he erupted with the slightest provocation. Just breathing too loudly could set him off. Liam started spending a lot of nights at my house after Child Protective Services decided there wasn't enough of a case to do anything about the bruises showing up on nine-year-old Liam's arms. I don't know exactly why they didn't do anything, or what evidence was missing, but my guess is that it was because the CPS agent was married to one of Liam's dad's drinking buddies. After that, my parents took him in whenever he needed it, no questions asked.

Liam seemed a little sad, and I couldn't stop thinking about Lilith. I decided that I needed to distract us both.

"Did I tell you that Ruth Jacobson thinks that terrorists are responsible for the weird weather?" I asked him, trying to lighten the mood.

The laugh that burst from him echoed through the surrounding trees, startling a few birds that were perched in their branches. I laughed too, but only because his laugh was completely ridiculous. It was always just a little louder than it needed to be, and if he didn't control it, would turn into an outrageous guffaw. Honestly, more people laughed at his laugh than whatever was so funny in the first place.

"It's true. She heard someplace that terrorists are getting better at trying to destroy the world or something. She was so offended when Mae Hesser pointed out that it was impossible for them to control the weather."

Liam shook his head, his laughter dying down a little. "I'm not surprised. Remember when Ruth thought Jessie Spritizen stole her dog for some kind of sacrifice in the woods?"

I laughed, bouncing in my seat as I was prone to do when I got excited about something. "Yes! The dog ended up being next door with the Smyth kids because she forgot to lock her gate! She had the entire town freaking out. Best Halloween ever."

"It really was."

The laughter died down almost as quickly as it started. Liam's face suddenly looked very serious.

"We just had our last summer together, didn't we?" he asked, his voice low.

I didn't know how to answer him. I knew how I should answer him, but I just couldn't yet. So I lied to him again. "I haven't made any decisions yet."

"I'm not stupid."

I stared down at my shoes, tracing patterns in the sand with a stick. "I just want to keep my options open."

"I know. And I know you don't want to turn into your mom or whatever, but how cool would it be to get an apartment together in Portland? You can go to school and work nights. I'll paint and work at a job I hate. It would be perfect."

I sighed and rested my head on his shoulder, feeling

horrible. He had at least part of it right; I didn't want to turn into my mother. I knew how awful it sounded, but it was true. My parents were born here, and they would die here. Our house was two blocks from my grandparents, who also lived here their whole lives. Mom's dad, and his dad, and his dad before him all worked at the hay farm outside of town, the only farm in the area. My little sister was ten and already poised to spend the rest of her life here too. But not me. Time dragged on in this place like a fly in cold molasses. If I stayed, my only options were to marry some guy I'd gone to high school with and have a few kids, or never marry at all and end up working as a children's librarian. The idea of marrying one of the boys from school was enough to send me running.

Neither of us spoke for a while. What was there to say? He wouldn't let up, and I couldn't make him understand. I asked him once why he wasn't fighting to study art somewhere that appreciated art. He didn't answer. He never answered.

"Sitting here in the silence is crazy exciting and all, but it'll be getting dark any minute. Want to head out?" Liam asked, already standing up. He offered his hand to help me up.

"Yeah, we probably should. Movie at my place? Or we could go to the theater..."

Liam rolled his eyes. "You always want to go to the theater. There's nothing ever playing there that's worth the time, or the money."

"That's not true!" I protested. "Right now, there's *Mission: Impossible* and *Rear Window.*"

Liam looked at me like I'd lost my mind. "Since when do you like *Mission: Impossible?*"

"I don't. I just thought if I told you that was the only other option, you'd automatically choose *Rear Window*, thus allowing me to see it again."

"For the fortieth time."

"Details."

He stared at me for a moment and I flashed him my most ridiculous grin.

Fine!" he said, finally giving in. "We can see it... again. But I'm going to complain the whole time."

I punched the air in a gesture of victory.

"I don't even understand how you can still like it after seeing it this many times. Isn't it less dramatic once you know how it ends?"

I shook my head. "No more than any of the other horror movies we watch. Besides, you become increasingly dramatic all the time, so it makes up the difference."

"I hate you so much," he laughed.

"Uh huh. Sure."

CHAPTER EIGHT

EVIE

I AVOIDED LILITH AS MUCH AS I COULD FOR THE next three days, which was not easy. My entire body wanted to be near her, but I was still processing our last conversation.

My father was complaining about the problems at the farm caused by the early cold weather. The farm's owner was concerned that he might not be able to keep everyone on if it continued, that once they harvested what they had, he'd have to start laying people off sooner than expected. Every year, for some reason or another, the owner of the farm was coming up with reasons to lay the workers off early. It gave my father worry lines that created deep dips in his forehead, his mouth set in a frown. I loved my father, and I hated seeing him like this, but he refused to leave.

"It'll be okay, honey. We still have the bookstore, and maybe the weather will right itself before too long," my mother told him, trying her best to be encouraging. She was always the optimist. Whenever anything went sideways for anyone, she'd smile, pat their arm, and say it would all be better in the morning. I thought she was just being unrealistic most of the time.

"Maybe, but we need to be prepared for what could happen if it doesn't change by mid-October." He dropped his fork onto his plate with a clang and rubbed his face with his hands. I loved my father's hands. They looked so cracked and rough from years of hard labor, but I remembered them as the very gentle hands that touched my forehead to check for fevers, applied bandages to scraped knees, or held my hand in church when I was little.

"Can we just talk about this later?" my mother pleaded, her smile stretched tightly across her face, cutting her eyes at both me and my sister.

"Mom, it's fine," I told her. "We already know what's going on. It's all anyone's talking about right now." I used my fork to push my peas around on the white dinner plate with the pink roses around its border.

"Evie, please. This is an adult matter," my mother responded, waving her hands in front of her and scrunching her forehead, as if trying to fend off the conversation.

I put my fork down and looked at her. "Why not? It's not like we have anything else to talk about. I mean, unless you want to hear about conjugating French verbs, or how Bea wants to be Matilda in the school play. Besides, I'm eighteen years old. I think I can handle it."

"Oh, you'll be a lovely Matilda!" my mother exclaimed, her face relaxing, thankful for the change in topic.

Bea beamed at her and started to say something, but I interrupted with a loud groan.

"Mom, you're missing the point," I told her.

My mother took a deep breath and closed her eyes. This was usually an indicator that her mood was changing quickly, and her optimism was wearing thin. She clasped her hands under her chin and cocked her head at me. "What exactly is the point, Evie?"

"That you can't keep things from us, Mom. I'm not a child. I hear about everything that happens. If someone's dog gets fleas, I know about it. If someone doesn't bring their trash can in from the curb fast enough, I know about it. No one can hide here!"

I hadn't realized that I was raising my voice until my father brought his fist down on the table, hard. Everyone jumped, including me. Especially me.

"That will be enough," he said calmly, his voice low

and decisive.

I took a deep breath. "This is ridiculous. I can't wait to get out of here," I mumbled.

And that's when my mother turned on me. "You stop it right now. I am so sick of hearing you look down on this town, on us, on everyone here. I won't have it anymore."

I seethed with anger, but she couldn't tell. I had my father's ability of being simultaneously calm and angry. "I do not look down on you," I said, knowing that this was mostly untrue. "I am just sick of you thinking that because you never wanted to leave that I won't either. I've worked my butt off to do more than this town can give me. Don't you want me to go to a really great school, and do really great things out in the world?"

My mother sighed. She was becoming frustrated, but so was I. "I think it's wonderful that you have dreams, I really do. But dreams don't pay the bills, Evie. Why not stay here? There are decent jobs, good people. It's a great place to raise children. You'd have a good life."

Clearly, she didn't know me at all. "Because I don't want kids and a husband. I don't want those things. I don't just want 'good' – I want 'amazing.'"

I watched her eyes begin to glisten before she looked back down at her plate. My stomach churned with the familiar guilt that conversations like this inevitably brought on. I'd stand up for myself, it would somehow hurt her, and I'd end up caving and apologizing to her. I felt it happening again.

"Look, Mama, I'm sorry. I didn't mean to make you or Dad or anyone else feel bad."

"But you do," my father interjected. "Every time you talk about how much you hate it here, how you can't wait to run off, you make us feel awful and stupid for staying here. Maybe it isn't a big city with a bunch of opportunities, but it's a good town. Everyone here has always been good to us, to you, to your sister. When you won that essay contest last year, Henry closed the diner for an entire night to throw you that party. When you turned sixteen, people congratulated you in the paper. They love you here, Evie, and you won't find that anywhere else, not like this. And you repay that by talking bad about everyone who lives here, including your mother and me. Of course it makes us feel bad."

I'd never told my parents about school, about the way people treated me there. I never told them about the names they called me, the vulgar things some of the guys said in the hall. I didn't tell them that I rushed from class to class to avoid those people. The only people that were decent to me were Max Brady, the kids in Drama Club, Liam, and now Lilith. But not a single one of them really knew all of me.

But it didn't matter. My father stood up from the table and walked away before I had the chance to say anything else. He didn't raise his voice, not once, but he might as well have. The effect was the same; I felt like a jerk. As much as I hated living here, he was right. Aside from the kids my age, people treated me fairly well. But none of them knew me, not really, and they probably wouldn't like me if they did.

"I'm sorry," I said, my voice barely above a whisper.

My mother pushed back her chair and stood up. I saw Bea flinch a little. I hated when she had to sit through these arguments. All they did was upset her and make her anxious.

"I hope you get your scholarships," my mother said. "I hope they make you happy, because that's the most important thing, isn't it? But no matter how much you hate it, this place is a part of you that you can't wash off. This is your home. Besides, you don't know what's out there. Here, you're safe. We all look out for each other. Out there...anything could happen." My mother turned and walked over to the sink.

I leaned back in my chair. I wasn't sure if I felt more angry or guilty. Maybe I was angry at them for making me feel guilty. I didn't hate my family, but they didn't seem to care that I wasn't happy, not really. They didn't know how hard it was for me to just exist here.

"That's the point. Anything could happen out there. I know you get scared, but I'm smart and I'm careful. It isn't enough for me to see photos of the Eiffel Tower in

Paris or the temples in Japan. Can't you understand that? Can't you just support me?" I stayed quiet for a moment, waiting for her to say something, but she didn't. So I reverted to just saying whatever would make it better for her. "I probably won't get into any of the schools I applied to anyway, so maybe it won't matter."

I heard my mother take a deep breath and lower her head over the sink. "You've always been different, Evie. We all know it. From the moment you were born, people told me over and over that you had big things ahead for you. You've always been one to set your mind to something and then you'd get it. I guess I shouldn't have expected for that to ever change. If you want it bad enough, you'll get those scholarships, and you'll get out of here. Just know that no amount of being careful can keep you safe out there." Her shoulders shook so slightly that I almost didn't notice it. My mother hated crying in front of people, and she tried hard to hide it.

I pushed my chair back quietly and got up from the table. I'd clearly done enough damage for one night. I left the kitchen and climbed the stairs to my bedroom on the second floor. The door clicked softly when I closed it. I reached for my cell phone on the nightstand and sent a quick text message to Liam to tell him I'd gotten into yet another fight with my parents. He answered quickly, asking if I was okay. I didn't answer. Instead, I asked him if he wanted to hang out. He offered to meet me at the diner, so I tucked my phone into my back pocket, opened up my bedroom window, and climbed out.

That was the night that changed my mind. I was going to talk to Lilith again.

CHAPTER NINE

EVIE

LIAM STAYED QUIET, JUST STARING AT ME from across the table. His wide eyes and high eyebrows told me that he was waiting for me to speak, but I didn't. Instead, I sat with my hands folded on the table, bouncing my leg underneath it. I wasn't sure where to even start. This wasn't the first fight with my parents, but it might be the worst, and I wasn't in a hurry to lay all the details out on the table.

"What happened?" Liam finally asked me. He reached across the table to touch my hand, but I jerked it away. Normally, I probably would have let him be comforting, but not today. Today, I was hating myself.

"They said I was looking down on them, that I was

belittling this town and everyone in it," I said, looking down at my hands.

He sat back in his seat and I heard him let out a heavy sigh. I looked up at him, narrowing my eyes. He had something to say but didn't know if he should.

"I mean, do I do that? You'd tell me, right?" I asked. Liam was always honest with me, though this I was mostly hoping for empathy and confirmation that they were wrong. I didn't get it.

"Well, you do talk a lot of crap about everyone," he muttered reluctantly. My face must have registered my shock because he began speaking quickly. "I don't think you mean to come across that way, I really don't," he backpedaled. "I think you're just really frustrated about wanting out of here, and you deal with it by taking swipes at everyone else. You don't mean to be hurtful, but you can be."

I didn't say anything. I was too busy trying to keep the tears that were stinging my eyes from falling. I closed my eyes and took a deep breath, swallowing whatever sadness or hurt was threatening to come to the surface. I hated those feelings. I didn't deal with them unless I had to, and this wasn't one of those times. I probably had years of pent up anger and sadness in my gut. Truthfully, the last time I cried was probably my grandfather's funeral when I was seven. I guess I was a lot like my mother that way.

"You're right," I said, my voice barely above a whisper. "You're right. I do say those things." I jerked my head up and looked Liam in the eyes. "I just don't want to end up like them. They're good people, but I want more than this, and I don't know why they can't understand that," I said desperately, gesturing at the people in the diner. "I want to see places, have experiences. I want to see Europe and Asia. I want to write about those places. I don't want to be stuck here, where the only thing to talk about is this weird-ass weather. I want to feel like I can be myself."

"You will, one way or another, I'm sure," he said. "But why can't you be yourself? I thought you were doing a pretty good job."

I stared at him, my lips pursed. He looked back at me, his eyebrows knitted together in confusion.

"I don't know what I meant," I lied, keeping my eyes on the tabletop.

"What?" he finally asked.

"I hung out with Lilith the other day," I blurted out. I watched his eyes widen. I had no intention of telling him, but it just flew out.

"Are you serious? When? Where?"

"A few days ago, after school. I went to her house…"

"Oh, wow," he said. "What happened?"

I didn't know where to start. I didn't want to tell him how nervous she made me, how the way Lilith looked at me made me feel like I was spiraling. Instead, I told him

62

about the giant snake, and that she lived in that creepy old house outside of town. Then I told him about the God stuff and how weird things got.

"She's probably in a cult or something, and you just walked into her house. You're lucky you got out of there alive," Liam said.

I laughed. "A cult? Why not a trafficking ring?"

Liam didn't smile. "It's probably both, but that's not the point."

"Then what's the point?"

"The point is that you can't be friends with her. She's weird. She gives you weird looks."

"What are you talking about?" I asked, rolling my eyes. What I really wanted to ask was how she looked at me because I wanted to know if it was the same way I looked at her. But I didn't ask. "In case you hadn't noticed, we're weird. Also, you don't get to tell me who I can be friends with," I told him, shaking my head. "Besides, we don't even know her, so we don't know that she's some unsavory character."

"You've known her for, like, a week. I think that's enough time to figure out what kind of person she is," he said. "I mean, she's hot, but not hot enough to listen to all that...stuff."

"You think she's hot?" I asked, trying not to sound like I cared.

He shrugged. "Yeah, I guess. Why? Do you?" he

joked, flicking his straw wrapper at me.

I rolled my eyes for the hundredth time, trying to pretend the idea was absurd, but I definitely thought so too. We both remained silent for a few moments.

I looked up and toward the door when I heard the little bell above the diner door ring. Lilith walked in. I involuntarily gasped.

Liam turned around to see what I was staring at. "Oh, great. Of course she shows up."

Lilith smiled at me and took long strides toward our table. My breathing picked up and the pull in my chest became stronger as she got closer.

"Well, fancy running into you here," she said, still smiling at me.

"Well, it's one of only three places to go here, so the odds were pretty high," Liam said, crossing his arms over his chest and leaning back. The look he gave her was not at all friendly. He and Lilith just stared at each other, making me really uncomfortable.

"So…do you want to join us?" I reluctantly asked her.

"I would love to!" she exclaimed, sitting down next to me. I scooted over to make room. Liam was looking less happy, if that was even possible.

"What are we talking about?" Lilith asked, folding her hands on the table and leaning in.

I looked back and forth between Liam and Lilith,

the tension rising. Well, the tension on Liam's side. Lilith seemed just dandy. She was smiling – even if it seemed forced – and maintaining eye contact with Liam. He held his own.

"Not much," I said awkwardly, hesitantly. "School, my parents, me being a terrible person."

Up until that last part, she was just nodding along. Once I called myself a terrible person, her head snapped in my direction.

"What in the hell are you talking about? Who said that?" she pointedly looked at Liam.

"My parents. Not that Liam helped."

He finally broke his intense staring and looked over at me. "I never said you were a terrible person. I said you can be a little harsh," he said defensively.

"And what is that supposed to mean?" Lilith asked, a disgusted look on her face.

"What are you even doing here?" he asked her, not answering the question.

Lilith scoffed. "Well, I came to get food, but it looks like Evie needs a friend."

This visibly infuriated Liam. He leaned forward, set his jaw, and looked straight into her face. "She already has a friend. You aren't welcome."

Lilith feigned offended and opened her mouth to say something, but before she could, I leaned in and put my hands between them.

"Before you two decide to throw down, maybe you can chill out for a second. Liam, I know you didn't say that, but Lilith isn't bothering anyone by being here,"

"That's good to know," Lilith said, looking...hurt? Offended? I couldn't tell with her.

Liam looked at me. "If she's staying, I'm going to go."

It was my turn to be incredulous. "What in the fuck is happening right now?"

"Relax, it's fine. I need to get going anyway," Lilith said, patting me on the thigh and scooting out of the booth. I think I stopped breathing.

"I'd say bye, but I don't care," Liam responded.

Lilith raised an eyebrow and rolled her eyes before looking back at me. "Evie, call me later, yeah?"

With that, she sauntered away and toward the counter.

I turned on Liam. "I cannot believe you. What is wrong with you? You've never acted like that toward anyone before. Why do you hate her so much?"

Liam stared down at his hands. "I don't know. I just do. I told you, I think something's up with her."

I dropped it and began picking at the cold fries in front of me, Liam watching me carefully. Something about his behavior and his being adamant about me staying away from Lilith made him seem jealous. It made me uncomfortable. I looked up at him and he was just staring at the top of the table, his jaw clenched. His left hand was balled into a fist on top of the table.

"I should get home," I said, interrupting the very awkward silence.

"Yeah, me too, I guess," he responded through clenched teeth.

"Want to crash at my house?" I was kind of hoping he would say no. I felt bad for hoping for it when he quietly nodded his head.

We paid our checks and walked back to my house. During the twenty-minute walk, we mentioned school twice, but otherwise it was radio silence. This wasn't like us at all, and it made me feel as weird as his jealousy did. I hoped that a good night's sleep would put things back to normal.

It didn't.

CHAPTER TEN

EVIE

THINGS AT SCHOOL CONTINUED TO BE awkward around both Lilith and Liam. Liam was tense most of the time. At the mere mention of Lilith's name, he would become sullen or hostile. If he saw Lilith in class or at her locker, it was worse. I was trying to figure out how Lilith felt about me. I didn't want to decipher Liam's feelings as well. Especially since I had my own feelings to contend with. I was definitely into her, and while I wasn't confused about that fact, I had no idea how to proceed, or how to know if she was into me. Why couldn't there be any other gay kids to ask around here?

I wanted to talk to her again so badly without Liam

around, but I had no idea how to approach her. The thought of it made me excited, but also like I wanted to throw up on the floor. She didn't initiate conversation, and she didn't wait for me before or after class. She did, however, smile when she saw me, so she couldn't be mad at me, right? Whatever was happening between us, I felt it in the very center of my being. I didn't make that up, did I?

By our last class together that Friday, I couldn't take it anymore. The distance, the not knowing, where that last conversation at her house would've gone. I didn't even know what to say to her. So, I waited until the teacher wasn't looking and passed her a note.

> Hey,
> Sorry I have been weird, and that I have not talked to you since the diner. Are you busy this weekend? And please do not say anything around Liam. He is being super weird. —Evie

I watched Lilith read the note out of the corner of my eye. I watched a small smile tug at the corner of her mouth as she picked up her pen and scrawled something on the note before passing it back. As I hurriedly grabbed the folded paper from her, I crossed my fingers that she wouldn't tell me to get lost and try someone else.

Come by tomorrow night? I'll answer whatever questions you have. I'm glad you changed your mind. And no worries, it's our little secret. —L

Whatever questions I had? Was I just supposed to say, "Hey, I can't stop thinking about you, are you into me? And why are you always so cryptic?" No, definitely not. Instead, I crumpled up the note, shoving it into my backpack. Liam didn't need to know anything. If he asked what my plans were, I'd just tell him I was staying in and studying.

Later, he did ask. And I did lie. I wanted to tell him what was going on, but I also didn't want to fight with him. Mostly, I wanted to have this one thing, this one person, in my life that didn't have to include him. I wanted to see what that was like.

When I told him that I had something else to do, he'd raised an eyebrow at me, waiting for an explanation. All I did was stare back at him. When Lilith came over to get into her locker, my eyes involuntarily darted in her direction. She avoided making eye contact with me, so Liam shook his head and snickered. When Lilith walked away, I turned on him.

"Look, Liam. Whatever your problem is with her, or me hanging out with her, get over it. She didn't do anything to you, or to anyone else. Besides, she's in almost all of my classes, and I may need help studying in them at some point. Plus, she doesn't make me feel like a freak, which is pretty nice. So, whatever your problem is, suck it up."

He was stunned, and I didn't care to hear if he had anything to say in response. I grabbed my backpack, slammed my locker closed, and turned to walk away. After a minute, I heard his feet shuffling behind me. He didn't walk up to me right away, choosing to stay behind me a bit. I didn't feel bad for standing up to him about Lilith, but I didn't know why I couldn't do that for myself. Eventually he worked up the nerve to walk up beside me, sneaking glances out of the corner of his eye.

Liam stayed for dinner that night. It had been tense in the house since my last fight with my parents, but with Liam there, conversation seemed to flow easily. I made it a point to try being less critical about…everything. Liam told my parents about his new paintings. Bea nailed her audition and talked excitedly about getting to play Matilda in the school play. My father was asked to build an addition to an old barn at the farm, so he was going to have work for a bit longer. My mother got a new shipment of books at the shop. I had nothing to contribute.

Liam helped my mother clean up after dinner, so I took the opportunity to earn more points by helping Bea with her homework. My father excused himself to go watch television.

"Evie, what do you know about the new family that moved into the house out on Mulberry Road right outside of town?" my mother asked as she washed a plate. She was talking about Lilith. I exchanged a look with Liam, who rolled his eyes and put silverware into the dish drainer.

I shrugged. "Not much. Basically only that there's a family there now. The girl that lives there is in a few of my classes."

My mother nodded slowly. "What about her parents? No one seems to know anything about them, and no one's seen them in town."

I was quiet. I hadn't seen any evidence of her family while I was at her house. Lilith didn't talk about them.

"I really don't know about them either. I don't know her that well," I answered.

My mother nodded again. She and Liam finished the dishes in silence. Once my mother left the room, I looked over at Liam and found him leaning against the stainless steel fridge, staring at me, his look hard and suspicious. I pretended I didn't notice and asked if he wanted to go upstairs and watch a movie. Without a word, he followed me out of the kitchen and up the narrow staircase toward my bedroom. He closed the door behind us with a soft click.

"What do you want to watch? I've got *Scream*. We've seen it a million times, but it's a classic," I said, digging through my DVDs.

"What's going on, Evie?"

I spun around to see him standing near the door, arms folded across his chest, his jaw clenched.

"Nothing," I said, turning back to my DVDs. I let out a shaky breath as I looked through the titles. "I'm not sure what you're so upset about, but—"

"You can't go there. I don't trust that girl. Something's up, and you need to steer clear." He took a few steps toward me, dropping his arms to his sides. "Everything you told me the other night...I'm worried about you. Seriously, stay away from her."

I took a deep breath and turned around. "Yes, you've made that abundantly clear. But I'm fine. Everything's fine."

"Evie—"

"What are you even freaking out about? You keep saying that you don't trust her, but that feels like bullshit. Do you want me to stay away from her for me, or for you?" I paused, taking a breath. I didn't know what I really meant by that last part. He just felt a little too adamant, and it flew out of my mouth. "I can take care of myself," I said, raising my voice slightly.

He looked a little panicked.

"Look, I'm sorry. I didn't mean to yell at you. I appreciate you looking out for me, but you don't need to. What's going on with you, anyway? You're weirdly overprotective," I told him.

He blinked rapidly, looking like he'd been busted with the keys to a stolen car. His behavior was becoming frustrating and irksome, especially since he wouldn't tell me why. We stared at each other. He looked like he was trying to swallow a secret, and I probably looked like I was going to beat it out of him.

"It's nothing," he finally said, his voice a little shaky. "I'll mind my own business. And for the record, you didn't yell. I've heard you yell, and that definitely wasn't it."

I smiled a little. We were both hiding something, but neither of us trusted the other enough to say whatever it was we wanted to say. Instead, we tucked our lies back into our pockets and sat down to watch a movie.

CHAPTER ELEVEN

EVIE

I WOKE UP EARLY ON SATURDAY MORNING AND groaned when I looked at my alarm clock. This was usually my day to sleep in, but it didn't look like that was happening. As the fog in my brain began to lift, I remembered something and my stomach clenched. This was my day with Lilith. All at once, I was nervous, anxious, and excited. I told myself that I was probably making it out to be a much bigger deal than it was. What kind of earth-shattering wisdom could an eighteen-year-old girl possibly impart upon me? In my experience, probably not much. I'd probably get there only to have her tell me the entire thing was a joke.

Unfortunately, there would be several hours before

I'd know. I tried to fill the time by getting ahead on my homework. When I ran out of that, I tried helping my dad go through boxes in the garage. There was no amount of old cookbooks or yearbooks or baby books that made time go any faster. I even helped my mother cook dinner, and then I rushed through eating it.

"Hey, can I borrow the car tonight?" I asked, clearing my place at the kitchen table.

"Where, exactly, are you taking it?" my father asked, his voice sounding suspicious. It made sense. I never asked to borrow the car. Everything was usually within walking distance.

"I'm going over to Lilith's house. You know, the new girl."

My mother put her fork down and looked at me. "I thought you said you didn't know her."

"I don't. I'm getting to know her. We're going to hang out at her house, maybe catch a movie. It's not a big deal. If she didn't live right outside of town, I wouldn't ask, but I don't really want to walk home in the dark."

My parents exchanged a look, and then my mother gave a small nod in my direction.

"Fine," my dad relented. "Take your mom's Camry."

I shouted my thanks and headed for the door.

"And put gas in it this time!" he yelled after me.

It was a fifteen-minute drive to Lilith's house. I spent another ten sitting in my car, staring up at the huge yellow Victorian-style house trimmed in slick black. In the moonlight, it looked menacing, like something out of an old Hollywood horror film. It didn't feel like the same house I'd been in a week or so before. There were no lights on the road, and the only light in the house came from the large living room window in the front. The shadow of the house stretched across the lawn, reaching for me, beckoning me to come inside. It reminded me of a book by Shirley Jackson that I'd read the year before. The houses were different, but the energy seemed like it might be the same. A shiver traveled down my spine.

I took a deep breath, trying to shake off my nerves, and opened the car door. As I traveled the short distance across the lawn, a porch light flicked on and the heavy wooden front door swung open slowly. The creak of the opening door seemed unnaturally loud in the dark, empty air. Lilith stepped into the light, a hand on her hip.

"I didn't think you were ever going to come in," she said. Her ever-present half-smile made me wish I'd come in sooner.

Great, she'd been watching me from the window. I tried not to read too much into it, but I liked the idea that she might be eager to see me.

"Yeah, sorry. I was just texting my parents to let them know I was here," I lied, holding my phone up as if that would somehow make her believe me more.

Lilith winked, nodded, and then stepped aside to let me in. The house was warm, but something still raised goosebumps on my skin. I pulled the sleeves down on my shirt. The scent of cinnamon and clove was sitting on the air, the same as last time. The soft yellow light from the living room provided an eerie glow into the hallway, lighting a path. I took a tentative step toward the living room, not entirely sure what I might find at the end of it.

But I found nothing. Well, there was the snake in its enclosure, but that was it. Everything looked like last time. This time, however, there was a book on the coffee table that was upside down, holding the reader's place.

"Go ahead and sit down. Do you want anything to drink?" I have water, tea, soda, coffee," Lilith said.

"Soda's good," I answered. She disappeared down the hallway.

"So you're reading *Fahrenheit 451*?" I asked, picking up the book from the coffee table and examining the cover.

"For about the millionth time," I heard her shout from the kitchen. "I love it. Have you read it?"

"Not in a long time," I shouted back.

"You should give it another read," she said, her voice traveling down the hall, gradually getting closer. "You seemed so uncomfortable last time, I wasn't sure if you'd speak to me again, let alone come to my house." She reentered the living room with two soda cans.

"Honestly, I thought you were in a cult or something and I wasn't going to talk to you again," I told her, taking one of the soda cans from her.

She laughed, sitting on the sofa and crossing her legs under herself. "Well, at least you're honest."

"I try to be," I said, opening my soda. It gave a crack and a hiss. "But the more I thought about it, about what you said, the more curious I was. Liam was definitely not happy about it."

"Well, you don't answer to Liam, do you?"

I stared at her. I didn't think that I did, but if he called, I jumped to answer. If he wanted to hang out, I dropped whatever I was doing most of the time. But he did the same thing for me.

"No, I don't answer to him. We're friends, we're there for each other. We've been through a lot together."

Lilith cocked her head to the side, studying me. "He's in love with you, you know." Her voice sounded almost disappointed.

I choked on my soda. The bubbles hit my nose as I coughed, making my eyes water. What in the hell was she talking about?

"What in the hell are you talking about?" I asked after I'd recovered from my coughing fit.

"I noticed it at the diner. I thought it would be obvious to you. It's pretty obvious to everyone else.

People talk about it at school. I mean, they talk about you in general, but that topic definitely comes up."

The idea of everyone talking about me made me nauseous. I knew that they did, and I could probably guess what it was about, but I wanted to hear her say it out loud.

"What do they say?" I asked, bracing myself.

She shrugged and looked down, playing with the tab on her soda can. "They talk about how you've never had a boyfriend, and that the only guy you do hang out with is Liam. They talk about your decided lack of femininity, which is ridiculous. I think you're just fine," she said, peering at me. "There are…other things, but that doesn't matter. I mean, it wouldn't bother me whether they were true or not."

My stomach did a twist that was seeming to become ever-present when I was with Lilith. If I didn't know better, I would've thought Lilith was flirting, but I made the decision not to think much about it. I don't think I'd even realize a girl was flirting with me anyway. Lilith was probably just being nice. And there was still the question of this Liam thing. He was my best friend. There was no way people could think we were together. I shook my head, taking another careful sip of my soda.

"You're wrong. There's absolutely no way Liam is… what you said," I told her, steering the conversation back around to its original topic.

"Why not? You're smart," Lilith said, looking at me, her eyes scanning from my hair to my shoes, a strange look in her eyes, like hunger. "You're attractive. The two of you are always together. Most people assume that if you're not together now, you will be eventually."

I wrinkled my nose in disgust. "Gross, that's never going to happen. Anyway, I'm not here to talk about him."

Lilith smiled. "Then why are you here?"

I tried to swallow the lump in my throat and felt my body stiffen as I tried to look away from Lilith. I suddenly couldn't remember which reason brought me here: my interest in what Lilith was saying the last time, or my interest in Lilith.

"You want to know how I can help," Lilith said, choosing the answer for me.

I locked eyes with her and nodded slowly, thinking that might be the safest choice to go with.

"Long story short, if you want your autonomy, you have to let go of the idea that anyone can give it to you," she said, raking her hands through her hair.

My brow furrowed in confusion and I let out a joyless chuckle. "That's so confusing. I have no idea what you're even talking about."

Lilith leaned forward and I found myself doing the same, pulled to her like a magnet.

"Don't you?" she asked. "I mean, no one would blame

you for feeling like you need someone's permission to live your life. After all, who decides what you eat? Who decides what you wear, where you can and can't go, whether you have to go to school, that you have to go to college?"

"My mom, because she cooks. I do, I do, my parents, and everyone," I replied, ticking the items off of my fingers.

Lilith took my hand and a zap traveled up my arm. I might've pulled away if she didn't have a firm grip on me. She used each of my fingers to tick off her own points.

"True. But you choose your wardrobe in conjunction with what your parents, the school, and the people in town would approve of," she closed one of my fingers. "You have to ask before you can go anywhere, or at the very least, you have to be home by a certain time. It's always been this way for you." Another finger closed. "Your parents and the state force you to go to school, and if you don't, the truant officers are bound to show up eventually. And finally, society says you have to go to college," she said, closing the last of my fingers and holding my hand in her own. "But you seem to want to go, so we'll ignore that one. Frankly, it's all bullshit."

I stared at her, trying to process what she'd said. My skin felt like it was burning where Lilith was touching me. I'd never thought about any of these things in this way, but it seemed to make sense when Lilith said it. I didn't set any of the rules, and no one asked for my input, but I was expected to follow them. I did anything that I could to make everyone else happy, and that maybe that would make it easier for them to let me leave Benson after high school. But unless my parents paid or a lot of financial aid came through, that wasn't going to happen. No wonder I didn't feel in control most of the time.

"I'm totally powerless," I muttered, the realization hitting me like a tidal wave.

Lilith looked at me with pity. She reached forward and tucked an errant piece of my hair behind my ear. "But you don't have to be."

CHAPTER TWELVE

LIAM

I KNEW EVIE WAS LYING WHEN SHE TOLD ME she was too busy to hang out with me over the weekend. When I called her house half an hour ago, her mom told me where she was, so here I was, standing in the tall hedges outside of Lilith's house, watching the two of them through a large front window.

The way they interacted with each other bothered me. If I was honest with myself, I was jealous. I wanted to be Lilith. I wanted to be the one holding her hand. I wanted to be the one making her laugh. More than anything, I wanted to know why Lilith was holding her hand and making her laugh.

I hated the way they leaned in to each other, the

way they stared at each other a little too long. I watched as sadness and confusion washed across Evie's face, and then I watched Lilith being the one that comforted her. I couldn't hear what was happening, but the way she looked down, the way her hair fell in her face that way… something was wrong. I knew her better than anyone, and I knew when she was upset.

And then Lilith reached up and brushed the hair out of Evie's face, and Evie leaned in to it. It felt like I couldn't breathe.

I probably should've gotten out of there, but the masochist in me wanted to see what would happen next. I felt so stupid being twisted up and jealous and borderline obsessive.

I kept telling myself that I was only here as her friend, but as I watched Lilith touch Evie, I knew that wasn't true. I wanted Evie. I'd felt like this for years, and she acted like she didn't know. She never seemed interested in being with any of the guys at school. Maybe all of the rumors about her being gay were true. If they were, why hadn't she told me?

Since she never showed interest in anyone, it was easy to pretend she was mine. It was easy to pretend that she'd come around eventually. It never occurred to me that maybe she didn't like guys at all, not until I saw her with Lilith. But Lilith would never know her like I did. She would never know that Evie's favorite movie was It's A Wonderful Life, but didn't want anyone to know she liked happy endings. She didn't know that Evie knew all the words to "MMMBop" and would die from embarrassment if anyone ever found out. She didn't know that Evie cried like a baby when her childhood dog was hit by a car and died.

I looked up through the window again. Lilith was gone, and Evie was pacing in front of the sofa. I watched her glance at a mirror on the wall and smooth out her hair. She looked nervous, biting her lower lip.

And then I saw her look directly at me.

I panicked, re-positioning myself to make sure I stayed in the shadow. My heart was pounding, and I hoped she didn't see me. I felt my phone vibrate in my pocket. I pulled it out, trying to dim the light with my other hand as I hit a button and it illuminated. One text message.

Saturday 7:40 PM:

Get out of here, you perv. If Lilith sees you, you're dead

I paused a second and then turned away from the house. I took a deep breath, knowing that I should go home, but I needed to try.

Saturday 7:43 PM:

Come on, let's just
leave. Let's just
get out of here, grab
a pizza, and hang
out. I'm sorry I
gave you such a hard
time about this.
That wasn't fair.
So can you please
come back with me?

I watched her read the text. She looked out at me
and shook her head.

Saturday 7:45 PM:

Just go home,
Liam. We can hang
out tomorrow. If
you're sorry about
everything, you'll
understand that
I'm just making a
new friend.

I didn't bother responding. It was pretty clear that if
I was going to come out the winner, this wasn't going to
be the way. I needed to do something bigger.

CHAPTER THIRTEEN

EVIE

WOW, YOU LOOK INTENSE," I HEARD from behind me and I spun around. Lilith standing in the doorway.

"We had a visitor," I said, motioning toward the window.

Lilith tilted her head. "Oh?"

"Liam was outside, watching us. Can you believe that?"

Lilith arched a perfectly sculpted eyebrow. "Is that rhetorical?"

"Don't say it."

She laughed. "I don't have to. He's doing plenty on his own," she said. She sat down and motioned for me to join her. "Okay. You said you had questions. Ask away."

I took a deep breath. I didn't know where to start, but when I opened my mouth, words came tumbling out.

"We're both only eighteen. How in the hell do you have enough life experience that you can help me at all?" I realized my tone sounded angry, but mostly I was just frustrated. Lilith just sat there, not looking bothered at all. It was like she was expecting the question. For the first time since we'd met, Lilith had no expression at all, and it rattled me.

"I get it. The first thing you need to understand is that nothing is exactly the way it appears. Sometimes, you need to look a bit beneath the surface."

I rolled my eyes. "What is that even supposed to mean?"

We stared at each other. Lilith seemed to be looking for something in my face, but I didn't know what that could be. Instead, I sat across from her, mirroring her expression.

"I don't know that you're ready to hear this," she finally said.

My frustration was growing. "You've got to be joking. I'm as old as you are. You said you could help me, that you had answers."

She didn't say anything. She just sat there, and it was making me antsy. It was making me feel like she'd lied to me. I hated it.

"You've got to give me something, Lilith. I took a chance and decided to trust you. I lied to my best friend for you."

It was small, but something in her face changed. If I wasn't looking directly at her, I would have missed the flash of guilt in her eyes, the small catch of her breath.

"You know Mae Hesser?" she asked, breaking her silence.

"Everyone knows Mae Hesser."

"Did you know she had a son once?"

I looked at her in disbelief. "No, she doesn't. She's never even been married."

It was Lilith's turn to roll her eyes at me. "First, you don't need to be married to have children. That idea is outdated, and it surprises me that you think that way. Second, yes, she does. Well, she did. Long before you were even born, she left town for about a year. She was a lot like you actually, wanting to try out life in the big wide world. She was in her twenties when she left Benson. She found a little garden apartment, a job she loved, and she was making friends. There was also a co-worker that paid special attention to her. She thought he was funny, charming, and when he finally asked her out, she said yes. It turned out he wasn't that nice," she said, her voice lower. Something in the way that Lilith told the story made the hairs on my arms stand up.

"He attacked her inside of her home, right inside

the doorway. He didn't even wait for her to ask him to come in. He just shoved her inside and slammed the door shut," Lilith said, looking as angry and nauseated as I felt. "Several stitches from the knife he carried and nine months later, she gave birth to a bouncing baby boy." There was no humor, no lightness to her voice. It was pure hatred and venom.

I waited for her to say that she was kidding, that she was just trying to scare me, but it never happened. My brain struggled to wrap around it.

"That's not funny," I finally told her.

"It isn't supposed to be."

"Prove it," I demanded before I could stop myself. My voice came out ragged.

"You can always ask her," she said.

The shock and disgust should have been very clear on my face. How could she even suggest it? "No way. That's horrible."

"You want proof that you're more comfortable verifying," Lilith stated.

I nodded, not sure I even wanted to hear what was coming next.

Finally, she took a deep breath, seeming reluctant to continue. Then she leaned forward. In a conspiratorial tone, she said, "When you were six days old, you got sick. You were laying in your crib, and you laughed in your sleep, not a normal noise for a baby your age to have made. Anyway, one minute you giggled, and the next minute you weren't breathing at all. You got lucky - your mother was sitting next to your crib. She screamed for your father, and the 911 operator walked him through CPR until the ambulance came. They said your father saved your life. It never happened again, and the doctor said your parents were just extraordinarily lucky. You grew up to be completely normal."

I stared at her, my mouth slightly open. "No. My parents would've told me," I said, my voice barely audible.

"Would they?"

"How do you even know all this?" I asked her.

She shrugged her shoulders. "I told you, not everything is the way it appears to be."

We stared at each other for what seemed like an eternity, neither of us knowing what to say next. Finally, I couldn't look at her anymore. It was too intense. I turned my head, not knowing if I should stay or go. I didn't know if I should ask more questions or leave it alone. I wasn't sure of a single thing Lilith said to me. Then a wave of nausea passed over me. Maybe Lilith was lying to me. Maybe she didn't know anything, and couldn't help me. I felt embarrassed, disappointed.

"I have to go," I said, standing up automatically.

Lilith sprang up. "Please, Evie. Don't go."

I wasn't sure if I could open my mouth without vomiting, so I ignored her and headed for the door.

CHAPTER FOURTEEN

EVIE

O N THE DRIVE HOME I TRIED TO TALKED myself out of everything Lilith said about Mae, or about what happened to me. Unfortunately, while I laid in bed that night, it gnawed at me. What if Lilith was right? What if Lilith was a huge liar and couldn't be trusted, like Liam said? It kept me awake, and I watched the sun slowly light up the sky. By the time I heard Bea stomp down the stairs a couple of hours later, I'd made up my mind.

I was going to ask my mother.

I felt on edge all day. I did my laundry, cleaned my bedroom, watched a movie, but nothing made me less anxious. How was I supposed to ask her about this without feeling like a jerk? Who would want to talk about this?

On the other hand, didn't I have a right to know?

I waited until I was alone with my mother after dinner to try and verify Lilith's story. All through dinner, I kept staring at my parents, my eyes darting back and forth between them. I wanted to know if this was a secret they were intentionally keeping, or if they just didn't think to mention to me. It was most likely the latter. Regardless, I needed to know if what Lilith said was true. If so, I had more questions, and maybe she could be trusted after all.

After dinner, I offered to dry the dishes while my mom washed them. She seemed pleasantly surprised by the mother-daughter time. We talked a little about school, about Bea's play, about maybe going shopping in Salem the following weekend. The more that I put off asking what I really wanted to know, the worse that the feeling in my stomach would get, like a huge snake rolling and slithering through my belly. Finally, as Mom was preparing to wash the last plate, I took a deep breath, swallowed the lump in my throat, and turned to her.

"Mom, can I ask you a question?"

"Of course," she said, smiling.

I took another deep breath. "When I was a baby, like, a brand new baby, did I ever get sick?"

She hesitated. It was so slight that I almost missed the widening of her eyes as she washed the plate in her now-shaking hands. I watched as she slightly shook her head, squared her shoulders, and righted herself.

"All babies get sick," she said.

She wasn't going to make this easy. "True. I mean, did I ever get sick enough to go to the hospital?"

She put the plate down in the sink and turned to stare at me, wet vinyl-gloved hands propped on her hips.

"What is this about?" Her tone was sharp, one she generally reserved for situations where I, or Bea, was in a lot of trouble.

"I was just curious…"

She stared at me for a moment before answering. "Yes. Once."

Butterflies exploded in my stomach. "What happened?"

"Evie, please, I don't want to talk about this," she said, turning back to the dishes in the sink.

"Mom, I need to know."

She shook her head and frowned. "I don't know why you need to hear this. It's only going to upset you, and it was so long ago. You're fine now."

I stayed silent, keeping my eyes on her. Finally, she relented. I watched her take off the vinyl gloves, place them on the edge of the sink, and motion for me to follow her to the kitchen table.

"You were only a few days old when it happened. It was so odd because you hadn't even been sick. I don't even know if I'd call it 'sick.' That night, I put you in your crib and stayed up reading in the rocking chair next to it. When you did sleep, you slept so hard. Out of nowhere, it sounded like you were laughing. At your age, you shouldn't have even been doing it, but there you were. I kept watching you when you stopped, waiting for you to do it again, hoping to tease your father about missing it. But you didn't do it again. Before I knew it, you weren't doing anything. Your chest, it wasn't moving…"

Tears began welling up in her eyes. I'd never seen her look so helpless and scared. I reached out and touched her hand, something I hadn't done before, and it seemed to comfort her. She paused, trying to collect herself, and then she continued.

"I screamed for your father. He was terrified of breaking you, but the 911 operator walked him through CPR until the ambulance arrived. The hospital ran so many tests. You were covered in these things that measured your heartbeat and your breathing. You were so small…" She shook her head. "The tests came back, and you were fine. They couldn't think of any reason for it, so they said it might be sleep apnea or some other ridiculous thing that didn't make sense to me. We brought you home after a bit, and watched you like a hawk. It never happened again."

We were silent for a few minutes, both of us staring down at the table. I couldn't look at her. I felt horrible for handing her a shovel and forcing her to dig all of this up. Maybe this was why she was so adamant about me staying in Benson. She'd almost lost me once.

"I'm sorry, Mom. Can I ask you one more question?" She nodded. "Do you know if Mae Hesser ever lived anywhere else?"

She thought for a moment, wiping the tears from her cheeks. "You know, I vaguely remember someone mentioning that once. She was gone for maybe a year or so. The way I heard it, she got mugged on her way home from work or something, so she came right home again and never left. How on Earth do you even know about all this?"

"I just overheard it," I lied. "Seemed weird." I stood, kissed her goodnight, and headed for my bedroom.

Everything Lilith told me was true. I couldn't really substantiate the specifics about Mae, but the rest of it was true. How did she know all this? How would a total stranger who'd lived here for only two months know all of this?

I didn't know what was going on, but I needed answers. Normally, I'd go to Liam for help with this, but I knew that was a terrible idea this time. I was still mad that he was spying on me and Lilith, but even if I wasn't, he would never believe this. I didn't even believe it at first. After a few minutes of pacing and debating about what to do, I realized that I needed answers more than I was afraid to find them out.

I spent most of that night on my laptop. Liam sent a text wanting to hang out and apologizing for following me, but I ignored it. I also ignored the six texts that followed. He finally gave up, saying he'd see me at school the next day. He'd see me at school, all right…

I started my fact-finding mission with Google, the place anyone starts when they need information, even if it was something they should probably see a doctor for. If Mae was attacked, there had to be something out there about it. Those kinds of crimes always made the news, right? I knew that it would probably be hard to find since the names of rape victims weren't usually released by police, and the case pre-dated the internet, but it was worth a shot. I tried every combination of search terms that I could think of, including "home invasions." That one gave me 1,680,000 results, and the first page alone made me scared to be in my own house. Then I tried her name, hoping I'd come up empty. Unfortunately, halfway down page two, there it was, a scan of a very short article from a Salt Lake City newspaper from 1957. Mae was twenty years old.

Salt Lake City police
have identified the
man that they say
is responsible for
a sexual assault on
Clearwater Drive
on Friday, May 24. The
assault occurred in the
victim's home. While
a person of interest
is currently being held
for questioning, no
arrest has been made.
The victim, Ms. Mae
Hesser is recovering
at a local hospital and
has declined comment.

That was it. There were no other reports. I felt like my blood was boiling. Her name was in the article for everyone to see, and no one was arrested.

As for a baby, the only way I could know about that for sure was to ask Mae, and I wasn't doing it. It was bad enough that they victimized her a second time by printing her name in the article. I wasn't going to do it a third time by asking her to talk to me about it. It wasn't any of my business anyway. I wished I didn't know at all. I wished Lilith didn't know. I wished it never happened.

Out of the three things Lilith told me, I could verify two of them. I stood up and began pacing the room and chewing my fingernails, an old nervous habit. Agnes, my cat, meowed loudly, irritated with my pacing. To illustrate her point, she jumped onto my desk and knocked over a container that held my Lisa Frank pencil collection, sending the brightly-colored pencils everywhere.

"What the hell, Aggie? What is your problem?" I took two steps toward the desk and bent down to pick up the pencils. Agnes, in normal cat fashion, continued to bat them to her floor before finally jumping to her cat tree.

"You're a jerk," I told her. Agnes turned her back, curled up in a ball, and readied herself for a nap.

It abruptly occurred to me that Lilith might have known about Mae Hesser because maybe Lilith was from Salt Lake City. Maybe when her parents mentioned they were moving to Benson, Oregon, someone said they knew a woman from there. I rolled my eyes at the thought. Even given everything, it was still far-fetched. But could it happen?

In Benson, probably. In a place as big as Salt Lake City, probably not.

It really only left one other explanation. Lilith was obviously a witch.

CHAPTER FIFTEEN

LILITH

I KNEW EVIE HAD BEEN ABLE TO CONFIRM everything I'd told her when she spent the next week avoiding me like I had the plague. That didn't stop her from staring at me when she thought I wasn't looking. But I was always looking at Evie. I couldn't help myself. There was something magnetic about her that kept my eyes searching for her.

I also watched her arguing with Liam in the hall at school that Monday, accusing him of being a stalker. I assumed it was because Evie caught him watching us at my house. Since I was in Evie's line of sight, I tried to keep her from seeing me watch the argument too closely. If I was being honest, I was more than a little happy to see her put Liam in his place.

Liam was going to be a bigger problem than I originally thought. He knew to be suspicious of me, but he certainly didn't know what I was capable of. He was just another pair of hands trying to hold Evie to this place. Sure, he had his aspirations of being an artist in the Big City, but it wasn't going to happen, not for him. I knew all about Liam and his family. He was going to stay here, just like his father. Then one day I met Liam's mother Connie. She was lucky, getting out as soon as she realized her husband was a nobody going nowhere, and a kid's sticky hands clinging to her leg. "Mom, Mom, Mom" all day long. A husband who constantly stank of cheap beer, working overtime at the farm as often as he could, which wasn't often. Connie knew about him and the waitress at the diner. As soon as she found out, she began hiding away money until she saved enough to get out. She kissed little Liam goodbye before he left for school, fixed her husband's lunch, and sent him off to work. Then she grabbed her scuffed green suitcase and hightailed it out of Benson.

Not much changed here in this time between the time I came for her, and now. The only difference was that Connie didn't ask any questions. Evie was asking quite a few.

I knew I couldn't push too hard with her. Evie might be trapped, but she was stubborn. She wasn't like the others - not to me, and not to Jax. Something about her was important, but I couldn't put my finger on why Jax was so interested in her. It was more than just the pull I felt when we were near each other, more than the way I always wanted to touch Evie, or the way our eyes lingered on one another a little too long.

The rest of the week went by without any interaction between us at all, and it was making me jittery. Evie was making fewer trips to her locker between classes, but I knew she stopped there at the end of every day. That Friday afternoon, I decided to use this to my advantage, taking my time at my own locker. I pretended to be organizing my books, my jacket, rearranging my locker a little. Finally, Evie showed up.

"Hey, Evie," I said, trying to sound casual. I knew I needed to be cautious, like a hunter trying not to startle the deer in their scope. Her eyes darted to my face and then back to her locker. That was a start, I guess.

"Hello." Her response was supposed to seem flat, but I heard the almost imperceptible quiver in her voice. She was trying to sound like she didn't care.

"Big plans for the weekend?" I tried again.

She stopped moving, took a deep breath, and turned to face me. "What do you want?"

I felt the corner of my mouth turn upward. "I don't want anything. I'd like to be your friend, but I'm not going to force it. I don't beg." I immediately wanted to hit my forehead against the locker for trying so hard to act like I didn't care. I did care. I cared so much more than she knew.

This caught Evie visibly off-guard. It was clearly not the response she anticipated. I wanted to apologize. I wanted to tell her that I didn't mean it. Instead, I put on my jacket, grabbed my bag, and made my way to the double doors at the end of the hall. I decided to make my way to the diner, knowing Evie might end up there.

She did. She walked in alone and headed for the back where I was sitting and reading. As soon as I looked up, she froze in her tracks. I waited, assessing her body language. Evie was facing me, maintaining eye contact, positioned to continue toward me. This was good. When she didn't move for several seconds, I slowly raised my right hand, waved my fingers, and then looked back down at my book. Just as I'd hoped, I looked up again to see her standing next to my table.

"Are you following me?" she asked, trying her best to sound forceful. It came across as mostly fearful, which I didn't like. I didn't want her to be afraid of me.

"Of course not. I was here first. Besides, you made it pretty clear this week that you don't want anything else to do with me. Like I said, I don't beg for anyone's time, even if that includes you." Again, I wanted to kick myself. What was wrong with me? I hadn't meant to say it that way, implying that she was somehow bothering me. I hated it because the exact opposite was true. I absolutely wanted to beg her to stay, and the feeling shocked me. I wanted her to feel the same way, but there was a plan in place, and I was supposed to follow it.

"Fine," she said defiantly. She started to walk away, but something stopped her, and she turned back around. "By the way, I know what you are now."

I chuckled and closed my book. "Well, this should be good."

"You're a witch," she said quietly, placing both her hands on the table and leaning in. Her hair fell in a curtain, and I caught the scent of lavender and patchouli. I wanted to put my nose against the skin behind her ear, but forced myself to stay present, to pay attention to what she was saying.

A witch, that's what she'd called me. Well, it wasn't the first time I'd been accused of witchcraft. It was becoming clearer every day that most people had no idea that real witches were everywhere, and they weren't those floating movie witches.

"Why is it that when a woman is assertive, powerful, and knows more than someone else, she's automatically labeled a witch?" I asked, not expecting an answer.

"I don't know, but I know you're a witch."

"Evie, by those standards, maybe you are too. But, if you're not going to take this seriously, there's no point in continuing our exchange."

"Where are your parents?" Evie asked. "Why are there no family photos, no evidence that they even exist."

She had the defiance of a child refusing bedtime. It would be cute, if it weren't so damn annoying right now. Why did everyone want to know where my parents were?

I sighed. "My parents travel for work, and we don't like having our pictures taken." It was a lie I'd gotten very good at delivering. Sometimes I'd add a little bit of sadness, but not this time. This time it was a simple answer to a simple question.

"You've been here for, what, two months? No one has seen them. Not at the bank, not at the grocery, not anywhere in town," she said, continuing to challenge me. She slid into the seat across from me.

"They travel a lot."

She arched an eyebrow, waiting for a better answer.

I sighed again. Technology made this area of questioning so much easier than it used to be. "They do all of their banking online. They like to do their grocery shopping in the bigger cities because the organic sections are better. They do other shopping online. Do you have any other questions, Detective?"

We stared at each other intensely. Her face wasn't terribly far from mine, and I wanted to kiss her. The thought of it, imagining it, threw me off-balance every single time. Finally, the waitress interrupted.

"Um," she started timidly. "Do either of you need

anything?"

"Fries. Side of mayo. Soda," Evie ordered, her chestnut eyes locked with mine. I heard the waitress shuffle away.

"Do you really care about what my parents are up to, or what my house looks like?" I asked, my voice low, huskier than I thought it was going to be. I knew the answer, but figured I'd give her the chance to answer anyway.

"No," she answered, her voice almost a whisper.

I needed to grab control of this conversation again, steer it back on course before I did something I wasn't sure either of us were ready for. I took a deep breath and focused. "I didn't think so. So why don't you tell me what this is really about. And, by the way, I'm not a witch."

Her shoulders dropped and she leaned back.

"You seem disappointed," I said, a little amused.

"I am. I thought I was right. Plus, I've kind of always wanted to meet a witch. Like, a real one."

I waved my hand dismissively. "Oh, they're everywhere. There's that girl in homeroom, the one who wears the amethyst around her neck. She's a witch."

Evie nodded. "That makes sense, I guess," she said, more to herself than to me.

The waitress returned with Evie's order and set it down in front of her. I watched her dip a fry in the mayonnaise and pop it into her mouth. I spent a lot of time staring at her mouth.

"I researched so much," she said. "I think I actually reached the end of the internet. I couldn't find anything. Well, I couldn't find anything about you-know-who having a you-know-what. I thought maybe your family was from Salt Lake City and that maybe that's how you knew, but that didn't seem likely. Also, according to Google, you don't exist," she confided.

"Oh, I'm there. You just need to know where to look, what to look for."

"Then tell me," Evie asked, leaning toward me. "Tell me how to find out more."

I plucked a fry from her plate, ignoring my own. "All you have to do is ask."

"I thought that's what I was doing," she said, leaning back against the booth and crossing her arms over her chest.

I laughed. "You're not very good at asking for things. You're very good at demanding them though."

"Please, tell me how you knew about me and about—"

"Whoa, slow down, Speed Racer," I said. "Not here. You should know that by now. I don't know why I keep having to remind you."

I looked around and noticed that Mae Hesser was staring at us. When she noticed I was looking back at her, Mae didn't break eye contact. The look on her face said that she recognized me. This was probably not good.

"Well, excuse me. This is all very new," she said sarcastically. "What's the problem? You afraid people might find out about you?" she asked, narrowing her eyes at me.

I leaned in toward her. "I'm not worried what they'll find out about me because if you can't find it, they won't. What they're saying about you and me is a little interesting though."

"What is that supposed to mean?" I could hear the panic edging her voice. Her body tensed.

I shrugged and took another fry from her plate. "In a small town, we're big news these days. There's a lot of talk about how you traded in your male BFF for the strange new girl." She didn't say anything, but I watched her eyes narrow in on me. "Evie, Liam's feelings for you aren't the only rumors going around. Like, very specific rumors. But I told you all of this."

I watched as her face went from confused to something I couldn't quite identify. For some reason, it made my stomach knot and I found it difficult to look her in the face. I regretted what I said, for the way I said it. I knew immediately that this wasn't something she was ready to deal with.

"Tell me again," she said, her voice low. I got the distinct impression that she was looking for something, but I didn't have a clue what it was.

I also didn't want to lie to her. I decided to just start and see how she reacted.

"Well, Liam's upset because you're spending so much time with me. Guys at school are jealous because I'm spending all my time with you. Girls at school are mad because the guys are paying so much attention to me and you," I said, keeping my voice low so that only she could hear me. Her eyes were searching my face for anything I wasn't saying, so I decided to just drop the hammer. "And a lot of people are wondering what's going on between us."

Evie looked worried, a little embarrassed. She took a deep breath and stole a quick glance around the diner. When she realized no one was looking at them, I saw her shoulders relax.

"I didn't mean to upset you," I told her. "People are assholes, honey. You should hear the things they say about each other. Don't worry about them, okay? With any luck, you won't have to deal with them for much longer. And it isn't any of their business anyway."

We locked eyes and my stomach dropped. The look in Evie's eyes, the sudden intensity of it…I'd seen that look before – curiosity, hope. I was more confused than I'd been a moment before.

"Yeah, I guess you're right," Evie said, nodding slowly and looking downward.

"Not what you were hoping to hear?" I asked, the

confusion evident in my voice. She quickly raised her head and met my eyes.

"No, that's not it," she said. She was lying, but I didn't want to press yet. "I just can't wait to get out of here."

CHAPTER SIXTEEN

LILITH

EVIE NEVER ASKED ANYTHING ELSE, INSTEAD she went home.

I paced my living room for close to a half hour that night. Why didn't I ever feel any closer to completing my assignment whenever I spent time with her? Why didn't I ever feel like I was getting anywhere with her at all? We just danced around things, each too afraid to ask the other what we really wanted to know: what's happening between us? Instead, I was spending far too much time trying to decipher what each minute twitch in her face meant, what was veiled in each of her responses. As much as I wanted to say that she was an easy read, I was wrong. She was an enigma of the most frustrating kind.

I tried to give her space during school the next day, hoping she'd come to me on her own. She didn't. I did catch her staring a few times, but then her eyes would dart away quickly. She was so close to figuring me out. She had no idea how close. But she'd gone in a different direction, thinking that I'm a witch. I laughed to myself. If she only knew.

I was sitting in my dining room when I felt it, that overwhelming turn of my stomach that indicated that someone needed me. And that someone wasn't far away, I could feel that much. But I had no idea who it could be.

I got into my car and drove, letting the feeling guide me. It guided me to a two-story modern country house, if that was even a thing. The yard was impeccably maintained, with flower beds all around the perimeter of the house. Large windows were on either side of the front door, each with their own window boxes full of purple flowers.

Confused, I put my car in park and sat in front of it, staring up at it, recognizing it. I'd been here before. It was years ago, and some little things were different, but it was definitely the same house.

The curiosity was too much. I let my feet lead me up the walkway and onto the very tiny porch. I stood in front of the door, looking into its window, hoping to see something, anything, that might indicate why I was here without an invitation. Nothing came. So I reached up and knocked twice.

I could only assume that the woman who answered the door was Evie's mother. They looked almost nothing alike, but I knew her face. It was aged, but not enough that I didn't remember her from that night eighteen years before, screaming for her baby girl. The woman in front of me had light eyes, light hair, and a petite frame. I just stared at her. She stared back. There was no confusion – she was the same woman. But the pull in my gut wasn't for her.

"Um, can I help you?" she asked me, blinking rapidly. I opened my mouth to answer, but a small girl bounded into view.

"Hi!" she said excitedly. "I'm Bea."

The feeling in my stomach grew more intense. She was the one.

It was a little confusing. I'd never gone to anyone this young. I smiled down at her. "I'm Lilith, Evie's friend. You must be Evie's little sister. Is she home?"

"Yep! I'll take you, come on." She grabbed my hand in her tiny one and pulled me inside. I heard her mother laugh, close the door, and go into another room.

At the bottom of the staircase, I stopped and pulled lightly on her hand. Bea stopped and turned around to look at me.

"Hey, are you okay?" I asked her tentatively. "Like, has something happened to you?"

She stared at me for a moment before looking down at the carpet. "How did you know?" she asked softly. I was right.

"Just a feeling," I said, trying to give her a reassuring smile.

I stood behind Bea as she knocked lightly on a door to the left of the top of the staircase.

"Evie? Can I come in?" she asked softly.

"Uh, yeah," I heard Evie say from the other side of the door.

Bea opened the door slowly. A small cat with a bell on its collar went in first, followed by Bea. I took a step in after taking a deep breath. I'd never been in Evie's room before.

"Lilith?"

Evie's voice was so high-pitched that I half-expected dogs to start barking. I stared at her, trying not to laugh. She was sitting on a gray comforter, a yellow unicorn-covered pencil in her hand. She cleared her throat and tried again.

"What are you doing here?" she asked, her voice a little closer to its normal pitch.

"Your bedroom is not what I pictured," I told her, looking around. There were white Christmas lights hanging in vertical strands behind her headboard, a thick furry white rug at the foot of her bed, and dark gray curtains on the only window. I smiled as I walked over and touched a container of brightly-colored pencils with the reverence of a holy relic. These were things she loved, things that made her happy. I picked up a photograph of Evie and her mother on a boat, both of them smiling widely, the sun in their eyes. The smile is where she looked like her mother.

"Well?" Evie asked again. She looked nervous about me touching her things, so I stopped and clasped my hands behind my back.

"I thought I'd stop by and finish our last conversation, but I think someone needs you first," I said, gesturing toward Bea. She was staring down at her socked feet.

"Bea, what's going on?" Evie asked.

Bea looked over at me for encouragement. Out of the corner of my eye, Evie looked confused.

"Beatrice, what's going on?" Evie asked again, a worried edge to her voice.

"Just tell her, sweetie. Your sister can help," I told Bea. Bea nodded, and I looked over at Evie, who looked suspicious of me.

I heard Bea sigh. "There's a boy in the play with me. Well, he's not really in the play. He helps the teacher when we practice. He hands us the props." Her voice was so soft, and she was stalling.

"And you like him...?" Evie asked, confused about

what was going on. Bea's head snapped up and looked Evie straight in the eye, a look of anger and disgust on her pale freckled face. Bea might've looked just like her mother, but there was a lot of Evie in that personality.

"No, I do not! I hate him. He hides my stuff, throws the props at me, and always tells me that I'm the worst part of the whole entire play. Wednesday, when it was just me and him in the room where we wait 'til we have to go on stage, he kicked me. Real hard. Just because I told him to stop hiding my stuff."

"Show her," I said to Bea. She hesitantly raised the right side of her daisy-covered dress, revealing a nasty purple softball-sized bruise on her thigh. Fire shot through my entire body at the sight of it. Evie leaped from the bed. Something about the way that Evie reacted made me sit down. It felt a lot like being shoved.

"Are you okay? Did you tell anyone? Did you tell Mom and Dad?" Evie asked, examining the bruise, her hands shaking.

"No! I can't! He said if I tell anyone, it'll be worse. None of the kids like him. He's so mean, Evie. Everyone says he kills the cats by his house. I don't want him to kill me!" she said, panicked. My gut twisted. I wanted to rip that kid's arms from his body.

Evie rubbed Bea's upper arms, trying to calm her down. She was breathing fast, her eyes wide, her face pale. "No one is going to kill you, Bea. I'll tell Mom and

Dad with you. They won't let him hurt you again."

Bea shook her head emphatically. "No. I won't tell. I just want to know what to do."

Evie stayed silent. Her jaw was set, her teeth grinding together. She was furious, and it looked good on her. She looked over at me, and I tried not to smile at her.

"Bea, who is this kid?" Evie asked, turning her attention back to her little sister.

"Jimmy Parker," Bea said reluctantly.

"Okay, no Mom and Dad," Evie said. "But I'm taking you to rehearsal tomorrow, okay?"

Bea sighed and her face relaxed a little. Beat flung herself forward, her slender arms wrapping around Evie's neck, squeezing tight. Evie hugged her back.

"Alright, alright, you're choking me," Evie joked, untangling Bea's arms from her neck. "You're like an octopus."

Bea laughed. Her mood seemed a little lighter, but it was obvious that she was still worried and scared.

"Okay, get out of here and let me talk to Lilith," Evie said, smoothing out Bea's hair. The energy vibrating off of Evie was protective. I could feel it as I watched Bea smile and nod, leaving the room and closing the door quietly behind her.

Evie turned to look at me. The corner of my mouth turned upward involuntarily. She looked a little taken aback by it.

"What is the matter with you?" she asked me. "You look amused by all of this."

"I'm sorry, I don't mean to be," I told her. "I'm not amused and it isn't funny. It's just that I like this side of you, all protective and full of fire." I was very aware that my tone was flirtatious. She just stared at me.

"You do?"

I rested my elbows on my knees, leaning forward. My top slumped off of my shoulder and it did not go unnoticed by Evie.

"Definitely. I never really thought that you were passive, but this just proves that I was right about you all along," I said. She looked confused, so I returned to the original topic. "Do you know this kid?"

She sighed heavily. "Yeah, I know him. Honestly, I'm not surprised. Jimmy's dad is awful," she told me, picking at her fingernails. "Emma, Jimmy's mom, is always covered in bruises. Everyone pretends not to see, but we see it. And instead of trying to help her, everyone just gossips about them." Evie shook her head and looked at me. "James is the worst kind of bully. Aside from hitting his wife on a pretty regular basis, he also tries bullying everyone else in his path. Most of us just try to stay out of his way."

I balled my hands into fists that rested on my knees. I hated men like this, always thinking they could do whatever they wanted to people that were weaker than them. I was seething, my blood feeling like it was boiling as I looked at Evie staring at the floor.

"I had the distinct displeasure of having a small run-in with him once at my parents' bookstore," Evie continued. "Emma purchased a book that she was pretty excited about reading. It was one of those paperback romance novels," she said. I wondered if she read those books too.

"Anyway, two days later, I was hanging out with Liam at the bookstore, and James came bursting through the door. Like, he knocked down the bells that hung above it. He threw Emma's new novel onto the counter, red-faced and ranting about how no wife of his would be neglecting her duties to read some stupid book," Evie said, doing an imitation of what I could only assume was this James guy.

"He wanted his money back. I, unable to keep my mouth shut as usual, didn't help the situation. I said, just loud enough for him to hear me, that his wife wouldn't need those books if he spent five minutes being nice to her instead of being an asshole. He didn't take that well. He didn't hit me, but he sure wanted to," she laughed without any humor.

"She should know that she doesn't have to put up with that from any man," I told her. "Your sister should know that too. So, what's your plan?"

I looked into Evie's eyes. That feeling from earlier,

that shove, was still radiating off of her, but it didn't send me reeling backward this time.

"But he isn't a man, Lilith!" Evie said loudly. "He's a twelve-year-old boy. But he won't do it again."

I smiled at her. "So you do have a plan," I cooed.

She sighed and looked at me. "I wouldn't call it a plan, but he won't do it again."

Something in the way she said that he wouldn't do this again made warmth race through parts of me that had been asleep for a very long time. I couldn't quite identify it, but it felt like...hunger? Excitement? A feeling that only happened in R-rated movies?

"What time are you and Bea leaving tomorrow?" I asked, my mouth dry.

Our eyes stayed locked.

"Noon," she said softly.

It was quiet for a few beats, and then I jumped up, unable to sit in whatever this feeling was for much longer without doing something – anything – about it.

"I'll see you at noon," I said.

I stood and walked briskly from the room, my heels clicking on the hardwood. I felt her eyes following me, so I gave her exaggerated hip swings all the way to the door. Just before closing it behind me, I turned, gave her a coy smirk, and winked. I stood just outside of the door for a moment, taking a few deep breaths.

"What in the hell just happened?" I heard her say

out loud. I smiled to myself and made my way to the staircase.

CHAPTER SEVENTEEN

EVIE

I TOSSED AND TURNED ALL NIGHT AS I THOUGHT about Lilith. Whatever happened between us in my bedroom that evening had me too wound up to sleep. The worst part was that I'd see her the next day, and I didn't know how to act around her anymore, or if I was reading too much into it.

I didn't know anything about her, not really. The only thing I did know was that she somehow had a lot of information on people in Benson, on me, by no discernible means. I knew what her parents did for a living, if that was even true. I knew that she was smart, funny, and beautiful.

I knew that every single time I was around her, it

made my insides hum, my heart race, and made me worry that I was always going to say something stupid.

I rolled over in bed and tried to adjust my pillow. From where I was laying, I could see out of my window. I could see gray wisps covering the moon. I wondered what Lilith was doing and then rolled my eyes at my own ridiculousness, rolling over onto my back. However, the sound of my cell phone vibrating hard against the surface of my desk sent a jolt through my entire body and my thoughts right back to the present.

I took a deep breath and tried to steady the heart that was threatening to burst from my chest. I glanced quickly at my bedside clock to see that it was two in the morning. I thought about ignoring my phone, but what else was I doing? Certainly not sleeping.

I pushed a button and my phone lit up. There was one text message, and it was from Lilith. I smiled involuntarily.

Saturday 2:02 AM:

What's your favorite color?

She sent me a text at two in the morning to find out my favorite color? I felt myself smiling again, glad that she appeared to at least be thinking about me too. I pursed my lips and quickly typed a response.

Saturday 2:04 AM:

You woke me up
for this?

I sat up in bed and leaned against the wall it was
bumped up against. I was suddenly too jittery to lay
down. I pulled my knees up to my chest and bundled my
comforter around me, waiting for her to answer.

Saturday 2:07 AM:

You weren' t asleep.
And you didn' t
answer the question.

I laughed quietly. I hated talking about myself, not
that I ever really got the opportunity with anyone but
Liam. No one ever cared about my favorite color before
now. Most of my conversations with kids at school,
when they did happen, were surface stuff. Occasionally
someone wondered why I didn't have a boyfriend, why
I didn't go to a particular party, or to just ask something
rude. I guess in a town this small, no one really needed to
ask those things. People just seemed to know.

I didn't know what to tell her. It wasn't some generic
green or sky blue. I took a deep breath.

Saturday 2:10 AM:

This is embarrassing,
but you know that
color the sky turns
right at sunset?
That crazy fiery
orange and red?
That' s my favorite.

She was definitely going to think I was a nerd.

Saturday 2:12 AM:

I love that so much.
It' s so specific.
Are you sure Liam
is the only artist?

I smiled down at my phone. Whatever was happening between us, I liked it. I didn't feel like this around anyone else. With everyone else, I didn't worry about looking stupid or saying the wrong thing. They didn't like me anyway, so it didn't really matter. I didn't get excited about seeing anyone the way I did with her, while simultaneously feeling scared to death. I wanted to reach for her any time she was around, and I certainly wished she was sitting next to me on my bed in the middle of the night.

Saturday 2:17 AM:

Hey, did you fall
asleep?

Just as I was typing out a response, my phone started vibrating in my hands. She was calling me. I immediately held my breath, not knowing whether I should answer. I just stared at her name on my phone for a second.

And then my thumb accidentally pressed the button to answer it, and I think my heart actually stopped. I just stared down at it, hearing the faint sound of her voice saying my name. I shook my head, let out the breath I'd been holding, and put the phone up to my ear.

"Evie? Are you there?"

"Yeah, sorry, I'm here," I said into the phone, trying to keep my voice as quiet as I could. The last thing I wanted was to wake up everyone in the house. "You know it's almost two-thirty, right?" I closed my eyes, and immediately regretted sounding like I didn't want to talk.

"Do you want me to let you go?" she asked.

"No!" I said a little too frantically. I cleared my throat and tried to calm down. "I mean, no, you're okay."

I heard her laugh. "What are you doing right now?

"I'm sky-diving. What do you think I'm doing?"

Her laugh came through loudly this time, and it made me smile. I liked that she thought I was funny.

Liam was the only person that thought I was funny. Well, Bea did, but she was a kid.

"Do you want to go for a drive?" she asked me.

I wanted to scream that I would be ready and outside in five minutes, but the idea of being alone in a car with her in the middle of the night...I wasn't sure that I was ready for that yet. So, I talked myself - and her - out of it instead.

"We're going to see each other in, like, nine and a half hours," I said, letting out a fake laugh. I hated myself a little for doing it.

She was quiet for a moment, and when she finally spoke, my stomach flipped. "But I want to see you now," she said, her voice quiet.

I closed my eyes. I was so out of my element with this. I'd never even gone on a date before, let alone with a girl.

"I want to see you too," I said quietly, the words coming out before I could stop them.

"Then let me come get you. You can sneak out, right?"

I could, but I didn't tell her. I liked Lilith. More than liked, I felt somehow connected to her, and those weren't feelings I was ready to deal with. So, I lied to her.

"I have to go," I whispered. "I hear my mom coming. I'll see you at noon."

And with that, I hung up on her. Right away, I regretted it. I took a deep breath and hit the button to call her back.

"Hey," she said sadly after two rings. I felt awful.

"I'm sorry, I feel so stupid. Yes, I can sneak out. Do you still want to go? I totally understand if you don't —"

"I'll be there in a few minutes," she said, happily interrupting me. And then it was her turn to hang up on me.

We sat awkwardly in Lilith's car as we drove through town. I didn't know what to say. For some reason, this was harder than just sitting in her living room, or sitting in my bedroom with my parents downstairs. Was it this awkward for other kids? Was it awkward for someone like Lilith?

"What are you thinking about over there?" Lilith asked.

I opened my mouth to answer and then closed it again. I couldn't tell her what I was thinking, could I?

"Nothing really," I lied. "Just thinking about how small this town is. Do you realize it took us exactly twenty-three minutes to drive through the entire thing?"

She laughed, which made me smile.

"I didn't realize you were timing us," she said, still laughing.

"I didn't realize that I was."

It was quiet for a moment, and then Lilith's voice

filled the space. "Wanna drive outside of town, rebel girl?"

It was my turn to laugh. I was no rebel. A rebel wouldn't survive long in this place. But something about the way she said it made me wish I was.

"Careful," I joked. "Next thing you know, I'll have us robbing banks and heading for Cuba."

"Would that really be so bad?"

"Robbing banks? Yeah. Yeah, it would be."

I saw her shake her head. "No, weirdo. Taking off to someplace right now."

It didn't sound bad at all. Nothing sounded better than the thought of telling her to hit the gas and head for the border with nothing but the clothes on our backs. I could see the entire thing in my head, clear as crystal. Windows down, singing along to old eighties hair metal on the radio, speeding down the highway, wind blowing my hair everywhere.

But I wasn't that girl. Any trace of humor I had a moment ago was gone. Now I just wanted to hide under my blankets. So, I faked a yawn.

"I should probably get home before someone realizes I'm missing. My mom likes to make impromptu check-ins when she can't sleep," I lied. I was lying a lot lately.

Even in the dark, I could see sadness and disappointment fall over Lilith's face.

"Yeah, okay," she said.

"Hey," I said, elbowing her and trying to lighten the

mood. "We'll see each other in a few hours, right?"

She nodded and turned onto my street.

CHAPTER EIGHTEEN

EVIE

I ROLLED OVER AND IMMEDIATELY remembered how I'd probably blown it with Lilith just a few hours before. I looked at the clock, and it read 10:58 AM. I had two minutes before my alarm would go off. I groaned, pulling the blankets up over my head. How was I supposed to face her today? I couldn't look her in the face, that was for sure.

Before I knew it, Stevie Nicks was blaring from my phone, signaling that it was time to get up. If Lilith was still coming, she would be here soon, and then we'd be on our way to confront Bea's bully. Before my feet had a chance to hit the floor, my phone alerted me to a text message.

Saturday 11:01 AM:

I'll be there in an
hour. Maybe we can
talk after?

My stomach dropped. It was Lilith. Before I could overthink it, I typed a quick reply saying that would work, and forced myself out of bed. I stumbled sleepily over to my dresser, yanking open the top drawer with a yawn. I sighed heavily as I looked at the contents of the drawer. It was nothing but old thrift store and band T-shirts, half of which I inherited from my dad. I closed the drawer and walked across the room to my closet. I groaned in frustration when I realized that all the closet contained were two floral dresses my mother bought me over a year ago, sweaters in various shades of gray and black, and my winter coat. I grabbed a pair of jeans and a red zip-up hoodie in the very back of the closet, and then I pulled a ratty Rolling Stone T-shirt with a partially-torn seam at the collar out of my dresser.

I was showered quickly and stood staring at my reflection in my bedroom mirror. Did I just comb my hair and go? Put on mascara? Also, why was this so hard? She knew what I looked like. I sighed heavily and decided to comb my hair and then put on the mascara. I definitely looked more awake. I was dressed and ready with half an hour to spare.

I was eating a bowl of cereal at the kitchen table when my mother walked in.

"Hey, Bea says you're taking her to rehearsal today?"

I nodded, my mouth full of cereal.

"Okay...why?" she asked, sounding understandably suspicious of my motives.

"I need to go to the library anyway, so I thought I'd do that while she's singing or dancing or whatever they do in there." Honestly, I was a little surprised at how easily the lie came. My mother continued staring at me.

"Okay," she said hesitantly. "Do you need the car?"

"Thanks, but Lilith is actually picking us up. We have a couple of tests next week to study for, so we're studying together. If we need more time, I'll probably drop Bea off after rehearsal and head over to Lilith's, if that's cool."

My mother nodded, still looking suspicious of me. After a few seconds, she left the kitchen, and I let out a breath I didn't realize I'd been holding.

I finished eating, put my bowl in the sink, and went to see if my sister needed help getting ready. By the time we had her script in hand and tracked down her left shoe, I heard Lilith's car horn outside. We called our goodbyes to our parents and ran out to Lilith's copper-colored CR-V.

"Hello, ladies." Lilith's eyes were covered by large round sunglasses. Her car smelled like new leather. She was smiling, so I took that as a positive sign and smiled nervously back at her.

"Hi, Lilith," Bea said cheerfully from the backseat.

"Hey, Bumble Bea. You ready to take care of this bully business?" Lilith asked her. I did a double-take at Lilith's use of my nickname for Bea. Had I used that when Lilith was around?

"Yeah…but what if it gets worse?" Bea asked.

"It won't. Your big sis is going to make sure of it, aren't you, Evie?"

I grunted my confirmation. The trip to the elementary school was short, but each second we got closer, my blood boiled that much more. I kept reminding myself of this kid's age, but also who his family was. He was likely raised to think this was okay, that he could do anything he wanted. That would not be the case after today.

We pulled up to the school behind a few of the parents all dropping their kids off for rehearsal. Lilith put the car in park, shut off the engine, and looked over at me, smiling.

"You ready, Killer?" Lilith asked, winking at me.

I rolled my eyes, but I had to fight so hard to keep from smiling. I still wasn't sure whether I was blushing or not. "Um, Bea, we'll walk you in."

Bea sighed nervously and walked inside with me and Lilith. There were kids everywhere, most of which were singing different songs at different decibels. I wasn't sure how long my ears could take this. Lilith, on the other hand, was even worse than me at masking her disgust. I elbowed her in the ribs, motioning to the parents eyeballing us. Lilith put her hands up in apology and plastered a look on her face that was probably supposed to be contentment or something, but it mostly looked like someone trying to hide their annoyance.

"Do you see him anywhere around here?" I asked Bea.

"There," Bea said, grabbing my hand. She pointed to a skinny boy, a little taller than almost everyone else, with shaggy dirt-brown hair. He looked just like his father.

"Okay, why don't you go get ready? Lilith and I will be here right before you get out."

Bea nodded nervously and let go of my hand. She walked over to where a group of girls greeted her with excitement. Well, at least Bea had friends here.

"That's him," I told Lilith, an edge to my voice.

"That's the bully?" she asked me.

Before I knew what was happening, my legs carried me in Jimmy's direction. I didn't bother asking Lilith to come with me.

I walked up to him and he looked nervously up at me. He knew exactly whose sister I was. Then I leaned down and whispered in his ear.

"If you touch my sister again, if you touch anyone again, if you so much as look at my sister funny, I will make sure your father finds out. I will make sure that everyone knows what your father does to your mother, and to you. I'll make sure he knows that you're the one who told."

I watched Jimmy's eyes widen as I kept talking. "Maybe you'll get lucky and your dad will forgive you and stop being an asshole. Or maybe they'll be finding pieces of your mother all over Benson."

As the words came out of me, I felt sick, but I couldn't stop them. He was a twelve-year-old boy and I was telling him his father might murder his mother. But still, the fury in me, the lava bubbling in my veins, it took over. I couldn't stop it.

The fear on Jimmy's face was evident on his face. He stared straight at me, not blinking, not moving.

He didn't even blink when urine began to soak through the front of his pants and down his legs.

CHAPTER NINETEEN

EVIE

IT SOUNDED LIKE I WAS UNDERWATER. VOICES were muffled, and the blood rushed through my ears as I walked toward Lilith. My heart was pounding as adrenaline flooded my entire body. Lilith grabbed my arm and said we had to go just as the commotion started. I watched as frantic parents and teachers approached the boy. He was staring at me, wide-eyed and shaking. I held his gaze as a brunette woman touched his shoulders and presumably asked if he was okay. He just kept looking at me until he disappeared behind the swarm of gathering teachers and parents. My stomach rolled and lurched as I watched them walk down a hallway.

I looked at the clusters of adults whispering to each

other as Lilith pulled my arm. I thought I heard Lilith say something from her spot next to me, but I couldn't make it out. She sounded so far away. I felt heat rise up through my body and scorch my cheeks. As soon as I felt the wave of nausea crash over me, sure that I might vomit, Lilith was pulling me by the arm through the glass doors of the school entrance, the heels of her boots clicking rapidly on the pavement. The voices of panicked parents spilled out behind us onto the walkway, but were cut off almost immediately by the closing doors. It wasn't until we were inside Lilith's car that my voice came back.

"What did you do?" she asked, her voice a little... cautious? Curious? I couldn't figure out her tone. "I mean, what did you say to him?"

I didn't answer. Instead, she stared at me for a moment before turning the key in the ignition. She hit the gas pedal, sending me slamming into the back of my seat. I saw her sneaking glances at me, waiting for some kind of explanation as she maneuvered the car out of the parking lot and merged into the traffic on the main road.

"Evie? Please."

"I didn't do anything," I lied, not taking my eyes off of the road in front of us. I couldn't tell her what I said to Jimmy, not now. What would she think?

"That's a lie," she said. Her voice was very matter-of-fact.

I didn't say anything. I couldn't argue with her.

"Is he going to be okay?" I asked, my voice quiet. It was all I could think to ask. I needed reassurance that I hadn't scarred that kid for life.

"How would I know? I don't know what happened. But honestly, do you care?" Lilith asked.

The question caught me off-guard, as most of her questions seemed to. I hadn't had any time to think about that, about whether I cared what happened to Jimmy. I watched the orange and red trees whir past us. I replayed the last twenty-four hours in my head. The bruise on Bea's thigh, Lilith asking me what I was going to do about it, whispering the threat in Jimmy's ear, the look on his face. I knew that I should care. He was just a kid. But so was my sister, and the memory of that bruise on her thigh…

"No. I don't care." The realization spilled from my mouth before I could stop it. I said it more to myself than to Lilith, and I felt something inside me shift. Something in me felt a little lighter, but also like a fire just starting to flicker into existence.

"Well, there's that, I guess," Lilith said, pulling her car into the small gravel lot of Leo's Pizzeria. There was only one other car in the parking lot, a beat up red Ford truck. I groaned. The owner of that truck was the last person I wanted to deal with.

It belonged to Liam's father.

"What?" Lilith asked, shutting off the engine.

"I think Liam or his dad might be here. We should

go someplace else. I don't want to deal with either of them."

Lilith unbuckled her seat belt. "Look, we're going to have to deal with your boyfriend sooner or later."

"He's not my boyfriend, Lilith. This, you know."

"Oh, relax. I was just kidding, I'm sorry. You're just so tense all the time."

"I am not," I said defiantly. Okay, so Lilith wasn't the first person to ever accuse me of being wound a little tightly. It was becoming obnoxious. "What do you mean by 'we' anyway?"

She didn't answer. Instead, she opened her car door and stepped out. I sat in place for a moment longer before getting out and following her. I had a very strong sense of dread as we walked across the empty parking lot toward the front of the restaurant. A little bell on the door alerted everyone inside to our entrance. As I suspected, Mr. Donovan, Liam's father, was sitting at the counter, talking way too loudly to Leo, the owner. I tried to lead Lilith to a table out of his eyesight without letting him know we were there, but I wasn't fast enough.

"Well, well, well," Liam's father said loudly. "If it ain't Miss High-and-Mighty." He wasn't ever quiet about his dislike of me. For some reason, he seemed to believe that I thought I was too good for Liam.

"Come on, Lilith, let's sit back there," I said, trying to ignore him and pull her away. The volume of his voice made it clear that he'd been drinking, and I wasn't interested in listening to it.

"Oh, so now she won't talk to me!" His voice boomed through the entire restaurant.

I sighed and rubbed the bridge of my nose. I muttered an apology to Lilith, but she was already turning toward Mr. Donovan.

"What is your problem?" she demanded, hands on her hips, staring him down.

I touched her elbow. "Please, Lilith, let's just go." She pulled away from me and continued staring at him, waiting for an answer.

Lilith's demeanor seemed to catch him by surprise. He was quiet for a moment, swaying every-so-slightly on his stool. It had been awhile since I'd last seen him. Years of heavy drinking had taken its toll on him. His eyes were puffy and the space under them had what looked like purple bruises. His white T-shirt was stained and stretched snugly across his bloated stomach.

Just then a huge guffaw erupted from him, a laugh so similar to Liam's that it was unsettling. His belly shook, and he reached up to rub his graying beard.

"Well, what do we have here?" he asked, mostly to himself. His eyes traveled up and down Lilith's curves. He licked his lips and looked like he wanted to devour her. I immediately wanted to rip his tongue out at the root and punch him in the throat. Lilith wrinkled her nose in disgust.

"It's never going to happen," Lilith told him. "Do you honestly think that any woman would want you? Just take a look at yourself, drinking yourself into a stupor every day and every night, stinking of cheap beer and self-loathing. I find you abhorrent. Evie finds you abhorrent. Your son avoids you any chance he gets. He's probably living in a tree somewhere to avoid you since Evie's mad at him. So just turn around, eat your food, and go home. Sleep it off. And keep your eyes above my nose."

My mouth hung open. Leo stopped wiping the counter with his dirty gray rag to watch the exchange. Mr. Donovan, on the other hand, was as red as Lilith's hair. His breathing was heavy, his fists clenched.

"Lilith, stop. Come sit down," I begged.

She never broke eye contact with him. "What, Evie? Is he going to hit me like he hits Liam? Like he hit Connie?"

All at once, the air was sucked out of the room. The shock of her question was evident on the face of Liam's father. Memories and questions flashed quickly across his face and in his eyes. He wanted to know how this very new girl knew his wife. I wanted to know as well.

"How...?" he stuttered.

"Oh, please, Bruce. Everyone knows. And maybe, if he's smart, your son will follow in his mother's footsteps and leave you here to rot."

Mr. Donovan's expression was confused. His eyes looked almost sad. He opened his mouth to say something, but nothing came out.

"Lilith, stop it," I said sternly, gripping her arm and pulling her away. Lilith put her hands up in surrender.

"I'm hungry now anyway," Lilith said, following me to a table in the back.

"Well, I'm not," I said.

From behind the counter, Leo looked uncertain about whether he wanted to take our order, but he eventually walked over, not taking his eyes off of Lilith. It was like he was waiting for her to jump all over him with some dark secret he'd been hiding. When all she did was look at him and smile, he visibly relaxed. A pretty girl like Lilith was disarming, to say the least. We ordered drinks. Lilith decided against the food when she looked at the frustrated expression on my face.

"Okay, you know I have to ask," I said after Leo walked away. My jaw was aching from keeping it clenched. "What in the actual fuck was that?"

Lilith blinked, her face void of any expression. "What was what?"

I waved my hands around the room emphatically. "Um, all of everything. Me, Mae Hesser, Liam's parents. Do you need a list?" I searched Lilith's face for…I didn't know what I was looking for. Regret? Embarrassment? A hint about how she could possibly know any of the information she just spouted? Instead, I found Lilith staring back at me, a look of impatience on her face from this line of questioning.

"That was nothing. That was me protecting you, and protecting Liam's mother."

"Protecting me from what? And how do you even know Mrs. Donovan?"

"You can ask me all the questions you want once you tell me what you did to that kid."

I groaned and rubbed my face with my hands. I didn't know what to tell her. I didn't know what came over me and made me say those things. "I don't know, Lilith. I really don't. I don't know what came over me. Nothing's made sense since I met you."

She stayed silent for a moment, just staring at me before she spoke again. "You're free to walk away." She sounded almost hurt.

I stared across the table at her. My heart dropped into my stomach. I didn't know what to say. It was true, I could just get up and walk out the door and never speak to her again. I could pretend none of this ever happened. I could pretend Lilith didn't even exist. I could pretend that she hadn't called me in the middle of the night because she wanted to know my favorite color. The thought of pretending any of that made me feel like I'd taken a punch to the gut.

"How am I supposed to walk away from you?" I

asked her before I could stop myself.

Lilith smiled a little, but she didn't look happy. Her eyes looked so sad. "I hope you won't. I hope that once you learn more about me, about what I can offer you, what I represent, that you won't run screaming for the hills."

I was confused again. "What you represent?"

Lilith leaned in, the smile on her face changing. Her eyes flashed with something I wasn't sure I recognized.

"Freedom. Independence. Never letting anyone make your choices for you again. Doing whatever you want when you want. You have power."

She stared at me.

For the first time, I wasn't scared - I was intrigued. "Power? I have power?"

Lilith nodded. "You sure have something, I'm just not sure what it is yet."

I didn't say anything, and neither did Lilith. We just stared at one another, her words hanging in the air between us. My thoughts raced too fast to make sense of them, each question in my head fighting to be asked first. Finally, after a few moments, I knew what I wanted to ask.

"How? What do I have to do to...find my power?"

Before she could answer, Leo strolled over with our drinks. He sat them down on the sticky tabletop and walked away, but not before casting suspicious glances at us. Neither of us touched our glasses right away.

"We can't discuss this here, and we still need to pick up your sister in a bit." Lilith unwrapped her straw and dropped it into her glass. "Are you worried Jimmy might tell people what you said?"

I couldn't stop worrying about it.

"I don't think he'll say anything," I told her. I was pretty sure he wouldn't.

"Well, I'm sure he won't be bothering Bea anymore. Aren't you happy about that?"

I nodded slowly, rolling her words around in my head.

"I am happy." It struck me for the first time that this was true. Earlier, I'd told Lilith that I didn't care what happened to Jimmy, but that wasn't true, not exactly. I didn't care whether Jimmy would be okay, and I was happy that he was so terrified.

"Good," Lilith said, interrupting my thoughts.

When we returned to the school to pick Bea up from rehearsal, she came running outside, a huge smile plastered across her face. She jumped into the back seat, cheery and red-faced from the cold. She was talking a mile a minute.

"Whoa, slow down, lady," I said, laughing. "Say that again?"

"Listen! We were all getting ready in the dressing room when Sammy Collier ran in and told us that Jimmy Parker peed his pants! They had to call his mom and everything! Sammy says Jimmy's crazy now 'cause he won't talk or nothing, but I think he's just scared. Our teacher said he has to go to the doctor now," Bea explained, buckling her seat belt.

Lilith and I exchanged a knowing look.

"If he bothers me again, I'll just call him —"

"You won't call him anything," I told her. "You don't get to bully him back." Just because I was suddenly of questionable moral character didn't mean she had to be.

"I know," Bea said quietly, sounding a little disappointed.

"Yeah, you just be the best Matilda ever, and forget about that kid," Lilith said, winking at Bea in the rear view mirror.

"Yeah!" Bea exclaimed.

A few minutes later, we pulled up in front of my house.

"I'll just walk Bea inside and then we'll head to your place," I said, unbuckling my seat belt. As I reached for the door handle, I heard Lilith unbuckling.

"I'm going to meet your parents," she said.

I don't know why, but this felt like a bad idea. "Um… didn't you meet them last night?"

She didn't say anything and just got out of the car.

Before I could object again, I was following Bea and Lilith up the front walk. Bea burst through the front door, yelling for our parents. We found them in the family room. Bea immediately began telling them all about what happened in rehearsal, particularly about Jimmy Parker. I watched my mother's eyes widen in alarm.

"Is he okay? Evie, were you there?"

"No," I lied. "I guess we left right before it happened." I suddenly remembered Lilith standing beside me. "Sorry, Mom, Dad, this is my friend, Lilith."

Lilith reached out and took my mother's hand. "Hi, Mrs. Franklin." And then Lilith paused, staring intently at my mother. There was a weird look on Lilith's face, and I couldn't make sense of it.

"It's nice to see you again, Lilith," my mother said warmly. "Though I still can't figure out why you look so familiar," she laughed.

Lilith smiled, nervousness creeping into her features. It piqued my interest. "I just have one of those faces, I guess," Lilith said. They stayed silent, just examining each other's faces, still grasping each other's hand.

"And this is my dad," I said, interrupting whatever was going on. Lilith reached out and shook his hand, trying unsuccessfully to seem more composed than she was a moment ago.

"It's good to meet you, Lilith," my father said, smiling. "That's a really pretty name. What brings your family to Benson?"

My mother patted the spot next to her on the blue and cream plaid sofa. Lilith sat next to her, seemingly avoiding eye contact.

"Thank you. My parents travel a lot for work, and this was more centrally located for both of them." The story came out so easily that I wondered if it was true. But even traveling parents come home occasionally, and hers never seemed to.

"Wow, that's interesting. What do they do?" my mother asked, genuinely interested.

"My mother is a flight attendant, and my father works for the government."

My mother seemed impressed. "That must be exciting! I've – we've – never been outside of Benson for more than a night or two," she laughed. I felt sad for her. I wanted my mother to have adventures.

"I guess it is, for them. They're gone a lot, so I suppose they enjoy it."

"That's got to be rough for you." The tone of my mother's voice changed into something more motherly. "Eighteen and all alone in that big house. At least you have a friend now," she said, smiling up at me.

"That I do," Lilith said, looking over at me, winking at me in a way that felt uncomfortable with my parents in the same room. I immediately felt my face flush.

"Okay, so we can all stop staring at me. Lilith, are

you ready?"

"You two don't want to stay for dinner?" my mother asked as Lilith stood up.

"Sorry, Mom, we already ate," I lied. Lilith, who I assumed was still hungry, shot an annoyed look at me.

Before my mother could respond, we were walking out the door.

CHAPTER TWENTY

LILITH

WE WERE HALFWAY TO MY HOUSE when the dark sky cracked open. The rain hit the windshield hard, like the car was being pelted with nails. As loud as it was, I barely noticed the rain. I was too distracted by sneaking glances at the girl sitting next to me, her head bobbing along to the radio.

I heard a ping and looked over to see Evie looking down at her cell phone, the light from the screen illuminating her face.

"It's Liam," she said, dropping her head against the headrest. She was biting her lower lip, looking like she didn't know whether to respond to him.

"You can always tell him you're with me," I teased.

I surprised myself by wanting him to be jealous that she was with me and not him. It would serve him right, trying so hard to keep her away from me. The look she gave me from the passenger seat told me that she didn't think I was funny. She took a deep breath. I looked away, focusing on the road.

"Text him back," I said, making the decision for her. "Tell him you're studying and you can't talk right now. If you don't, he'll come looking for you, and we don't need that right now." I didn't necessarily like making decisions for people, but Evie seemed confused a lot of the time lately.

"Yeah, you're right," she agreed, typing quickly on her phone.

I was well aware that Evie and Liam had been best friends their entire lives, and that the relationship was important to Evie. I didn't want to be responsible for coming between them, but Liam was making it very difficult. I knew how he felt about her, and I knew that he seemed to feel some sense of ownership over Evie, which made me angry. I also knew that Evie didn't feel that way about him. As far as I could tell, there hadn't been anyone she was interested in at all. In the month I'd been a student here, I'd heard all of the rumors about Evie. Some of the students thought that she and Liam were secretly dating. Others thought she was stringing him along. But most of the students thought that the reason Evie had never had a boyfriend was because she is gay. Once she started spending time with me, those rumors only became more persistent. But if Evie was aware of them, she did a great job of hiding it.

For me, it was becoming more difficult to ignore whatever was happening, and I didn't really want to. I've had entanglements with other people during my long existence, but I had the feeling that all of this was new territory for the both of us. It didn't help that neither of us was acknowledging it. I wanted to reach over, to put my hand on her thigh, and just keep driving out of this town. But first, she needed to figure herself out, and then we needed to talk.

I pulled into my driveway, trying to park as close to the front steps as possible. The rain was coming down in sheets, and it was cold. It was the end of September and the temperature was already in the mid-forties. I shut off the engine and we both jumped out of the car, covering our heads and trying to dodge bullets of rain. I quickly unlocked the front door and we were greeted by a rush of warm air. I kicked off my boots in the hallway and headed in the back toward the kitchen. I heard Evie's footsteps right behind me.

"Hungry?" I asked her, flinging open the refrigerator door. There was nothing in it. "Well, I hope not. There's nothing in here, unless you like mustard." I turned around and found her leaning against the door frame, her hair and her shirt soaked. I felt my skin turning red.

"I think I'm good on the mustard front, but thank you," she said, raising an eyebrow. "You could've eaten at Leo's, you know."

I smiled at her. "While I appreciate your permission, I figured you just wanted to get out of there." I grabbed a can of soda from the fridge and popped it open, handing it to Evie. I grabbed another for myself. "I still want pizza though. Does Leo's deliver out this far?"

"Yeah, probably. But in this weather, and on a Saturday night, the wait might be an hour or so. He only has one driver."

"You in a hurry?" I asked, locking eyes with her before taking a sip of my soda.

The right side of Evie's mouth curved upward. "Not tonight."

In the forty-five minutes that it took for the pizza to arrive, there wasn't much talking. I spent most of the time watching the expressions on Evie's face: thoughtful, curious, self-conscious, amused, back to thoughtful and curious. I liked the way that Evie chewed on her bottom lip when she was thinking something over, or when she was trying to keep a thought from spilling out. I liked the way the light in the room laced itself in Evie's hair, creating flecks of gold. I wondered if she knew she was as beautiful as I thought she was, but I didn't think she'd be comfortable with me asking.

I watched Evie tear the crust from her slice of pizza in half, her brow furrowed.

"You look like you have a question, but the words are stuck in your throat," I told her, putting a piece of pepperoni into my mouth. I watched splotches of red creep up into Evie's cheeks.

"They're not stuck…I'm just not sure what to ask first."

I nodded. I was used to this part. Some people asked so many questions, others asked nothing at all.

"It's a lot to take in," I told her.

"Exactly."

"So, where would you like to start?"

Her eyes quickly met with mine. If I had my way, we'd only talk about her. None of the rest mattered to me.

"You seem to have a lot of ties to a town you say you haven't been to before," she blurted out.

"I never said that," I told her, refusing to let go of her gaze.

"Didn't you?"

I didn't answer. The redness in her cheeks began to disappear, and something in her seemed to switch on. She began looking more confident than I'd ever seen her look. She didn't look away from me, she was leaning in, elbows on the table, looking me in the eye. I think she enjoyed challenging me, the banter between us. A feeling that could only be described as the butterflies everyone talks about took flight in my stomach.

"Is that why my mother recognized you?" she asked, shattering the silence in the room.

I didn't know how to respond, so I made something up. "She met me the night before, remember?" I asked her, shrugging my shoulders. "Besides, this place isn't exactly a sprawling metropolis. She was bound to meet me sooner or later."

"Why are you here? Why are you so involved in the lives of people here?" Evie asked.

I leaned back in my seat across from her and sighed audibly. I was overcome with the need to tell her everything. I wanted to tell her about Jax, about everything I'd been involved with over all these years. But even I didn't know everything. I didn't know why Jax sent me for Evie. I was always given just enough information to complete my tasks, and no more. Then I moved on. I suddenly couldn't look Evie in the eye anymore.

"You can tell me," Evie said, her voice barely above a whisper.

I looked up at her again. "My life, Evie…it's really complicated. I don't know if you could understand. I don't know if you would stick around."

"Try me." There was no hesitation in Evie's voice and

it was soothing.

I nodded to myself, looking around the room and trying to find a place to start. I took a slow, deep breath.

"I work for a man named Jax. I've been working for him for a long time. Actually, I don't know if 'work for' is the right term. He lets me do my own thing as long as I agree to complete particular tasks when he needs me to. He gives me a name, a location, a quick rundown, and I'm on my way." I had no idea how much of this I was allowed to tell her, but I needed Evie to know who I was, what I was. "When I work on my own, I find women who need something, who need me, and I help them take back their lives. I help them by showing them how to help themselves," I explained.

"And what do they want, these women?" she asked. I could hear the slight tremble to her voice. She wasn't sure if she wanted to hear my answer.

"The requests are always pretty much the same. Revenge, justice, payback, vengeance. I show them how to take action."

"What did Mae Hesser want?"

I took another deep breath. "Mae wanted a couple of things." I stayed quiet for a moment, not sure how to proceed. Evie's raised eyebrow urged me on. "The first thing she wanted was vengeance. The helplessness and desperation she felt had taken root and turned into an almost obsessive need. She wanted to destroy the man who hurt her."

"And you…helped her?"

I nodded. "She also needed help with the baby." I chanced a glance at Evie, who's face went pale.

"What did you do?" she asked.

I couldn't look at her. "The baby lived for three days, and then it didn't anymore." I felt nauseous. I realized then that I didn't want Evie to know any of this about me, about who I used to be. I didn't do those things anymore. I was suddenly terrified that Evie would get up and walk out and I'd never hear her voice again.

But she didn't get up. She continued to lean in, waiting to hear more. "And the man?"

I shook my head. "You don't want to hear that part."

I watched her eyes widen. I had no idea what images her mind was conjuring up, and I didn't want to ask. Instead, she asked me about her own story.

"Jax doesn't ask me to do something very often, but when he does, it's important. There's usually a very specific reason behind it, but he doesn't always let me know what it is. When he sent me here, I had fewer details than usual. It felt rushed. I was told that a child was born here, and I was supposed to…take care of the situation."

Evie looked confused, and I couldn't blame her. "Take care of it?"

I nodded. I couldn't even look at her now. I couldn't bear to know if she was appalled by me, or afraid of me, or angry at me.

"That's why my mother recognized you," Evie said, more to herself than to me.

"It's possible," I told her. "It's probable, though we never spoke. Jax told me to get in and get out, so I kept my head down. I posed as one of the EMTs. Your mother... she was hysterical. I saw you, so tiny and so helpless. I was prepared to do what was asked of me. You...you were supposed to die, Evie. I was supposed to make sure that you didn't make it."

Her eyes were huge and round, staring at me. She was afraid of me, and it made my stomach turn. But she wanted to know, and I needed to tell her.

"I took you from another EMT to transfer you into the ambulance. But the moment I held you, something in me recognized something in you. It was like I knew you, which was impossible. You were an infant," I explained. "I don't know why Jax wanted you to die, but I needed you to live. So, for the first time, I went against what he wanted. I needed to keep you alive and safe with your mother. I haven't had anything to do with babies since that night. I just couldn't bring myself to keep doing it."

Evie looked completely taken aback, like she had no idea how to process anything I'd just told her. I couldn't blame her. I'd been trying to process it for years.

"That's impossible. We're the same age. You would've been a baby too," Evie said.

I took a deep breath. I was going to have to explain other things to her as well.

"Age is...irrelevant for me. It doesn't exist for me, not in the way that it exists for you. Look, I know this is a lot, and I'm sorry to lay it all on you at once. But I need you to trust me. I need you to trust that what I'm telling you is the truth. There is so much I can show you, things that would blow your mind. I just need you to trust me. You do, don't you?"

CHAPTER TWENTY ONE

EVIE

I STARED AT MY REFLECTION IN THE SHINY RED surface of the kitchen table. My stomach clenched, my pulse was racing. What was happening? What was Lilith saying, that we'd met before? This didn't make any sense.

"I want to trust you, so much. But none of this makes sense. Are you really okay with this, with helping women get vengeance on other people?"

Lilith shrugged. "Aren't women entitled to a little vengeance? Who am I to judge? Who are you to judge?"

I just stared at her. This was her response?

"You're so casual about it," I said in disbelief.

Lilith smiled a little. "Honey, my job isn't to police

how a woman uses her freedom, her autonomy, or how she gets justice, just so long as she gets it."

I continued to stare at her, not really sure what to say. "I don't think that I can do this," I finally said.

Lilith straightened her spine, a look of panic on her face. "But you don't even know what 'this' is yet. Besides, just because that's the route of someone else doesn't mean that it has to be yours," she said. "That's the beauty. Everything will be the way you want it to be."

I wanted to stay. I wanted her to explain it all. I wanted her to take away all of the hopelessness I felt living here. I wanted her to tell me that I didn't have to know that people were whispering about me at school, or around town. I wasn't stupid. I knew what they were saying about me; they were certainly loud enough about it. It didn't matter whether it was true or not. In a town like this, once you had a label, it stuck with you. In places like this, where every decision was made based on what was in a bible, I wouldn't ever get to be myself. I knew exactly how they felt about people like me, girls without boyfriends, or girls who paid too much attention to other girls. I had no control over my own identity here. But with Lilith, I had a chance.

"I could be in control," I said out loud.

"Yes. You can choose to accept my help, and be the person you want to be," she said.

I smiled to myself, feeling a little relieved. And then

I saw Lilith's face: curious, concerned…mostly curious.

"I have to ask, and I need you to tell me this time," she said, her voice low. "Jimmy."

I took a deep breath and nodded knowingly.

"He's a bully," Lilith said, leaning forward. "Whatever you did, you don't have to be sorry. You did it to protect your sister."

I looked down. "The problem is that I don't think I feel sorry."

When I looked up, Lilith was nodding. "I can understand that. Just because you feel like you should feel sorry doesn't mean you will."

"Do you really want to know?" I asked.

"Only if you want to tell me," she said, smiling reassuringly.

I took a deep breath, weighing the pros and cons of telling Lilith this. If I told her, I risked her looking at me differently, and not in a good way. If I don't tell her, would this always be hanging between us? If I was being honest with myself, I needed someone to tell me that what I did was okay, even if it wasn't, and I felt terrible about it. But I took another deep breath and stared out of the window on my right.

"I told him that if he touched my sister again, I would let his father know. I told him that I would tell everyone how his father treats him and his mother." I paused before finishing, trying to gather my courage. "I told him that there was a chance his dad might forgive him, but that there was also a chance that the police would find pieces of his mother's body all over town…"

Lilith was silent. I was terrified to look up at her. When she finally spoke, I was more than a little surprised by her reaction.

"Well, I think you probably got the message across," she said, somewhat laughing.

"I said that to a twelve-year-old boy. What is wrong with me?" I asked, more to myself than to her.

"There's nothing wrong with you. You were protecting someone you love. We should all be so lucky to feel that intensely about someone. Don't be so hard on yourself. You saw what he did to your sister. I'm sure you don't want that happening to anyone else. Little boys who do these things grow up to be big monsters who prey on any weak person they can find. This is one of those cases where the ends justify the means."

I didn't say anything.

"Do you really want what you said would happen, to happen?" she asked me.

I felt the muscles in my face tense. I didn't want that to happen at all.

"Yeah, I didn't think so. Besides, it's not like you hope it will actually happen. You just wanted to scare him."

"Well, I certainly did that. With a side of humiliation."

I saw Lilith roll her eyes. "Details," she said, waving

her hand dismissively. "He's lucky it wasn't me that confronted him."

I didn't understand her reaction. What I did was not okay under any circumstances, but she made me feel like it was, and I was somehow grateful for that. I stared at the girl in front of me, wondering what she might've done. Her story about Mae Hesser and the man that attacked her…just how violent could she get? And how long would it be before she turned on me? Was that even something I needed to worry about? It was obvious that her temperament could change from hot to cold in no time flat, and that she might be dangerous after all.

Regardless, something was pulling me to her like a bug lamp. Unfortunately, those lamps zapped anything that got too close.

"Make a decision, Evie. In, or out," Lilith said.

"Just like that? I don't even know what I'm agreeing to."

Lilith turned and headed out of the kitchen toward the living room. After a moment, I followed her. I turned into the room to see her pulling the lid off of Samael's habitat.

"Oh my God, Lilith, can you leave that thing in there until I'm gone?"

Lilith ignored me and lifted the snake out. The snake immediately wound itself around her arm.

"My name next to God's," Lilith mused, her nose

close to the serpent's. "That's not something I hear every day. I'm sure he doesn't either," she laughed, glancing upward.

Something about the sound of her laugh eased me, soothed me some, though I wasn't sure if it should. It wasn't enough to eliminate all of my confusion, my fear, or my doubt, but the richness of it reminded me of something. It was almost like the feeling of wrapping myself in a warm blanket that's fresh from the dryer. Or maybe the thrilling and terrifying feeling of that slow climb of the first hill of a roller coaster. A person should want to get off, to get back down to safety, but the rush of falling so fast was one that couldn't be passed up. And I found myself more and more willing to take that plunge from some high place with her more and more everyday.

"So…the other women that you've helped. Were any of them…important to you?" I wasn't sure what I was asking. I wanted to know if she'd been with any of them. I wanted to know if she'd loved any of them. I wanted to know if I was somehow special.

"They are all important to me." Lilith said, glancing at me with a smirk. "Tell me what you really want to know, Evie." she asked, her voice soft.

I stayed quiet. I suddenly didn't know if I was ready for this conversation. I still didn't have a handle on where I was with all of this. I thought about every encounter we've had since the day we met. Was she always being flirty? I didn't have a lot of experience with this, not with girls, not with anyone. Was this complicated with everyone, or was I just overthinking it?

I stared at her staring at the snake. Whether or not she was interested in me, there were some things that confirmed my feelings that she couldn't be a bad person. She helped women stand up for themselves, and helped them get what they wanted. I stared at the way her long red hair fell around her shoulders. I saw the way that she and the snake seemed to be so connected...

That's when something clicked. I wasn't sure why I was now remembering something I'd read online during a research project about goddesses from mythology last year, an article about a goddess who wanted equality and freedom, who helped women. Someone who was said to be the first wife of Adam, a wife who was replaced by Eve in the garden. I wasn't sure why this mattered, but I made a mental note to dig through Google again later.

Lilith returned Samael to his habitat and closed the lid. When she turned around, she just stared at me, like she was waiting for me to say something, anything. But the way she looked at me, her eyes full of worry, and of something akin to wanting, made me feel like I was both falling apart and coming together. How was I supposed to explain any of that to her when I couldn't adequately explain it to myself?

She began slowly walking toward me, and with every

step she took, my heart pounded that much faster. By the time that she was sitting on the coffee table in front of me, her hands pressed firmly on my knees, I felt like I couldn't breathe. The feeling of her hands on me felt both calming and dangerous. There was that word again: dangerous. I wanted so badly to look at her, but if I did, the choice about whether to stay with her would be the least of my concerns.

When I finally did force my eyes up at her, everything inside me, every bouncing cell and my racing heart, all calmed instantly. She didn't look frightening. She never did. She was the girl who winked at me in front of my parents, the girl who stole my fries even when she had a plate full of her own. She was the girl who always smelled like figs and the only person who made me nervous. She was nice to my family, even to Liam. She was the girl who just wanted me to be happy.

She leaned toward me, her face just inches from mine. I"m sure my breathing stopped.

"Let me help you get what you so desperately want," she said, her warm breath wafting over my face. I couldn't even remember what I'd wanted before this, but I had a feeling we might not be thinking of the same things.

"You don't have to stay here," she said. "We can leave together. We can help others like you, like Mae, like your sister. Just say yes."

My stomach flipped. Lilith's eyes danced excitedly,

something flickering in them. The intensity of the way she looked at me, the pressure of her hands on my knees, made me forget any reason I might've had for saying no.

"Okay," I said, my voice dry and raspy. "I'm in."

CHAPTER TWENTY TWO

LILITH

I STARED AT HER FOR A SECOND , NOT SURE I heard her correctly. But the look on her face, the resolve, the way that she stared into my eyes, the way she didn't shrink away when I touched her knees, I knew I heard her just fine. She said yes. She chose me. Well, she chose what I was offering, but I hoped that maybe it had a little to do with me. I hoped that she was really choosing me.

Hope. I felt like I was using that word a lot lately. I didn't hope for anything, not normally, but with Evie, I was hoping all the time.

She was sitting next to me on the sofa now, staring straight ahead. This was awkward. We couldn't just sit here, not speak, staring at the wall.

I blinked rapidly, trying to tear my eyes from her face. I slowly removed my hands from her knees and I saw her deflate a little. I felt the now-familiar tug in the center of my chest, the buzz in my veins. Maybe part of her choice was about me after all.

She looked nervous, so I tried to steer the conversation to something else.

"Where's your favorite place?" I asked her. I wanted to see everything she loved before we'd leave here for good. I wanted to see the places and the people who made up the person in front of me. I wanted to see what made her happy so that maybe I had a chance of giving her the same one day.

She opened her mouth to answer, and then seemed to think better of it. After a few seconds, she turned her body toward me and shrugged.

"The only place I can think of is the cove, but I don't know. It's where Liam and I hang out a lot, and he'd probably kill me for taking you there," she said, looking down.

"I don't want you to do anything that would cause you two to argue," I told her. "I know how important your friendship is with him." I was surprised at how much I meant it. I didn't like him, but he was her best friend and I had to accept it.

"I mean, he would probably never know," she said,

trailing off.

"Are you sure?"

She looked up and smiled. "Let's go."

As I drove toward Evie's cove, the only sounds in the car were Hozier playing through the speakers and Evie giving me directions. The streets were fairly empty for a Saturday evening. Benson was a strange town. It wasn't necessarily just because everyone was so nosy, but aside from school, I never really saw too many teenagers wandering around. Even restaurants seemed to be sparsely occupied. I'd been to a lot of small towns, and none of them ever seemed this empty. It was also weirdly cold, and the foliage around town looked more like we were weeks away from winter instead of weeks away from the actual start of autumn.

"Turn in here. We'll have to walk the rest of the way," Evie said, gesturing to a small gravel pull-off with a long streetlamp.

"This isn't what I was expecting," I said.

"You thought there would be a valet?" she joked.

"Oh, ha, so funny," I said sarcastically.

I parked near the head of the trail she was pointing to and turned the engine off. I looked over at her, her face barely illuminated by the light from the parking lot lamp. I wanted to lean in, to smell her skin up close, and I had the feeling she was thinking about it too. It made me nervous, and I was never nervous...normally. Just as I was about to bite the bullet and close the distance, I heard the click of her undoing her seat belt.

"We should go," she whispered, staring at my mouth. Leave it to Evie to change my entire course.

"Yeah, okay," I said, trying to hide my disappointment. I was glad it was relatively dark and that she couldn't see it on my face.

We both got out of the car, and I let her lead me to the head of the trail. The walk was only a few minutes, and it wasn't an easy one. It was close to pitch black, and I was tripping over every branch, every low bush. My face was stinging from the number of branches hitting me in it, and I could barely see Evie in front of me. She slowed down so that I could catch up, and I held on to the back of her jacket for the remainder of the walk.

Just as suddenly as we were enveloped by the trees, they parted, expanding into a beach-like area. I could immediately see what she loved about it. It was small, intimate, and the stars were so bright. The moon was almost full and cast light and shadows across the space. The small ripples from the river licked against the rocks at its edge. The cold breeze off of the water wrapped its way through the trees causing goosebumps all over the surface of my skin.

"This is beautiful," I said out loud. "How long have you and Liam been coming here?"

She walked over and took a seat on a large fallen log. "Since we were kids. Liam found it one day, and we started coming here a lot. I don't think anyone else knows about it."

"Well, I do now," I said, sitting as closely to her as possible, my thigh pressed against hers for both warmth and, well, just being close.

She smiled. "Yes, you do now."

"Can I ask you a question?"

"Yeah, sure," Evie said, looking out at the water.

I followed her gaze and took a deep breath, not really sure I wanted the answer to my question, but I needed to know. "Do you really not have feelings for Liam?"

Even in the dark I could tell that she didn't really want to have this conversation. I didn't want to force it, and I don't know why I needed to know. I heard her take a deep breath.

"I love Liam, I do. He's been my best friend for my entire life, and I can't ever imagine him missing from it. But I'll never love him the way you mean. I also think that you might be wrong about how he feels. We're just friends," she said.

"What about anyone else?"

"I don't know how to answer that, not right now," she said, staring forward.

I remained quiet. I didn't know what to say. She didn't know how to answer that right now? What did that even mean?

"What about you?" she asked me.

"Oh, I don't have feelings for Liam at all," I joked, trying to lighten the mood.

She laughed and elbowed me in the side. "You know I mean."

I elbowed her back. "I know what you mean," I told her. "Yes, there's someone, but I'm not sure if anything will come of it."

I saw Evie bite her lower lip and look downward. She looked hesitant.

"I get that," she finally replied. "Love is weird."

I laughed. "That's an understatement."

She chuckled, and then became a little more serious. "Okay, it's your turn. Where's your favorite place? You've probably been to so many places."

I nodded. I'd definitely been to a lot of places, but only one stood out.

"There's a place in Scotland called the Isle of Skye. It has a place called the Fairy Pools. It's beautiful. There are cliffs and waterfalls, and the water is so blue and green, like piles of emeralds and sapphires. It's so peaceful there. You would love it," I told her.

"Wow," she whispered in the dark. "It sounds incredible."

I smiled. "It's magical. Maybe I'll take you one day." The thought was out of my mouth before I could stop it. I couldn't promise her that, not right now. I was pretty sure we'd both just acknowledged that we didn't know where this was going, if she was talking about me.

"I'm sorry, I shouldn't have said that," I muttered.

"No, it's okay," she said. "I'd love to do that with you."

I think that was the moment that I knew I was completely lost.

CHAPTER TWENTY THREE

EVIE

"SO, WHAT HAPPENS NEXT? WHEN DO WE do…whatever it is we're going to do?" I asked, trying to ignore the awkward expectation-filled air between us. Fortunately, it was getting darker by the minute, so there wasn't the added pressure of having to look each other in the eye.

"I have no idea. We can go someplace else, if you want?" Lilith asked.

"That's not what I meant. I mean, when do you help me?"

I heard Lilith clear her throat. "It's more about making a series of choices, about feeling brave enough to do it. I'll be here to help you when you need it. But then, when you're ready, you can leave."

"How soon do we have to do it?" I asked. "Leaving, I mean." There was so much I needed to take care of first. I couldn't just disappear.

"There's no time frame," she said. I breathed a sigh of relief. "Having second thoughts?"

"No, I'm not. I just…you'll think it's stupid," I said, shaking my head. I could only make out some of her features in the dark until she turned her entire body to face me.

"Never," she said. "Tell me."

"I want to stay for one more Christmas. I can't ruin Christmas for Bea by leaving earlier."

"We can do that, I think. What about New Year's Eve?" she suggested. "Start the new year as the new you?"

It sounded so cheesy, and also so perfect. I could wrap up my old life and start my new one.

"I love it," I told her.

Lilith dropped me off at home later that night. When she pulled up in front of my house, we awkwardly sat in the car for ten minutes, both of us either staring at our hands or staring wide-eyed out of the front window. We did manage to talk about school, which was the most ridiculous thing to talk about. We finally said goodnight and she waited until I was inside to drive away.

The house was dark when I walked inside. I could see the blue flickering light from the television in the family room, and my father asleep in the recliner. My mother and sister were likely asleep in their respective bedrooms. I walked quietly up the stairs and to my bedroom at the end of the hall. I closed the door behind me with a soft click, locked the door, and flipped on the light switch next to it.

"Shit!" I yelled out. Adrenaline sent a zap that felt like electricity through my limbs. Liam was sitting on the floor, his back against the side of my bed. He was scowling and I could see that his fists were clenched. He looked ready for a fight.

"You were with her, weren't you?" he asked.

I stared at him, not sure where this was going to go. "With who? Lilith? You have to get over whatever your problem with her is. She's a new friend, that's all."

"Since when?" he asked. He was clearly exasperated.

I kicked my shoes off in the corner of the room closest to my door. "Since I decided that my entire world world can't just revolve around you, or my family, or this stupid town," I hissed, trying to stay quiet. The last thing I needed was to wake up everyone in the house.

He looked a little hurt, but no less pissed off. It tugged at my chest a little. I didn't want to hurt him. He was my best friend. We'd been together through everything. But how much longer was I going to let the feelings of everyone else dictate my own?

"You don't own me. We can have friends outside of this tiny circle," I said, stepping closer to him. "It's not even a circle. It's like a line or something."

He just stared at me from his spot on the floor. It was a little unnerving. He looked so cold, his face stone. In all the time I'd known him, he'd never looked like this. He looked just like his father. It made me step back, unsure of what to expect. I'd never been afraid of him, ever, but now I wasn't so sure.

"Liam? Are you okay?"

And that's when it happened. Before I had a chance to react, he was on his feet. He grabbed me, hard, and his lips collided with mine with so much force that it nearly knocked me over. His eyes were clamped shut, but mine were wide, looking around the room, frantically searching for a way out of this. I tried to yell in protest, but it just came out as a grunt, my words smashed against Liam's mouth. My chest tightened with panic. What was happening? Where was this going to go?

No no no no no! My brain was firing at the rest of my body, trying to fight him off. This wasn't what I wanted at all. I tried to pull back, but he gripped my upper arms even tighter, and I gasped at the intense pain of it. His fingers dug in so hard that I thought he'd break right through my skin. Tears stung my eyes, blurring my vision, and bile rose up in my throat. Stop stop stop stop, I screamed internally. He let go of one of my arms, only to twist it painfully into my hair, smashing my face painfully against his own. He pushed himself against me, my back slamming so hard into the wall behind me I was sure there would be bruises. I raised my hands to push him back but he let go of my hair and pinned my arms against the wall. For a moment, I wished we'd just break through the plaster so that I had a shot at getting away.

Finally, my brain went completely blank and my instincts took over. All at once, my knee slammed up and into his groin while I pushed him away at the same time. When I shoved him away, I stumbled over something and fell to the floor. Liam was folded in half, looking at me, his eyes wide with shock.

We stared at each other. I didn't know the boy in front of me, breathing heavily and looking like he'd attack again as soon as he recovered. I was panting hard. My entire body was burning, aching, at the places his hands had been. My back was throbbing. My bottom lip felt wet, so I reached up and touched it. There was a smear of blood when I looked at my fingers. Anger boiled up in me and I felt my face twist into something that might bite back.

"Get the fuck out," I growled, my teeth gnashed together and tears pouring down my face.

"Evie, I'm—" he gasped, taking a step toward me.

"No!" My voice was quivering and I raised my hand with the blood on it. My hand was shaking uncontrollably. The person in front of me wasn't my best friend. I didn't know this person.

"Get out," I told him again.

I watched confusion wash over his face. This was clearly not the response he thought he was going to get. Normally, I'd care that I hurt his feelings, but not now. Now, I pulled myself to my feet and backed up against the wall.

I watched the realization of what he'd done replace his confusion.

"Oh, God, Evie, I'm so sorry," he said, taking a step toward me. My jaw clenched shut. I tried to back up but with my back pressed up against the wall, the pain was excruciating. I watched his chin quiver and he nodded, his eyes dropping to the floor.

My crying was gaining momentum now. I was trying so hard to wait until he was gone, but my heart was broken and my body was in pain. Looking at him was making me want to vomit, but I was afraid to look away. I watched him pick up the hoodie he'd thrown on my bed and make his way to the window.

I'm so sorry," he whispered as he climbed out. He didn't even look back at me before he descended out of my view.

My body racked with sobs, and I was sucking in air

like I'd been underwater for too long. I felt like I couldn't breath, and my arms, my mouth, my scalp, and back felt like they were on fire. Then there was a soft knock at my door.

"Evie? Honey? Are you okay in there?" It was my mother.

I tried to pull myself together. I closed my eyes and took a deep breath. "I'm okay, Mom. I'm sorry if I woke you."

"Are you sure? I thought I heard crying."

I closed my eyes and leaned my head back against the wall. "I'm okay. The book I'm reading is just really sad." I bit my sore lip to keep myself from screaming that no, I wasn't okay.

It was literally the worst lie I'd ever told, but she seemed to buy it. She told me to let her know if I needed anything and that she was going back to bed. But I didn't know how to tell her that it felt like there was no ground beneath me, that nothing felt real. I didn't know how to tell her that my bedroom no longer felt safe, and that in a matter of minutes my entire life was different, and I couldn't even go to my best friend about it.

I didn't know how to tell her or anyone else that I'd been attacked in my bedroom by my best friend while everyone who loved the both of us were fast asleep.

CHAPTER TWENTY FOUR

EVIE

LIAM CALLED SEVERAL TIMES ON SUNDAY morning, but I didn't answer a single one of them. I ignored his texts as well, and there were so many of them that I contemplated turning my phone off. I didn't know what to even say to him. Every single time I saw his name flash on the screen, my stomach clenched. On one hand, I knew that I was absolutely justified in feeling the way that I did, but on the other...he was the boy I watched bad movies with, shared fries with at the diner...the boy who cried for weeks after his mom left. The fact that I felt bad for him made me even angrier.

I wanted so badly to call Lilith, to know what she would do about this. But if I was honest about it, I knew exactly how she'd react. She'd be infuriated. Lilith would want to take care of it on my behalf. She would make sure it never happened again.

I screamed, burying my face in my black- and gray-striped pillow.

"Wow, dramatic much?"

I must've jumped ten feet in the air. It felt like live wires through my entire body and I almost fell off of my bed. I looked up to see Lilith's figure in the doorway, arms folded, propped against the door jam.

"What are you doing here?" I asked slightly panicked, running my hands over the front of my t-shirt as I struggled to sit up. She chuckled, stepping into the room and closing the door behind her.

"Saw Liam at the diner this morning. Looked like someone ran over his puppy. Thought it might have something to do with you."

I sighed heavily and made room for her on the bed next to me. I watched her cross the room, every movement she made so fluid and graceful that it made me want to throw up. Or maybe it was her mention of Liam.

"How did you know?"

She sat down and faced me, crossing her legs beneath her. "Seriously? His whole world revolves around you and painting. It wasn't hard to figure out. No one looks that depressed over acrylics."

I would've laughed if I wasn't still so upset.

"Okay...you too? What is going on? And what is up with your busted lip?"

I involuntarily sucked in my bottom lip. "Nothing. I think I bit it in my sleep or something," I lied, avoiding eye contact. If I just didn't look at her, there was no way she'd know.

Out of the corner of my eye, I saw her scan me. I closed my eyes the moment I saw her notice the bruises creeping out from beneath the sleeves of my t-shirt.

"What the fuck did you do to your arms?" she asked, pushing my t-shirt sleeves up a little bit.

"I didn't do anything. It's no big deal," I told her. But it was hard to ignore the purple shapes of fingers and hand prints and the half-moon marks from Liam's fingernails.

She looked at me incredulously. "The hell it isn't. What happened?" She gingerly touched one of the half moon bruises, carefully lining up her own small hand with the memory of Liam's large one, and I pulled away, pulling down my sleeves as far as I could get them. I watched her face change. She wasn't angry. She looked worried. But it didn't take long for her to put two and two together.

"Tell me, Evie," she said, her voice soft but demanding. "Now."

I stared down at my lap for a minute. As much as I wanted to call her a minute ago, now that she was sitting in front of me, I just wanted to forget about it. Instead, I took a deep breath and blurted out the entire ordeal. Her face remained unmoving, and I was worried that I wasn't actually saying the words out loud. But then I noticed her hand twitch in her lap.

"I think someone needs a lesson in boundaries."

I jumped up from the bed, facing her and gesturing emphatically. "Nope. We're not doing that. We're just going to leave it alone, hope it blows over, or that maybe time travel suddenly becomes a thing. No 'lessons'." I was pacing back and forth now, my go-to method for dealing with anxiety.

"Killing him is an option," she said calmly.

I shot her a glare and continued pacing. Lilith stood up, stepped in my path, and gingerly placed her hands on my shoulders. I felt my entire body suddenly relax.

"We'll do it your way," she said softly. Her eyes were focused on me, demanding my attention. "Are you okay?"

I looked at her, her face was genuinely concerned, and felt hot tears stinging my eyes. She furrowed her brow and moved in to hug me, but I winced, involuntarily hissed, and jerked away.

"What's wrong?" she asked, pulling back and removing her hands from my body, looking me up and down.

"It's nothing," I said, trying to downplay it. Lilith looked at me, knowing better than to believe me.

"My back hurts," I reluctantly explained to her.

Lilith looked at me for a second, staring me in the eyes so I'd understand her next move. I nodded my consent. She carefully walked around me, and I felt the fabric of my shirt rising up to reveal the remnants of last night on my back. I wanted to pull away, to tell her to mind her own business, but I didn't. I held my breath instead.

"I'll fucking kill him," she said through clenched teeth.

"I'm okay, really. Please, can we just talk about something else? Please?" I asked her.

Lilith looked more furious than I'd ever seen, well, anyone.

"You want to change the subject? Have you seen your back?"

I shook my head. I hadn't seen it. I didn't want to. If it looked half as bad as it felt, I'm not sure I'd be able to hold myself together. I looked at her, pleading, begging for her to let this go, for now. I knew she wouldn't let it go forever, but her face changed. She now looked... helpless, sad. She looked how I felt.

She took a deep breath and then finally gave in. "Okay. This is your call. Just know that I probably have a machete or something if you change your mind."

I smiled a little. I couldn't help myself.

"So what do you want to talk about?" she asked.

"I literally have no idea," I told her.

She moved over to my bed and sat down. She patted the seat next to her. I sat down.

"We can just sit," she said quietly.

"That would be good," I said, a tear rolling down my cheek.

Lilith turned her head toward me, raising her hand to tuck a wayward piece of hair behind my ear. This was a move that was becoming familiar and comfortable, and it still made my breath hitch every single time.

"I'm so sorry this happened," Lilith whispered. She leaned her forehead against my head. "Whatever you need, when ever you need it, I'm here."

I didn't say anything. I didn't need to. She knew without me having to say a word, but I was so grateful to have her here right now.

CHAPTER
TWENTY FIVE
EVIE

I SPENT A WEEK KEEPING AS MUCH DISTANCE as possible between me and Liam. It was harder than I thought it would be. He was absolutely everywhere. Lilith stuck close, walking to every class with me, driving me home. We were together more often than not, but I didn't mind it. Being with her kept me from thinking too much about everything else.

Unfortunately, when I shut my locker door, Liam was standing on the other side of it. My stomach bottomed out.

"You have to talk to me eventually," he said, his head lowered but his eyes still looking directly into mine.

"No, actually, I don't. I don't even know what to say

to you," I replied, my voice shaking a little. I grabbed my backpack and started to walk away. I heard his footsteps behind me.

"I'm sorry, Evie. I thought you were into it," he said, stepping into my path.

I immediately wanted to punch him in the face. It felt like fire was spreading through my stomach, into my limbs, up into my cheeks.

"Are you high? Into it?" I repeated, fighting to keep my voice low. "Seriously? You really are clueless. When have I ever expressed that any part of me was into it, into anything more than being friends? Was it the part where I was trying to fight you off? Oh, maybe it was the part of me trying to get away from you. Or maybe it was this—" I looked around to make sure no one was watching before I raised the sleeve of my shirt a little, just enough to show him the deep purple imprints of his fingers on my skin. "What part of any of this made you think that I was into it?" If I couldn't stop seeing it, I wanted to know that he couldn't either.

I watched his eyes widen and well up with tears. He looked horrified, and it made me involuntarily soften and that made me angrier.

"No, you don't get to do that. You don't get to do that to me and then stand here crying. If you think any part of that is acceptable, you can go fuck yourself. I want you to leave me alone," I said quietly. He visibly deflated, but

I straightened my back. "I don't want you to call or text. I don't want notes in my locker. I don't want you hanging out and waiting for me. I want you to leave me alone. And maybe you need to talk to someone about why you felt compelled to attack me."

He opened his mouth to say something but seemed to think better of it. I watched him gather up just enough courage to ask her how long I needed.

"As long as I need," I replied.

With that, I adjusted my backpack, stepped to the side, and walked away from my best friend. I saw Lilith waiting near the school exit, looking impressed. She began a slow clap as I approached her.

"It isn't funny," I shot at her. I could feel my heart breaking all over again for a friendship that might never recover. Lilith put up her hands in resignation and opened the door for me.

"I'm sorry. I won't say another word," she promised, her face apologetic.

And she didn't say another word. She didn't mention Liam's name again. In the car on the way to the store to stop for snacks before going to her house, she kept stealing glances at me. I appreciated her concern, but it was making me crazy.

"You know, constantly watching me is more annoying than you actually asking me what's wrong," I finally said, looking out of the passenger side window. She cleared her throat, adjusted in her seat, and faced forward.

"I know, I'm sorry. I should know by now that you can take care of yourself. I'm just used to swooping in and…rectifying these situations."

I smiled to myself. I secretly liked that she cared enough to be a little overprotective, but I didn't need a bodyguard. I needed her to be normal with me. I needed the girl that winked at me and laughed at my stupid jokes.

I sighed and leaned my head against the headrest. This wasn't how I wanted my first kiss to be, not with Liam, not like that. If I was being honest, I wish it had been with someone like Lilith, and I didn't know what to do with those feelings right now. Every time I thought about it, I simultaneously felt excited, guilty, and terrified.

We pulled into the busy grocery store parking lot and got out of the car. As we entered the store, the bright fluorescent lights made me cringe. They always seemed way too bright, and it always took me a few seconds for my eyes to adjust.

It only took a moment to notice the looks. The cashiers at the front, mostly kids from school, were watching. Nathaniel, a man from my parents' church, stocking the shelves was moving slower, sneaking glances at us. Before I had a chance to over analyze it, I felt Lilith link her arm in mine.

"So, what are we getting?" she asked.

I involuntarily smiled at the gesture. She hadn't really been like this all week, touchy and affectionate, and I didn't realize how much I'd missed it. I felt a little lighter.

"We're heading for the back," I said, dragging her toward the back of the store and passing by Nathaniel.

I steered us through the store, dodging displays and other customers. As we passed shopper after shopper, arms linked, I started to notice that people were looking at us. There were two women in the produce area, Bonnie and Madeline, whispering and watching.

"Hey, are you okay?" Lilith asked, pulling on my arm a little to get my attention.

"Huh? Um, yeah. It just…does it feel like people are staring at us?" I whispered.

Lilith looked around. When Bonnie noticed us looking back at her, she sneered, shook her head, and walked away, Madeline trailing right behind her.

"I tell you what, Bonnie, these kids need church. That's what's wrong with 'em," I heard Madeline say.

They were talking about us. My heart started pounding. At school, I could ignore people thought I was…different, chalk it up to gossip-hungry adolescents. Here, out in the world with adults watching and whispering, I didn't know how to deal with it.

My heart was racing. I looked around and could've sworn that everyone else was whispering, and it seemed so loud. Everything seemed so loud. I couldn't breathe. I wanted to drop the cupcakes in my hand and run.

"Hey, what's going on?" I heard Lilith ask, her voice low. She was leaning toward me, trying to get me to look at her, but I couldn't.

"I want to leave," I whispered. My voice was quivering and more high-pitched than normal. I felt dread quickly taking over.

"Okay, we can go. I'll pay for this stuff. You go to the car, okay?" Her voice was so calming, so reassuring. It made me want to cry. I was afraid of people seeing us together, and she was making sure that I was okay.

I nodded and she handed me her keys. I kept my head down. I was practically running through the aisles and had to force myself to slow down. I almost ran directly into Madeline, and I heard her scoff at me. When I finally reached the front doors and they slid open, the cold air hit me in a rush, alleviating some of the nausea I was starting to feel. I walked over to Lilith's car, unlocked the passenger door, and ducked inside.

A few minutes later, Lilith walked out, a plastic shopping bag in her hand. She looked frustrated, and I was worried that she was upset with me. When she opened her car door and got in, I couldn't look at her. She put the key in the ignition and the engine roared to life, but we just sat there, the heat blasting through the vents.

"You going to tell me what happened back there?"

she asked. Her tone was soft, not the way I'd interpreted her expression a minute before. That didn't make my guilt disappear any faster.

"Nothing, I just didn't feel well," I muttered, looking straight ahead. I saw her shake her head out of the corner of my eye.

"That's bullshit. What's wrong?"

I looked out of the passenger window and rubbed my hand over my mouth. She didn't care what people thought about her. I thought I didn't either, but it turns out that I cared a lot.

"I'm never going to be able to breathe here." I was speaking more to myself than to Lilith. "I will always have to be someone else here."

I heard her sigh. "You've always been different from them, Evie. If you stay here, and it's absolutely your choice, they will suffocate you. They will twist and bend and break you until you're one of them. You're special, you're not like them. There is more that you're supposed to do, that you're supposed to be, but that won't happen in Benson."

I turned to look at her, letting the tears fall down my cheeks. Crying about this made me feel weak, like I needed rescuing. She reached up and brushed the tears away with the back of her index finger.

"I can't stay here," I whispered.

"I know. That's why we're leaving."

CHAPTER
TWENTY SIX
LILITH

W E RODE BACK TO MY HOUSE IN silence. Halfway through the drive, I reached over and laced my fingers with hers. I didn't know what else to do. Neither of us said anything, and we didn't look over at one another. When we finally got to my house, we sat next to one another on the sofa, still silent. After about half an hour, she reached down into the shopping back at my feet, and pulled out the pack of cupcakes she'd chosen at the store.

"Cheer me up," she said, looking over at me while fighting to get the package on the cupcakes open.

"Cheer you up," I repeated. "Hmm. Samael once ate a neighbor's cat. At least I think he did."

I looked over to see her eyes widen. I shrugged, and then a laugh burst from her like an explosion. I laughed at her.

"I'm sorry," she said, trying to stop. "I'm sorry. It isn't funny but..." She just kept laughing. After a minute, her laughter started to die down and she shoved half a cupcake into her mouth.

Just as I opened my mouth to lecture her about how she needed a meal that didn't consist of frosting, my cell phone rang. I glanced over at it and saw Jax's name. I rolled my eyes.

"Sorry, I need to take this," I said, picking my phone up. "I'll be right back."

She nodded and I walked quickly out of the room while hitting the answer button.

"Hello?" I asked, the confusion in my voice evident.

"Make her an offer," he said bluntly.

"What?"

"Make her an offer. Tonight," he instructed.

"I don't understand. She's normal. Like, couldn't be more normal. Why do you want her?"

I heard his dry humorless chuckle in my ear. "Oh, please. She's far from normal. You really should've noticed by now. I want you to make her the offer tonight. I'm sure she'll take it."

I leaned against the wall in the hallway. "And what makes you think she'll do it?"

"After tonight, there's no way she'd say no. She already said yes to your help. She'll say yes to this. Don't make me tell you again."

Before I could say anything else, the line went dead. How was I supposed to do this? How was I supposed to ask her to spend the rest of her life with Jax and me and so many others?

"Hey, is everything okay?"

I turned, surprised, to see Evie poking her head into the hallway. I forced myself to smile.

"Yeah, totally. I was just coming back in."

She smiled at me and my stomach flipped. I hoped that when I made Jax's offer, she'd stay with me. I smiled back at her and followed her into the living room.

Evie plopped back down on the sofa and went to eat the other half of her cupcake.

"I don't know how you eat that junk. You might as well be sucking on sugar cubes," I said, sitting down next to her.

"Because sugar cubes are not this delicious," she said, waving it in front of my face. I pulled away.

"I'm serious. I don't know how you're not bouncing off the walls."

She swallowed hard and nodded. "Give it time," she joked, widening her eyes. "Besides, this cupcake isn't going to kill me."

"I know, but it wouldn't kill you to ingest a vegetable

either."

She nodded and put the junk food back in its bag. I watched as she curled her legs underneath her and tried to look more serious and focused. I smiled and rolled my eyes.

"I know it's really early, but what are you doing for the holidays?"

I looked over at her, my eyebrows raised. "Yeah, it's definitely early. It's only the end of September."

Evie narrowed her eyes at me. "I know that. Answer the question."

I chuckled. "No plans. I never have plans. I don't usually even know where I'll be."

She gasped dramatically. "You have to spend it with us, especially Christmas. We have a huge, gaudy tree. My mom is the worst at wrapping gifts. Bea and I stay up all night watching movies. You have to be there."

I stared at her. Less than an hour ago, she was panicking because people were watching us in the store, and now she wanted me to spend the holidays with her family. I didn't know if this was a normal thing for people, but it seemed weird.

"Are you sure about that? Earlier..." I started.

Her smile faded and I wished I'd never asked.

"I mean, I'll just tell my parents that your parents won't be home. Liam used to spend some holidays with us. It'll be fine."

I turned my body toward her and studied her face. I wanted to ask her why. I wanted to ask her what we were to each other. I also didn't know if I wanted the answer. What if I was reading too much into it? Over the years, some of the women I'd helped…it wasn't unusual for them to think they were attracted to me, to think that they wanted more from me. It sometimes made me get out faster. But this time, this time was different. I was willing to stick around for months, just because she asked me to. I wanted to know why she was here.

But I didn't ask her any of this. Instead, I smiled at her and told her that I would love to spend the holidays with her and her family. She grinned at me.

It felt like a good time to make her the offer.

"So, I wanted to ask you something," I started.

"Okay…"

I wasn't even sure how to start, so I decided diving in was probably best.

"What if I could offer you something bigger than just getting out of Benson? What if you could give to others what I am offering you?"

Evie's head tilted slightly, seeming to weigh what I was asking her. She was interested. At the very least, she was curious to know more.

"What makes you think I want to help anyone?" she asked.

"I don't know. Just a feeling, maybe. Maybe it's the

way you want to protect Bea. Maybe it's the way you didn't want to terrify a twelve-year-old boy, but you did it to help someone weaker than them."

"Okay," she said, adjusting herself to get more comfortable. "But Bea is my sister. Why would I want to help strangers?"

I smiled at her. "Like I said, just a feeling. So, what do you think?"

"What exactly does this involve?"

I took a deep breath. "Look, you already know that I'm…different. You would become different too. There's a little…ceremony. It just formally allows you to dedicate yourself to this." I felt nervous. I wasn't sure how to explain that it was actually a pretty in-depth ritual, and that it involved more than just me.

"I'm not killing anyone," she blurted out.

I bit my bottom lip to keep from outright laughing.

"No murder, got it." I laughed at her, and Evie relaxed a little.

Just like that, somehow, I knew that I had her. Jax would be pleased, but I wasn't so sure yet if I was.

CHAPTER TWENTY SEVEN

EVIE

I STAYED QUIET AND LET LILITH EXPLAIN because I wasn't sure where this was going.

"You could travel all over the world helping women like you, like Liam's mother, like Mae Hesser, like your sister."

I was definitely curious, but I had one question that I needed to have answered.

"Will I be with you?" I asked. "I mean, while I'm helping all these people, will I still be with you?"

As soon as I asked the question, I regretted it. What if she said no? While she'd never indicated that she didn't want me to stick with her, she didn't outright say it either.

"If you want to be," she answered, the edges of her

lips turning up in a smile.

I smiled at her. I didn't really know if that meant she wanted me to stay with her, so I hoped for the best. "I do."

The air between us remained silent for a few minutes, but it felt charged with electricity, the same electricity I always felt with her. Between us, it felt like a million possibilities just waiting to be grabbed on to. Unfortunately, I wasn't sure what they were. It felt like we were constantly dancing around what we were to each other, but I knew that I couldn't do anything about it as long as we were here. I didn't know what else to do.

"I just need time," I said, hoping she'd know what I meant. I still needed a little more time with Bea, with my family.

"I know. I mean, you didn't want to leave until the new year anyway. We'll figure it out," Lilith answered.

I could live with that, and I hoped she could too.

"Okay, so how do I help people?"

Lilith shrugged. "It's not that complicated, once you get the hang of it."

"Once I get the hang of it?"

Lilith curled her legs underneath her. "I don't really know how to explain it. After the ceremony, things change a little," she explained. "You'll start getting these… intuitive feelings. It's a little different for everyone. I get mine in the pit of my stomach."

I was a little floored. "It's different for everyone? How many people are there like you?"

"Like me? None, but there's a huge group of us. Everyone does something different, and we don't really get involved in anyone else's thing."

I was surprised by all of this. All this time, I thought it was just going to be us, doing our own thing. And now, it was a group, probably with a boss.

"Okay…that's a little weird, but I'll go with it," I told her.

She laughed. "It's not so bad. We rarely see each other. You and I could travel to wherever we're called, help who we can. When we aren't helping anyone, we go where we want to go."

That sounded a little better, a little more exciting.

I left her house late that night and crept up the stairs to my bedroom. The idea of sneaking up there made me uncomfortable and a little freaked out, remembering the last time I'd done it. I hoped Liam wouldn't be up here this time. When I opened my bedroom door to find it empty, I sighed with relief.

On the ride home from Lilith's, I remembered that I still hadn't Googled the information I remembered about that goddess also named Lilith. I hit the power button on my laptop and changed into my pajamas while I waited for it to boot up. I pulled my hair up into a pile on my head as I sat down at my desk.

I pulled Google up and typed in "goddess Lilith," not having any idea what might pop up. I was immediately met with 10, 500,000 search results, and I wanted to scream. Then I remembered that if it wasn't on the first page, it probably didn't matter.

There was so much information on that first page. There were pictures at the top of women with horns, or women surrounded by zombies or something. There were articles about demons, goddesses, Jewish mythology, and something about the first wife of Adam. I clicked on the link to that article. It made that Lilith sound horrible. The Lilith I knew wasn't anything like this. Another article said she was a symbol of power for women. That seemed to make sense. Other articles called her a serpent goddess, a demon child-killer, a feminist icon. I was even more confused. These were all myths and legends. The girl I knew was real.

I sat back in my chair and stared at the wall in front of me. I was trying to compare the person I knew with the information on the internet. She helped women, an article said she was a feminist icon and symbolized power for women. My Lilith - I smiled at the thought of it - had a huge snake named Samael, and an article mentioned Lilith was a serpent goddess. Another article called her a child-killer, and there was that time she was supposed to kill me, and may have killed Mae Hesser's baby...

I was overwhelmed.

Thinking of the snake, I did a quick Google search for him too. I knew it was stupid, but with everything else...

And there it was, at the very top of the first page: Samael was Hebrew for "venom of God," just like Lilith said.

Well, my life had just become exponentially more complicated.

I didn't even give it a second thought. I just put on my shoes and a jacket over my pajamas. I needed to talk to her now. It couldn't wait. I need to see her, to ask her about everything I'd just read. Without any thought to how I was going to get there, I opened my window and climbed out.

CHAPTER
TWENTY EIGHT

EVIE

I WALKED THE ENTIRE WAY TO LILITH'S HOUSE.
It was colder than I expected and the trees along the empty road stretched like hands reaching across the sky, blocking me in. My breath came out in puffs in front of me and my hands were freezing. I wished I'd have thrown on a sweatshirt and a coat instead of this flimsy jacket.

There were no street lamps on her road, and it was way creepier in the pitch-black night. I thought I heard howling in the distance and almost peed my pants. The night life was probably not for me.

When I finally saw her house looming ahead of me at the end of the road, I sped up my pace. I was practically running. The house was dark and I felt a little bad for banging on the door at...

I looked at my phone. It was two in the morning. I decided I'd ask for her forgiveness later.

I ran up the three steps to the porch and pounded on the door. A few minutes later, a very annoyed looking Lilith opened the door in an over-sized t-shirt that hung off one shoulder and a pair of very short plaid shorts, her hair mussed around her head. Did she even know the temperature outside? Did she always sleep dressed like this?

"What in the hell...?" she started. When she saw that it was me, her eyes flew wide. There was confusion and then concern. She searched my face, and I saw her look behind me, presumably searching for a car.

"Evie? Is everything okay? Get in here, it's freezing." She said to me, slight panic in her voice.

"I need to know who you are," I said, not moving from my spot.

She reached forward, grabbed my arm, and pulled me inside, closing the door behind me.

"You'll need to be more specific, darling. I've been called a lot of things over the years, and only a few of them have been good. But if you're looking for some existential answer, who are any of us, really?" she rambled.

It was way too late at night for her to be talking about existential answers. I rolled my eyes and walked back toward the kitchen without asking while she rambled on, not making a whole lot of sense. Someone needed to remind me not to wake her up in the middle of the night anymore. She was a talker.

I walked straight over to her tea kettle, filled it up at the sink, and then put it on the stove.

"Yes, please, help yourself," Lilith said, her voice sleepy and sarcastic. I heard her pull out a chair and sit down at the kitchen table.

I ignored her and began opening and closing cabinets, looking for tea.

"You said you're not the devil, and you said you're not a witch, but then you might be some serpent goddess or a baby-killing demon who was married to Adam. Like, *the* Adam. I'll come back to that later..." I rambled off, finally finding tea in a cabinet across the kitchen. "Who keeps tea this far from the stove?" I asked aloud.

"I do. And what are you talking about? Where did you hear any of that?" Lilith asked, and I noted a tinge of nervousness to her voice.

I stopped, turned around, and stared at her. "I Googled you."

Her eyebrows shot upward. "Oh, is that what they're calling it now? You'd think I would remember doing that with you," she said, winking.

I rolled my eyes, blushing, and turned back around, waiting for the water to boil. "That's..." I cleared my throat, "that's not what I meant…"

"I think this means you owe me dinner now."

I couldn't look at her. My face felt like it was on fire.

We didn't say anything for a minute. Finally, the tea kettle whistled and I removed it from the burner. I turned the stove off and poured the steaming water over the tea bag in Lilith's yellow mug.

"Do you want tea?" I asked over my shoulder.

"No, thank you," Lilith said.

I turned around and leaned against the counter, finally feeling like I could look at her.

"Are any of those things true?" I asked, looking her directly in the eye.

Something flashed across Lilith's delicate features and was gone in an instant. She looked…uncomfortable? Uneasy? Embarrassed? Scared?

"I don't know how you'll react," she said, staring back.

"Yeah, me either, so try me."

She laughed to herself. "I didn't lie to you when I said that I wasn't the devil or a witch, though you sure wouldn't know that by the ridiculous representations of me on television and in movies."

"What do you mean?"

"In some cases, people think I possess women. Some think I'm a female version of Satan. Oh, and I'm a cult leader."

"Ah, so that is what's really happening here," I joked.

Lilith rolled her eyes and laughed. "Anyway, I wasn't exactly forthcoming with the correct information when you asked, I know that. I assumed you'd eventually figure it out, not quite so quickly, but yeah, eventually, but I wasn't ready for you to know everything about me. Not yet."

I waited for her to continue, but she didn't. I groaned in frustration and exasperation. Without a word, I walked out of the kitchen and into the living room. I heard her footsteps behind me.

"You just make yourself right at home, don't you?" she asked as I took a seat on her couch.

"You're changing the subject. Tell me what I'm missing!" I implored.

All at once, she opened her mouth and blurted out something I wasn't expecting.

"I'm technically a demon," she said with such speed that I thought she might be broken.

I took a deep breath and stared at her blankly, waiting for her to say that she was joking. When she didn't, I calmly placed my mug on the coffee table and stood up.

"Well, it was nice seeing you tonight. I'm sorry I woke you up. I'm going to go home now," I said. My voice was surprisingly calm, even.

As I started to walk past her, she grabbed me by the wrist, a look of desperation on her face.

"Please, don't leave," she whispered. Something about the look on her face, the way her eyes widened, pulled hard at the center of my chest. I couldn't make my feet take another step.

"If you would just let me explain, please," Lilith begged, still holding on to my wrist.

"I'm listening." I whispered after a moment of silene.

I let her pull me by the wrist over to the sofa. We sat down and she handed me my mug of tea. I took it with my free hand because she wasn't letting go of the other.

"So did you choose to be a demon?" I asked, not sure I believed her yet.

She finally let go of my wrist.

"I don't really remember, but I think so. I mean, everyone does, usually when we don't have many other choices."

I knew about choices, I didn't have many in this town. And there is a part of me that would do anything to get out of here. I sighed heavily.

"You understand, don't you?" Lilith asked, piercing through my thoughts. Lilith sounded surprised.

"For the record, I think you might need therapy, but I get it," I told her. But then something else occurred to me.

"Okay, so you're not the devil, but you are a demon. What's the difference? Don't demons work for the devil? How does that work?" I asked. I'd grown up in church, but I still didn't know the hierarchy of Hell.

"No, I don't work for the devil. The devil, in biblical terms, is just someone who defied God. Demons, on the other hand, are the only beings that have a knowledge that human beings don't have. Human beings aren't even capable, the entire concept is really difficult to explain."

I nodded. "For the record, I'm really smart." Lilith laughed, and it made me smile. "Okay, so... other stuff I found. I did find a mention of Samael, but I didn't dig too much. I learned that your name has a few creepy meanings. I think my favorites were 'ghost' and 'night monster.' Also, there was some stuff about...Eve..."

"Eve..." Lilith repeated, her voice trailing off. She looked confused.

I waited for her to say something else, but she just stopped talking. She looked sad and confused.

"Lilith? Did you know her?" I couldn't even believe I was even asking the question.

"Hmm?" she said, snapping back to the conversation at hand. "Sorry, I'm good. Honestly, I don't think so. If I did, she clearly didn't make much of an impression."

"You seem sad," I muttered. I didn't know how or why, but for some reason, whatever she was feeling, I was feeling.

"I'm fine, really."

I didn't believe her, but I let it go. After a moment, I had another question.

"Lilith…how old are you, exactly?"

She rested her head on the back of the sofa. "Exactly? Honey, that's a lot of math."

"Am I going to become a demon?" I asked, not sure if I actually wanted the answer.

Lilith shrugged and looked at me. "That's really up to you."

"Is that what the ceremony is about?" I asked.

Lilith nodded.

And finally, it was time to ask the question that I was scared to ask. "Have you done this with anyone else?" My voice was low, barely above a whisper. She probably thought I was talking about just the ceremony, the offer, but I wasn't. I was talking about whatever was between us. I was just too afraid to ask directly.

"I've only done the ceremony one other time," Lilith replied, her voice low, her eyes closed. "Didn't go well."

I didn't smile. I didn't do anything but stare at the girl across from me who might be a billions-year-old demon. Two months ago, I'd have never stayed for this long, listening to this. But I really only had two choices: I could stay here in Benson and rot, or see what life Lilith was offering.

My decision was made. It was always going to be Lilith.

"I don't want to go home," I whispered.

She looked at me for a long moment, her eyes

serious. "Then stay with me."

The wind rushed out of me and I laughed nervously. "My parents would love that, I'm sure."

Lilith looked disappointed. She had no idea how much I didn't want to leave.

"Can I at least drive you home?" she asked.

"I would appreciate that. It's ridiculously cold out there," I told her. "Also, I really am sorry about waking you up. I should've waited until tomorrow."

She looked at me, her eyelids heavy. "I'm glad you didn't. I like having you here."

On the drive home, she held my hand again. It was kind of an absent-minded thing. Mostly our hands brushed each other, and she just held on. Whatever it was, it was becoming comfortable. This time though, I notied the ring on her middle finger.

"Where'd you get this? You wear it a lot."

Lilith took a quick glance down at our entwined hands. "Oh, the ring? I've had it for so long. Jax gave it to me ages ago."

I didn't really feel the need to press it any further. I had all kinds of weird things that seemed to pop up out of nowhere, things I picked up at carnivals that would come through or that my mom would buy online.

Lilith pulled up in front of my house. It was still

dark. At least my parents didn't know I was gone. I turned to look at her and tell her goodnight, but she was already looking at me, like she was expecting something. I felt a little breathless. I wanted to ask her if she felt the same way.

Instead, I thanked her for the ride, apologized again, and just…sat there. The air was charged, but we were both too afraid to make a move. I figured she'd have more guts than me, but it turned out we were both cowards.

Then, at the exact same time, we moved to close the distance between us. This was it. A kiss that I wanted, one that I'd waited my entire life for, one that would be the beginning of something good.

And maybe it would have been if we hadn't tilted our heads the exact same way at the exact same time. Our noses slammed into one another, and then our foreheads. I wanted to die. This had to be the single most humiliating moment of my life. The only saving grace was that it was dark.

It felt like I was watching a car crash, and I was glad she couldn't see the shade of red I must have been. So, without a word, I got out of the car, walked into the house, and decided that the next thing I'd Google was how to get into the Witness Protection Program.

CHAPTER TWENTY NINE

EVIE

I DIDN'T SLEEP AT ALL THAT NIGHT. I LAY IN bed, staring at the ceiling and replaying everything that happened. Especially the almost-kiss. I wanted a do-over on that, but after our heads collided, any trace of courage I had was gone. How was I supposed to talk to her at school on Monday? What if she called?

I heard something hit the floor. I sat up in bed to try and find the source of the sound and saw Agnes batting around a yellow highlighter she'd knocked off of my desk. I groaned and glanced over at the clock on my nightstand. The glowing red numbers indicated that it was 4:37 in the morning. Frustrated, I threw the thick comforter to the side. I hissed when my bare feet barely touched the floor, jerking them back up. It was obscenely cold. I reluctantly tip-toed to my dresser and pulled out a pair of thick wool socks. I put them on, grabbed my pink fluffy robe, and tried to quietly open my bedroom door. It squeaked anyway.

I quietly descended the stairs, hoping my dad wasn't asleep in the recliner. I cautiously ducked my head into the living room so I wouldn't give either of us a stroke, but I was relieved to find it dark and empty. Well, I was a little creeped out. Why did everything look like monsters in the dark? All this talk about demons was making me paranoid and jumpy. I heard my stomach growl, so I stepped to my left toward the kitchen.

I didn't bother turning on the light, my logic being that if I turned on a light, I had no shot at ever getting to sleep. Instead, I opened the refrigerator door, it cast a bright light over the kitchen, throwing shadows in all of its corners. I grabbed a string cheese from the fridge, an apple from the bowl on the island, and ran on my tip-toes back to the living room. Seriously, what kind of demon was I going to be if I couldn't even handle my own kitchen in the dark?

I grabbed the remote control from the end table on my left and settled into my dad's recliner. I flipped through the channels, finally settling on old reruns of *Law & Order: SVU*. I hadn't watched this show in years, and yet the next two episodes were somehow ones I'd already seen. Go figure.

When I heard my mother come downstairs a couple of hours later, I was still sitting there, wide awake.

"Evie? What are you doing up?" she whispered, stepping beside the recliner to see what I was watching on the television. "Have you been here all night?"

"Just the last few hours. I couldn't sleep, so I came down here," I answered, yawning.

She patted my arm gently. "Come into the kitchen. I'll get breakfast started."

I got up and followed my Mom into the kitchen. I sat at the island and watched her almost dance across the kitchen, somehow making the task of cracking and whisking eggs look elegant and celebratory. That was the thing about my mother – she could make the most mundane tasks look fun. It had been that way my entire life. She made games out of cleaning my bedroom or doing the dishes.

When it came to cooking for her family, every bit of her heart went into it. I felt a lump rise in my throat and tears well up in my eyes as I thought about the homemade chicken soup she would make when Bea or I was sick. I thought about my mother's easy laugh, the scent of her weird green apple shampoo.

I'd spent my entire life taking all of this for granted, taking her and my father for granted, and in three months...

Would my decision change everything for them? Would it change my parents, change Bea? Would my mom still be carefree, dancing through the kitchen and making laundry seem fun? Would I ever see them again?

"Baby? Are you okay?"

My mother's voice broke through my brain fog. "Yeah, I'm okay. I think I'm just exhausted."

A few minutes later, my father and my sister were both coming down the stairs. Bea, with her usual boundless energy, plopped into a chair next to me. My dad sat next to her. My mother put a platter of bacon on the table, and Dad and Bea immediately started fighting over a particular piece. I smiled. My heart ached at the familiarity of this scene.

Mom sat a plateful of scrambled eggs in front of me, steam rising from the plate.

"Thank you. These look delicious," I told her, looking up at her. Her eyes sparkled. I'd never noticed that before.

I was determined to soak up as much time with them as I could over the next two months. As much as I wanted out of Benson, it was never about running away from my family. Regardless of who or what I would be at the end of this ritual, I was always going to miss these three people more than anything in the world.

But I wasn't willing to walk away from Lilith. Before, it was just about getting out of Benson, seeing things, living a life. It was about getting to be myself. I didn't know what that meant at the time, but I was starting to figure it out. And Lilith was wrapped up in it.

"So, are you hanging out with Liam today?" my father asked.

I turned toward him. "Um, no, probably not," I said, looking back down at my eggs.

"You've not been hanging out with him much lately," my mother said. "Did you two have a fight?"

I huffed. "Something like that," I muttered.

"You should apologize, work it out," my father said.

"Why do you think I started the fight?" I asked him.

He stared at me. "Because you usually do."

"Well, it wasn't this time. This was one hundred percent on him." I was now feeling a bit less sentimental.

"What happened?" my mother asked.

I sighed heavily. "Nothing I want to talk about. "

"Well, you should still call him," my father said sternly.

I stared down at my plate, trying to keep my temper in check. Logically, I knew that they had no idea what happened, and I wasn't going to tell them. But the fact that they didn't seem to be on my side was a little infuriating.

I dropped my fork onto my plate with a clatter. "I am going to go shower. I need to go to the library," I lied. I didn't wait for a response. I pushed my chair back away from the table, got up, and left the kitchen.

As I stomped up the stairs to my bedroom, I realized that if it weren't for Bea, I'd leave with Lilith tonight, maybe even right now. And to think that I was just doing an entire internal monologue about how much I was going to miss them.

I went into my room, slammed the door, and let out a yelp when I turned around. Lilith was laying on my bed, reading one of my books.

CHAPTER THIRTY

LILITH

WWHAT ARE YOU DOING HERE?" EVIE whispered harshly.

I bolted up right and almost threw her book. I composed myself fairly quickly as she locked the door and stepped closer to me. She was still wearing the tattered pink robe, plaid pajamas, and thick socks from hours before. She looked cute, her hair still piled into a mess on top of her head. She also looked like one of those nerdy Rom-Com girls in the 1990s. I tried not to laugh.

"Well?" she asked again, looking at me expectantly.

"I'm sorry, but you weren't answering your phone and I had this feeling—" It definitely wasn't a lie. The twist in my gut had me in my car and headed in her direction within minutes.

"A feeling that I wanted someone waiting on my bed to give me a stroke?" she asked, interrupting me.

I sighed. She could be really obnoxious at times. "No," I said. "I was checking on you."

She tore her robe off angrily and threw it in the chair by her desk. "Yeah, everyone's just checking on me. Is Liam here to check on me as well? Is he hiding in the closet or something?"

I had no idea what was going on, but it seemed like I'd walked in on something. "No…What's going on with you? Did you hit your head? Did someone try to poison your Cheerios? You've got to give me something to work with."

Evie flopped down on her bed and looked up at me. She looked angry and sad, all at the same time. I didn't even know that was possible. I scooted over next to her and just waited for her to tell me.

"It's my parents," she said, sighing. "They think I should call Liam and apologize."

Her mood made sense now. "Do they know what happened, why you aren't speaking to him?" She shook her head. "Do you want to tell them? I'll go with you." She shook her head again.

"Honestly, I just want to get out of here, leave Benson and not look back."

My heart started pounding and my breath caught in my throat. I let it out slowly.

"We can, you know."

Evie nodded, still looking at the floor. "If it weren't for Bea, I'd pack a bag now."

I hesitantly reached up and put my hand on her back. After last night, I wasn't sure if that was okay, until she leaned over and rested her weight against me. I wasn't sure what to do next. All of this was very new, but somehow familiar, like I'd always known her. I didn't know how to be there for her the way she needed. I only knew how I would ordinarily handle it. But obliterating Liam didn't seem to be an option.

"So, what's the deal with this ritual ceremony thing?" Evie asked, bursting my thought bubble.

"What do you mean?"

"I mean, is this a *Deadpool* situation?" she asked, pulling a pillow to her chest and leaning back against the wall.

"Okay, I don't know what that means. The only thing you're turning into is a better version of yourself," I said. I leaned back against the wall next to her.

Her laugh rang out, lightening the entire mood in the room. It was like tiny bells and twinkling lights or the last day of school before summer vacation. I was guessing on that last one, but it was magical nonetheless.

"No offense, but you sound like that Rachel Hollis

lady. Next you'll be telling me that I'm living my best life and all that stuff."

"Well, I have no idea who that is either, but in a way, you will be. You'll be stronger, more powerful. You'll be more assertive, more confident, more…everything," I explained.

"So it is kind of a *Deadpool* situation," she replied.

"You're so weird."

"So what aren't you telling me?" she asked. Her expression wasn't distrusting. It was curious.

"There are a lot of things I'm not telling you just yet. But really, you shouldn't be such a worrier. It'll give you wrinkles." I touched a red-tipped finger to the space between her eyebrows, rubbing it lightly. "I won't let you walk in blind. You'll know exactly what you're walking into before the ritual. I just need for you to be patient, something you're clearly not very good at."

"Hey, I'm fine with patience. I just don't like being lied to."

I winked at her. "I'm not lying," she said. "I'm just withholding information a little bit longer."

"For the record, that's the same thing, but I'll wait."

For the rest of the weekend, all I did was think about how Evie's parents thought the situation with Liam was somehow her fault. I had a million things to say to him, and a million things I wanted to do to him. So, on Monday morning, I got to school early and found him at his locker, sitting on the ground and reading a tattered copy of On the Road.

When I stepped in front of him, he looked up, rolled his eyes, and groaned audibly. "What do you want?"

"You really may want to reconsider your tone. Lucky for you, I'm not here to tear your arms off. And believe me, I could," I told him.

He ran a hand through his shoulder-length wavy brown hair. "Then why are you here?"

I rested my hands on my hips. "I'm here about Evie."

He closed his book and sat up straighter. "Is she okay? What happened?" His tone was worried, but I wasn't willing to let him off the hook just because he was suddenly concerned about her.

"She's about as well as anyone would be if their best friend assaulted them."

I watched him clench his jaw as he turned his eyes downward. "I tried to apologize."

"Mm, no, you didn't," I said, shaking my head. "You told her that you thought she wanted it, which is basically not what any woman wants to hear after something like that."

He stayed silent. There wasn't really much he could say. He knew that I was right, that he did say those things to her.

"I want to apologize to her, but she won't even speak to me," he muttered.

"I'd love to feel sorry for you and everything, but I've been too busy making sure that the actual victim is okay."

He scoffed at me. "You mean you're trying to get rid of me so that you can have her, right? That's what you're doing, isn't it?"

"Oh, you don't need my help. You're screwing this up all by yourself."

His blue eyes widened and he started to stand up. "No, you are screwing this up. Things were fine before you got here," Liam said, taking a big step toward me. He leaned down, his face inches from mine, but I didn't flinch. I was used to worse men than this.

"Wow, you really are your father's son, aren't you?" I said, my voice only loud enough for him to hear. I watched his face redden. He was angry.

"What's going on?"

Liam and I broke apart quickly and snapped our heads in the direction of the voice. Evie was standing there, her backpack slung over her shoulder, staring at us. She looked nervous, cautious.

"It's nothing," I said, reaching up to touch her arm and steer her away. She pulled her arm out of my grasp.

"No, it's definitely something. What is going on?" she asked again.

Liam and I shot a look at one another. I opened my

mouth to tell her a lie, to tell her I was asking about an assignment or something, but Liam jumped in before I had a chance.

"So you're with her now? You're telling her everything?" he asked Evie, thrusting his thumb in my direction.

I wanted to immediately take off my boot and hit him in the head, impaling him with the heel. But the look in Evie's eyes, the complete betrayal when she looked over at me...

I crumbled. "Evie, I didn't—"

"I trusted you." That was all she said before she turned and walked away, back down the hall and out of the front double doors.

I immediately turned on him. "You're dead, do you hear me? You are dead."

Before he could answer, I was running down the hall after the only human being in the world that meant anything to me.

CHAPTER THIRTY ONE

LILITH

EVIE, COME ON, PLEASE TALK TO ME!" I shouted to her. I was pacing her in my car as she walked in the direction of her house. "Please. It isn't what you think it is. I never betrayed you. I didn't say anything!"

She laughed and shook her head. "You sound like every cheating guy ever," she said, continuing to stare straight ahead, arms crossed over her chest.

"Okay, that's just...I'm not a guy, and I definitely didn't cheat on you."

She stopped walking and spun to face me. I slammed on my breaks and against the back of my seat at the same time.

"No, you didn't cheat on me, because *we aren't together*," she said, putting a lot of emphasis on those last three words. And those three words stung. It was precisely in that moment that I realized I wanted to be with her. I knew there was something happening, but I didn't realize how badly I wanted it until she said we weren't together.

"I know, but if you would just listen to me, let me explain—" I didn't even bother finishing my sentence. The way her eyes watered when she looked at me, the way she ran her hands through the front of her hair, I didn't need to. Whether or not I did what she thought I'd done didn't matter. What mattered was that I'd hurt her.

"Do you have any idea what this is like for me? As long as I'm here in this stupid backwards town, I can't be myself. It isn't that I don't want to be with you. I *can't* be. You have all the freedom in the world, but it isn't like that for me. I can't hold your hand or ask you to prom or introduce you to my parents as anything other than my friend. And to think that you told someone before I did—"

"You want to take me to prom?" I asked, confused.

She closed her eyes and sighed. "Theoretically? Yes. But I need you to focus."

I didn't know how to respond. She was absolutely right. If things got messy, I could just pack up and walk out of this town and never give it another thought. But

Evie had a life here. She was born here, had roots here, had family here.

"Then let's go," I said, throwing the car in park. I turned off the engine and got out of the car. I stepped up to her and grabbed her by the shoulders, making her look at me. "Look, I want to be with you. So, if you need to leave for that to happen, let's go. We'll do the ritual tonight and be gone in the morning."

I saw her chin tremble. "You know I can't do that," she said quietly.

I dropped my hands from her shoulders. "Why not? How much time do you really need? This is the rest of your life we're talking about, the rest of our lives. This is everything you've ever wanted and I'm handing it to you. Haven't you already been preparing for this your entire life? Why are we waiting another two months?" I asked her. And then it occurred to me that maybe it was something else entirely.

"Are you worried about us?" I asked her. "About what could happen?"

She stared at me. I couldn't read her expression. I didn't know whether I was right or wrong, and I hated it. She took a deep breath and closed her eyes.

"I'm afraid to make a mistake. I'm afraid that leaving is a mistake, I'm afraid staying is a mistake. I'm afraid to leave Bea without anyone. I'm afraid of being with you. I'm afraid of everything. Lilith, I don't know what I'm doing."

I nodded. I didn't know how to reassure her. I knew that I'd made the right choice for myself, but it was a big choice. Neither of us knew what life would be like after her ritual, after we left Benson.

"I don't know what to tell you. I can't promise you that leaving will fix everything. But I know that staying will fix absolutely nothing. If you want to leave now, we'll do it. If you want to wait two months, six months, a year, I'll wait. I'll wait for you."

I watched Evie swallow hard and then nod slowly. She seemed to be mulling something over. I couldn't read her, and I didn't know what to do. So much had happened, so much was said within the last five minutes, and I didn't know where we stood on any of it.

"I need a minute," Evie said, turning around, walking away, and sitting on the curb. She looked so nervous, bouncing her right leg frantically, chewing her thumbnail. Every now and then, she'd rub her face with both her hands. I just stood there, hands at my sides, staring at her face, trying to figure out what she was thinking. After a few more minutes, she stood up and started pacing back and forth. This was making me nauseous. Then, as quickly as she started, she stopped. She turned and began walking in my direction.

"Okay," she started. "Tomorrow night. Let's do it."

"Are you sure?"

She gave a single quick node. "Yep. I can't wait anymore. Bea will be okay. I need to do it now."

"Okay," I said, my stomach swirling. "I'll get everything ready. You do what you need to on your end."

Evie took a deep breath and nodded. "I'll be ready."

CHAPTER THIRTY TWO

EVIE

I SPENT THE REST OF THE MORNING AT HOME alone. Both of my parents were working and Bea was at school, so I relished the quiet. I needed to think. In twenty four hours, I wouldn't be sitting in this house anymore. I wouldn't be sitting in this town anymore. With everything that happened recently, I was fine moving up our ritual timeline from New Year's Eve. I just didn't care anymore. I couldn't keep living like this.

And then there was Lilith. She wanted to be with me. She told me she did. And I said the same thing to her. It all felt very matter-of-fact, but it was there, everything we'd been too afraid to say. I did not feel any less anxious about it.

I was flipping through channels, trying to relax, when my doorbell rang. I contemplated ignoring it, but it rang again. I groaned, pulled myself out of the chair, and threw the remote where I was sitting. I grabbed the doorknob and opened the door, not having any clue who would be on the other side. When I opened it, I saw Liam standing on the porch, his back to the door.

He spun around when he heard me open it. "Hey, you are here," he said, sounding relieved.

I stayed in the doorway, not inviting him in. I just stared at him, not saying a word.

"I just wanted to make sure you were okay. You and Lilith kind of bailed today. Can I come in?"

"No."

He looked surprised by my response for some reason. He really was dense. "Is she here?"

I sighed, annoyed with him. "That's none of your business."

He nodded and looked down. "I just wanted to see if you were okay. You didn't seem okay."

"And you have no idea why, I'm sure," I said in a monotone voice.

He inhaled deeply. "Oh, no, I figured that one out."

"So, what do you want, Liam?"

He leaned against the porch railing. He looked nervous. He wasn't making eye contact, kept looking at the ground. It made me nervous.

"While your friend pisses me off, she made a good point today."

I crossed my arms over my chest. "She usually does. She's very annoying that way. What did she say?"

He rubbed his hand over his mouth and finally looked me in the eye. "She made me realize that I never apologized to you, not really. Evie, I'm so sorry. What happened that night…that never should've happened."

I tilted my head and stared at him. I wanted his apology, I needed it, but it bothered me that Lilith had to tell him to do it. So, instead, I asked him something I needed to know.

"Why did you do it? I never led you on. I never acted like I wanted that, but you did it anyway. What made you think that you had any right?" I took a slow, deep breath to try and settle myself, to try and keep from crying.

He was back to looking at the ground.

"Look at me," I demanded. He raised his head, his eyebrows knitted together. He seemed to be trying to come up with an answer.

"I don't know," he said after a beat or two. "If I'm being truthful, maybe you were right, maybe I was jealous. I mean, I've been…I've had feelings for you for a couple of years. Like, more than just friends. And then Lilith showed up…"

"This doesn't have anything to do with her. This is about what you did."

He nodded. "You're right. I don't know why I did it, and that's the truth. Maybe I panicked. Maybe I thought if you knew how I felt, you might feel the same way."

I dropped my arms to my sides. "You could've just told me. There are so many things you could've done instead of forcing yourself on me."

"I know. I guess I just felt like you were mine, that you weren't hers."

"I'm not anyone's. And I'm definitely not something that you're entitled to."

"I just got scared."

This was ridiculous. I wanted to be able to forgive him, but he was just giving me excuses. His apology wasn't about me. He wanted me to reassure him, to tell him it was okay, and I would be damned if I was going to tell him that it was all forgiven.

"Well, I'm glad you got that off your chest," I told him. "Feel better?"

"Are you with her?"

We were back at this. "Jesus, Liam, when are you going to let that go?"

"It matters to me," he said.

"Well, it shouldn't. It's none of your business who I am or am not with. Now I'm going to go back inside. There's somewhere other than here that I'd like to be."

"Evie…"

I turned and went back inside, shutting the door on

him.

"Evie, you have to talk to me!" I heard him shout through the door.

I didn't have to talk to him at all. I wanted to tell him that he was lucky I even let him say that much. Instead, I just went back into the living room and turned the volume up on the television.

Dinner that night was awkward, to say the least. It was probably only awkward on my end, but still, that made a difference. I didn't know whether I should tell them that I would be leaving the next night with Lilith, or if I just shouldn't say anything at all. I almost blurted it out while my mom was putting a platter of rolls in the center of the table, but I managed to keep myself under control.

"You okay?" my father asked when I didn't realize he was passing a plate to me.

I blinked rapidly, trying to focus. "I'm good. I think I just haven't been sleeping much lately and it's catching up with me. I came home early from school today to try and get some rest, but it didn't work. I'm sorry I didn't call either of you."

"That isn't like you. You haven't missed school in... years," my mother said. "Are you sure that's all it is?"

I forced a smile. "Yeah, that's all it is."

"Okay. Just…tell me when you're not feeling well," she said.

During the rest of dinner, my irritation at my family from the day before began to soften. I didn't know for sure if I'd ever see them again. At the very least, it wouldn't be for quite some time. I ate slowly, making it a point to remember everything. I tried to engage in the conversation. I laughed when Bea told a story about accidentally putting her costume on inside out at rehearsal the day before. I assured my father that everything was going to be okay when he told us that shifts were being cut at work. I even offered to help my mother with the grocery shopping after school the following day.

I thought that leaving would be easy, but it was proving to be a little harder than I anticipated.

CHAPTER THIRTY THREE

EVIE

AFTER SCHOOL THE FOLLOWING DAY I WAS leaning against a shopping cart while my mother asked how Bobby, the son of the butcher, and his family were doing. Bobby was a couple of years older than me, and he was already married with a kid. His family had been in the butchering business for generations. Yet another casualty of Benson. I immediately wanted to kick myself for thinking it. I didn't want to spend my last day in Benson being an asshole.

I didn't know exactly what was prompting my change in attitude. Maybe it was because I might never see any of this again. Maybe I loved this town and the people in it a little more than I wanted to admit.

Maybe I was having second thoughts.

"Thank you, Bobby! Tell your mother I said hello," I heard my mom say cheerfully. She turned and put three large bundles wrapped in butcher's paper into the cart.

She put an arm around me, and I stiffened a little. Things were so strained, at least on my end, since the other day. I didn't know if I should hug her back or just not do anything at all. But, before I could overthink it any further, I wrapped my own arm around my mother's slender waist and leaned against her. She hummed contentedly.

"I am so happy to get to spend time with you today," my mother said.

"Me too."

We walked down the well-lit cereal aisle like this, our arms wrapped around each other. My eyes were immediately assaulted by an army of cartoon characters staring out at me from a wall of brightly-colored boxes. My mother grabbed a small box of Cinnamon Squares with a dancing cinnamon stick in a top hat on the bright red box. It was Bea's favorite. I laughed to myself because it used to be my favorite at her age too.

"What's so funny?" my mother asked, a smile spreading across her finely-lined face.

I shook my head, feeling more nostalgic than amused. "You've been buying that same brand of cereal since I was younger than Bea."

My mom looked at the box in her hand. "You might be right. I don't think I'd ever realized that before," she said, chuckling. "Maybe you'll both buy it for your own kids one day."

I laughed. "Well, maybe Bea will. I think that we can both agree I'm not quite the mothering type."

"I don't think that's true at all. You're so good with Bea, and you were always good with your cousins."

"So I'm a great cousin and a great sister. That doesn't make me a great mom."

My mother shook her head. "You don't think enough of yourself, Evie. I wish you did. You're so smart, and beautiful, and talented. Maybe your father and I didn't tell you enough."

I was taken by surprise. It was true, they never really told me those things, but I never expected either of them to admit it.

"That's why you want to leave, isn't it?" she asked me.

I didn't really know how to answer that one. "No, not at all. I just want more opportunities, more experiences, just...more. I can't forge my own path here, and I want to do that. I want to go someplace where no one knows me. I want to go out into the world and surprise myself, and be surprised. I want to meet other people. I want to see things in person, not just in books."

She smiled sadly, looking off into the distance. Something flashed across her face, just for a second. As soon as it was there, it was gone.

"Mom?"

"I used to want those things too, you know," she confessed quietly. She acted like the mere suggestion that she used to want something else for herself might be blasphemous. "I used to want to see every library in the world. It's so silly, isn't it?"

I shook my head. "It isn't silly. There are some incredible libraries out there."

"Yes, there are. But, you know, the first time I noticed your father staring at me from across the school cafeteria…all I could see were wedding bells and babies."

I laughed. As much as the idea of this for myself was nauseating, the way my mother smiled was sweet. All I wanted was my own shot at that much happiness and contentment. All I wanted was to feel fulfilled with my life, just like my mother felt about hers.

"You know your sister is going to miss you," my mother said, searching the cereal shelves for something. "She's afraid you'll forget about her."

I had no idea that Bea felt that way, and it made me sad. "No, that could never happen. I love Bea. And leaving doesn't mean I'll never be back."

"I know that, but she doesn't. She's just a little girl, Evie."

We both stayed silent while she continued her search for another box of cereal. The idea that Bea could ever be forgotten…especially by me.

"So what's on your agenda for tonight?" my mother asked, finally locating a box of fiber cereal and placing it in the cart.

"Oh, um, just hanging out with Lilith," I said. "We've got a test coming up."

"You two are spending a lot of time together. Is Liam going to be there?" she asked.

I shook my head. "No, he won't."

"I'm a little worried that you're ignoring your best friend to hang out with this new person."

"Liam and I got into it, so we're just taking some time to cool off, that's all," I said. It wasn't a total lie. I thought about telling her what happened, but decided against it. There were going to be enough questions when I left town. I didn't need to put another burden, another worry, on my parents.

As I wheeled the cart through the store behind my mother, I started to feel a little weird. The lights felt too bright, and it felt like the shelves were getting a little too close.

"Do you remember if we needed more oranges? I can't remember," my mother said.

I tried to answer her, but my heart started racing. She didn't notice as she picked up a bag of clementines. She put them in the cart and started to walk away, but I couldn't get my feet to move. I could hear her calling my name, but it sounded like she was miles away. The supermarket lights were still so bright. I looked at my mother who was looking back at me with concern. She took a step toward me. The blood was roaring in my ears and I put my hand to my chest. Was I having a heart attack? Is this what a heart attack feels like? My breathing started to become labored. I gripped the handle of the cart and started gasping for air. I could hear my mother calling out my name again, but I still couldn't answer. I could only stare at her, my eyes wide and my chest tight. I looked around the aisle frantically, trying to find a way out. Colors were swirling around me so quickly that I started to become dizzier by the second. I tried to use the cart to anchor myself, but the wheels began to slowly slide across the linoleum.

"Evie!" I heard my mother's muffled yell, but it was too late.

I was already falling backwards.

"Evie? Evie, can you hear me?"

My eyes fluttered open and I immediately became aware of the throbbing pain in the back of my head. I groaned, raising my hand to it. I looked at the face of my mother, who was bathed in a halo of fluorescent light. That's when I remembered we were in the grocery store.

"What happened?" I groaned again, wincing when

I touched the back of my head. It took me a moment to realize I was lying on the floor. I reached for my mother's hand to help pull myself up.

As I struggled to right myself, I realized that we were not the only two people in the aisle. A very small group was gathered, mostly employees, to see what happened.

"Oh my God," I muttered, fighting to get to my feet.

"Take it easy, Evie." My mother's voice was calm, comforting. "An ambulance is on its way, honey."

"A what?" I didn't think that this could possibly get any more embarrassing.

"You stopped responding to me and passed out. I wasn't sure what was happening, but Justin called an ambulance and stayed with us."

I looked over at the boy that my mother was gesturing to. I recognized the sandy-haired boy from one of my classes but I couldn't think of his name.

"Mom, I don't need an ambulance. I'm fine, seriously." I tried again to get to my feet just as two paramedics were rounding the corner and into my path. They quickly dropped down on either side of me and began firing questions. I knew the older paramedic, Bailey, as a customer in my parents' bookstore. I sold him several Science Fiction novels.

"Hey, can you tell me your name?" Bailey asked me.

"Evie," I answered.

"Good, Evie. Do you know where you are? What's

the last thing you remember?"

I thought for a second. "My mom was asking something about oranges," I said, a little confused. Bailey looked up at my mother who nodded.

"That's great. We're just going to run some vitals, make sure you didn't have a sudden drop in blood sugar or anything. Can you tell me what happened?"

"I'm not really sure," I told him. "Everything was fine, and then the lights got really bright and it felt like the walls were closing in. My heart started racing, things got blurry, I started breathing really hard, and I guess I just passed out."

While I was telling him all of this, another paramedic, someone I recognized but didn't really know, pricked my finger, then checked my pulse and blood pressure.

"Evie, have you had a panic attack before?" the second paramedic asked while putting away his equipment.

I shook my head, confused. "No, never."

"Is that what happened?" my mother asked, a slight panicked edge to her voice.

"I think so. Your blood pressure is a little low, but nothing to be concerned about right now. Your pulse is slightly elevated. Blood sugar is normal. Were you feeling anxious before this happened?" he asked.

"She has a big test coming up," my mother answered for me.

I nodded. Anxiety certainly made sense. I mean,

selling my soul or whatever in a couple of hours would give anyone anxiety, right?

My mother looked worried.

"I'm fine, really," I told her. "It's probably just senior year stuff, you know?"

My mother visibly relaxed. "You really shouldn't worry this much."

"My head hurts," I said, changing the subject. The first paramedic gingerly touched the back of my head, pushing slightly on a bump that was forming back there. I winced.

"It doesn't seem like a serious hit, but there's definitely a knot back there. We can take you to get it looked at, if you want." I shook my head. He nodded. "Then you should be fine with an ice pack," he said. "Just give us a call if the dizziness returns or you begin vomiting."

My mother started to object, but I said I'd give it a couple of hours and go from there. The paramedic had me sign a form, and they left. The small crowd began to disperse, apparently disappointed that I wasn't dying or anything.

"We should go home. I can do all of this tomorrow," my mother said, helping me up off the floor.

I shook my head. "No, it's fine. We're almost finished. We'll grab the milk and eggs and then go home. Really, I'm okay."

My mother opened her mouth to protest, but

stopped herself. Instead, she nodded, took the cart from me, and moved us slowly toward the cold section of the store.

CHAPTER THIRTY FOUR

LILITH

I LIT THE LAST CANDLE IN THE LIVING ROOM and looked around. The quivering flames cast shadows that danced off of the walls and across the ceiling. Evie sent me a text an hour before saying that she'd be here soon, so I thought that I'd use the opportunity to make the place a little homier, a little more lived-in. Evie was right, it did look cold in here, so hopefully she would find it more comfortable. I purchased a couple of art prints at a local shop in town, flowers from the florist near the grocery store, and was lighting scented candles that I had laying around.

The sound of the doorbell ripped through my thoughts. I took a last look around, tugged at the hem of my top to straighten it out, and made my way to the front door. I felt strangely nervous, like most girls might feel before a first date, or their prom, or whatever it was that human girls were into. After the previous day, it felt like a lot was riding on this. It was the first time we'd been alone since then.

I pulled the door open to find Evie standing there looking haggard. She was pale, tired, and disheveled in an over-sized hooded sweatshirt. I furrowed my brow in concern and motioned for her to come inside.

She shook her head. "I'm not staying," she muttered. Before I could object, she put her hand up to stop me. "I don't think that I can do this."

"What are you talking about? Of course you can. This is what you said you wanted," I replied, the panic starting to rise in my voice, started to coil around inside me like a snake.

"I've been thinking about it all day," she said, looking agitated and anxious. She was a little jumpy, unable to stand still without moving. "I don't know if I can leave my parents, leave Bea. She's so young, and my mom says Bea thinks I'll forget her. She's so young. She won't understand. And there's no plan. I don't know what happens to me, to us, once this is finished."

I took a deep breath and tried to quiet my own feelings about losing Evie in an effort to regain control over the situation. "But…isn't this what you want? This is your chance to get everything you've been dreaming about - traveling, a life of your own."

She covered her face with her hands. When she pulled them away, her eyes were glistening. "I haven't heard from a single school that I applied to. Not a single word, not even a rejection letter. I had a panic attack at the grocery store today. A panic attack. I literally passed out there on the floor! I'm not ready for this! This was a mistake."

It felt like I'd been punched in the gut. "Are you okay?" I asked, my own panic rising to the surface. "Please, come inside. Let's just talk about this."

She stared at me for a moment before nodding and stepping inside.

I let her lead us to the living room. She began pacing, so I stood in the entry of the living room, arms crossed over my chest in an effort to protect myself from whatever hurt was heading my way.

"Okay, so correct me if I'm wrong, but no one hears from college until the Spring, right? You're freaking out over nothing. Besides, if you leave with me, it won't matter. You're just nervous," I stammered, stepping forward and reaching out to touch Evie's arm. "That's normal. Everyone gets nervous until it happens. Once it's over, you'll be completely fine, I promise."

She shook her head. "I need more time. I need to think. I need to know that Bea will be okay without me."

"Bea's a strong girl. She'll be okay. You keep using her as an excuse, Evie. Do you really think a sister who talks a big game about leaving and then caves out of fear is really what's best for Bea? What kind of example is that for her?"

It was a low blow, and I could see by the look on Evie's face that it stung. Bea was the most important thing in Evie's life. I knew that implying Evie was a failure was probably not my best strategy, but subtlety didn't work well with her either.

"Look, Evie, I'm sorry," I said. "Bea will be fine. She isn't unhappy here. She doesn't want to leave. But you do, so what's going on?"

"I need time," she said again, her eyes downcast.

"You keep saying that. I don't know what that means. You've made the decision. I don't understand why you keep saying you need more time to decide about a decision you've already made." It occurred to me then that we might be skirting around the real reason she needed time. "This isn't about needing time to make a decision, is it? This is about needing time to be sure I'm the one you want to leave with. This is you not knowing if you really want to be with me."

Her lip quivered and she turned away from me. It was clear that I was right. I heard her taking gulping breaths, and when she finally turned back toward me, her cheeks were wet.

"I told you – I don't know what I'm doing, and I'm scared. It isn't about being sure about you. It's about doing this for the right reasons, and I can't be leaving just because there's a girl I want to be with. You can understand that, right? You of all people can understand?" She asked, pleading with me. "I need to do this for me, and right now I'm not sure if it's for you or for me. If I'm doing this to be with you and it all falls apart, I'm left with nothing, with no direction, with nothing of my own. If I leave for me, because of all of the things I want, then I have a life with you in it instead of a life that hangs on whether we're together."

As much as it hurt, I did understand. "I get it. This is why you keep putting it off? Why you've been having panic attacks, right?"

She looked confused. "I've only had the one panic attack," she said, moving toward the sofa and sitting down.

I followed her. "No, you've had at least two since I've been in town."

"What are you talking about?"

"You had the attack today, and you had one the other day when you and I were at the grocery. Don't you remember?"

I stared at her face as she remembered. "That wasn't anything like today. I didn't pass out or anything."

"You don't have to pass out to be having a panic

attack, Evie. That day in the store, you looked terrified. You were fine one minute, and then you started acting a little weird. You were frantically looking everywhere, you were breathing pretty heavily, and then you started freaking out and saying we needed to get out of there. Once we were out, you seemed to calm down."

"That was just because people were staring."

I nodded. "I know."

We were quiet for a few minutes.

"The grocery store seems to freak me out a lot," Evie said thoughtfully.

"Yeah, I'd say so. Why?"

She shrugged. "I honestly have no idea."

We sat staring at our hands for what felt like an eternity. What was there to say? She was having panic attacks about leaving with me. I was putting so much on her, and she kept telling me she needed time to sort things out. I kept pushing. I was doing this to her and I hated it. I knew that I shouldn't say anything else about it right now, but I couldn't help it.

"You don't have to do this. You don't have to do the ritual. You don't have to leave with me," I said. She looked up at me, her expression frustrated. "I am doing this to you, and it's the last thing that I want. So I'm pulling back. Whatever you decide, it won't be because I talked you into it. I'm here either way, but I won't say anything else about it, okay?"

"That's not what I meant," she said.

"It's what I mean."

With that, Evie scoffed, stood up, and walked away.

CHAPTER THIRTY FIVE

EVIE

HUMANS HAVE A WEIRD IDEA ABOUT Halloween," Lilith said as she looked through a costume catalog while sprawled out across my bed. I sat on the floor, back against the bed, attempting to make sense of my English homework.

This was the closest we'd been to normal for a few weeks. To say that the last month was awkward would be an understatement. Lilith and I still spent time together, but it was different. There was no more talk about the ritual, just like she'd promised. I did continue to think about it, to consider my options, but there was no forward motion.

"Are you about to give me a lesson on the

commercialization of a holiday with Pagan origins?" I asked, turning my head to look at her.

Lilith smiled at me. "Wow, I'm impressed."

I rolled my eyes. "I swear, you act like I live in some alternate universe."

"I think that some of the people living here do, but not you. You seem pretty okay."

I laughed. "Well, I'm glad you think so. I'd hate to disappoint."

"You? Never," she said.

She was quiet for a minute before she sighed. I took a deep breath. She was up to something.

"What is it?" I asked.

"What do you mean?" she asked, feigning innocence.

I put my book down, turned to face her, and propped my elbows on the bed. "That sigh means you want to ask me something, but you think I'll say no, so you pretend like it's important so I'll say yes."

She looked at me and smiled mischievously. "There's a party tonight."

"Nope," I said, turning back around.

"Oh, come on. It's Halloween."

"Weren't you the one just complaining about how people don't honor the holiday correctly?" I asked.

"No, that was you. Come on, Evie. We can go, you can be a stupid teenager for once. If you get drunk, you can stay at my house and your parents will never know."

I shook my head. "We weren't invited."

She was quiet for a second. "Um…I was…"

I didn't know what to say. My feelings weren't exactly hurt about not receiving an invitation, and I wasn't really surprised that Lilith did get one, but it was just another example of being an outcast here.

"I think you forget that those kids hate me," I muttered.

I felt her arm wrap around my neck. "I'll be with you the entire time."

I reached up and touched her arm. "I think that's great and all, but that's putting me in a really weird position, and I'm pretty surprised you'd do that."

She took her arm back. "I'm sorry, you're right. That was a shitty thing of me to do. I just thought we'd go, crash a party, start some rumors."

"There are enough rumors about me already, thank you very much."

"Hey, me too. They think I'm dating the hot girl," she said, nudging me with her shoulder.

I laughed. "I think you're insane. Besides, I have plans."

I felt the mattress bounce as Lilith jumped off the bed and sat in front of me. "Plans? What plans? You didn't tell me about any plans."

"I'm taking Bea trick-or-treating. I've been doing it every year since she was five. My parents take her to some very wholesome thing at church in the afternoon, and then I take her out that night to parade among monsters," I said, wiggling my eyebrows.

"Ooh, that sounds fun! Would it be okay if I tagged along? I've never done that before," she asked.

I doubted that Bea would protest. Bea thought Lilith was the coolest person she'd ever met. She'd walked Bea home after school with me a few times, and the two of them never stopped talking. It was annoying.

"I'm sure Bea would love that," I said.

"And you?" Lilith asked.

I smiled at her. "I think that would be fun. We leave in an hour," I told her.

"Awesome. I'm going home to change."

"Oh God, please don't wear a costume," I groaned.

"Oh, don't be so dramatic. I'm not wearing a costume."

When she moved to stand up, she stumbled and stopped herself inches from my face. I held my breath, not sure what was going to happen next. After that night in her car, we'd never come close to kissing again. I wasn't sure why, but it just never felt like the right time.

"Are...you okay?" I whispered, staring into her eyes.

Lilith's breathing picked up a little. "I'm okay."

After another second or two, she pulled back and stood up, leaving me on the floor, butterflies flooding my stomach.

"I'll see you in an hour," she said quietly before walking out of my bedroom door.

"Bea, hurry up! You'll miss all the good candy, and you know Mrs. Henny's goes fast," I shouted up the staircase.

"I'm hurrying! My wings are stuck!" she yelled back.

Before I could say anything else, a knock at the door distracted me. I walked the few steps and opened it to find Lilith standing there in fitted distressed jeans, an olive green t-shirt, and a leather jacket. Well, at least I wasn't under-dressed in my jeans, t-shirt, and flannel.

"You look comfy," Lilith said happily.

"I can never tell if that's a compliment," I said, looking down at myself.

"No, it's definitely a compliment," she winked.

I opened my mouth to thank her when I saw her eyes drift behind me.

"Whoa, little fairy! You look great!" Lilith said.

I turned to see Bea at the top of the stairs in her glitter-covered costume, complete with giant fairy wings.

"Thanks! My mom made it!" Bea said excitedly. She came bounding down the stairs, her wings almost taking out a family portrait from the year before.

"Thank you both so much for taking her out," my mother said, looking exhausted. "You have no idea how much I appreciate you doing this every year, Evie." She leaned over and kissed my cheek. I smiled at her.

"I like it," I told her. "I get all of her candy corn."

"Gross," Bea said, turning her nose up.

"Lilith, enjoy your first Benson Halloween!" my mother said.

"I plan to. Thanks so much," Lilith said smiling.

My parents took a photo of the three of us in front of the staircase, Lilith had one arm around Bea and the other around my waist.

"Oh, that's going on the staircase," my mother said as she checked the photo on her phone. I rolled my eyes.

"We'll see you later," I said, leading Lilith and Bea through the front door.

We dropped Bea back off at home two hours later, amped up on the candy apple she'd devoured on the way home. I was really glad I wouldn't have to deal with putting her to bed.

"Okay," Lilith started, linking arms with me as we walked down the front walk toward her car. The plan was to go back to her place, make a huge bowl of popcorn, and scare ourselves by sitting in the dark and watching horror films. Something told me that was about to change.

"I know you said no to the party, but what if we only went for, like, an hour?" Lilith asked, leaning against me outside of her car.

I stared at her, slightly annoyed at the change in plans but very much enjoying the feeling of her weight against me. "I don't even understand why you want to go."

"I don't know. I've never been to a stupid high school party. We can make fun of everyone drinking too much and sloppily making out in dark corners. You cannot tell me that won't be hilarious," she said.

I bit my lower lip. I was not going to tell her that I wanted to be one of those stupid drunk kids sloppily making out with her in a dark corner. "Fine," I finally said. "But I hate you."

"I know," she smiled, opening my car door.

We pulled up in front of Phillip Simpkins' house a few minutes later. It wasn't hard to miss. Orange and purple lights from the yard were pointed at the house making intermingling swirls of ghosts and pumpkins. As Lilith and I stood on the sidewalk in front of the house, I could see kids in the windows, spilling out onto the porch and the front yard. I felt a very deep sense of dread. I really didn't want to be here.

"I don't know why I let you talk me into this," I said to Lilith.

"It'll be fun. Just relax. I'll stay with you the entire time," she assured me.

"Oh, you better."

"Evie! Lilith! You came!" A visibly drunk Max Brady stumbled in our direction. It was hard not to laugh. "You never come to parties, Evie!"

"I never get invited!" I yelled over the music spilling out of the house.

He laughed loudly. "You're so funny!" Without another word, he turned and walked back over to his group. I shot a wide-eyed look at Lilith who just shrugged and laughed.

I reluctantly followed her up the walk and into the house. The music was deafening. I cringed. There were people everywhere. My anxiety rose exponentially.

I felt Lilith grab my wrist. "Come on," she yelled. "There's an empty corner over there!" She pointed to a corner in the dining room, dark and away from most of the people. I nodded and let her lead me in that direction.

We stood there for a few minutes just people watching. The popular girls stood in a group daintily holding red cups and sipping, careful not to spill anything on themselves. Football players were stereotypically doing shots in the living room. A few people were attempting to dance nearby. A few people were pointing in our direction and whispering. Not surprising.

"Hey, do you want a drink?" Lilith asked, leaning in and speaking loudly in my ear. I winced.

I nodded. It was the only way I was going to make it through this hour. Besides, the drinks were stationed just across the dining room, so I wouldn't lose sight of her. She squeezed my arm before stepping away, weaving through the crowd near us. It was then that I felt a hard tap on my shoulder.

I spun around to see Liam. I blinked a few times. This was not his scene. Once I was past the initial confusion at seeing him, fury bubbled to the surface. I made a quick glance in Lilith's direction, but she was carefully ladling something green into red cups.

"What do you want?" I yelled at Liam.

"I didn't expect to see you here," he yelled back.

"Yeah, well, I didn't plan to be."

And then he just stood there, staring at me.

"What do you want, Liam?" I asked him. My throat hurt from my yelling.

"Can we go someplace and talk?" he asked.

I looked at him incredulously. "No, we cannot go someplace and talk. I don't want to talk to you."

"Please, you have to talk to me."

And there it was, him constantly telling me that I had to talk to him. I didn't have to do anything. The fury that was bubbling inside me a moment ago was turning into something I couldn't place. It was like...anger and fire coming together until it was close to an explosion. I felt it in my stomach.

"I don't have to do anything!" I screamed. "Leave me the fuck alone!"

I watched his eyes widen, the force of my words sending him stumbling backward. A few people nearby stopped what they were doing to watch what was unfolding. Everything felt so vivid, so sharp, like suddenly I was staring at everything through brand new eyeglasses after getting so used to fuzzy vision. I became aware that I was in a dominant stance, my feet planted firmly on the floor, my eyes not leaving his. If he made a move, I was ready for it. I didn't know why he would, not in a space this public, but it didn't matter. I was ready.

CHAPTER THIRTY SIX

LILITH

I FELT IT BEFORE I SAW ANYTHING. ONE SECOND I was pouring some strong-smelling green liquid into cups, and the next I felt a powerful wave of something pour over the room. I turned to see Evie squared off against a terrified Liam. Even from where I stood, I could see Evie's chest rising and falling in deep, measured breaths. She wasn't afraid of him – she was going to kill him.

I dropped the cup in my hands and it went clattering to the floor. I was across the room faster than I thought possible, grabbing her arm and pulling her through the crowd of onlookers. The pulsating music seemed so out of place all of a sudden. I dragged Evie through the front door and down the porch steps, my hand firmly around her forearm.

"When we're in the car, you are explaining what the fuck just happened," I said, dragging her through the front yard.

She didn't say anything. She just let me pull her toward my car parked just around the corner past a stop sign. I hit the button on my keychain to unlock the doors, yanked the passenger side door open, and held the door until she was inside. Her face was frozen in shock. Whatever happened back in the house with Liam, she hadn't expected that reaction from herself. I closed her door and jogged to the driver's side.

As I pulled away from the curb, I didn't waste time. "Evie, I need you to tell me what happened back there. Did Liam do something?" I asked hesitantly.

I took a glance over at her. She looked like she was trying to remember something.

"I don't know."

"What do you remember?"

She waited a moment before responding. "I remember him tapping me on the shoulder, dezmanding that I had to talk to him. And then I felt this...rage. All of a sudden, he was stumbling away from me and he looked scared," she said. She grabbed my leg. "I didn't do anything to him, I swear. I didn't hurt him."

I put my hand on hers. "I believe you. It's okay. I'm

just going to take you back to my house for awhile, okay?"

She didn't say anything, but I saw her nod out of the corner of my eye. Neither of us spoke during the rest of the short ride to my house. I gripped the steering wheel while Evie stared down at her lap.

After I parked, I led her up my front steps and unlocked the door. I stepped aside to let her in, trying to get a look at her face. It was shielded by her hair. Evie walked into the living room and sat on the floor in front of the sofa.

"Do you want tea or anything?" I asked her.

She nodded. "Tea, please," she said, her voice barely rising above a whisper.

I was reluctant to leave her alone. Whatever happened back at the party, it was taking its toll on her. She looked scared and confused. I wished I'd never taken her to that stupid party. I was just trying to find us something new to do instead of always sitting on my sofa talking about serious life-altering things. As I put the kettle on the stove and waited for it to boil, I wished I could go back and stick with the original plan: horror movies and popcorn. If I had, there wouldn't be a freaked out girl sitting on my living room floor.

I jumped when the kettle whistled. I dropped a bag of rose tea into a mug and poured steaming water over it. I carefully carried the mug into the living room, handing it to Evie, and sitting cross-legged in front of her.

"Are you okay?" I asked her, touching her knee.

"I don't know," she said, blowing on the tea. "I wish I had a better answer, but I don't."

"No, that's okay. I'm sorry I dragged you to that stupid party. We should've just stayed here like we planned."

She was shaking her head. "Neither of us knew that was going to happen."

"No, I should've known. You said you didn't want to go, and I—"

"Lilith, it's fine. It isn't anyone's fault. I just wish I could figure out what happened."

"What did it feel like?"

Evie took a deep breath and a sip of her tea. "Like this surge of something in my stomach. Like...fire and power and some weird force."

I stared at her. Maybe Jax was right after all, maybe there was something special about her, something that would be important to him. I hated that he treated Evie like some kind of commodity, like everyone else in his life. She wasn't some random girl to me, especially not when she was sitting on my floor looking like she'd done something awful.

"It'll be okay. You were probably just panicking and reacted," I tried to reassure her.

"Couldn't be. I only panic at the grocery store," Evie joked, smiling at me over her mug.

I laughed. "There she is," I said, relieved to have her

back. "You know, we can still salvage this night. I'm happy to go make popcorn and we can watch *The Exorcist*," I offered.

"I would like that," she said.

CHAPTER THIRTY SEVEN

EVIE

THE WEEK RIGHT BEFORE A HOLIDAY WAS more stress than anyone should ever have to deal with. Thanksgiving was days away, and the previous two weeks were nothing but exams at school and finalizing menus with Mom at home. It was exhausting. Lilith, on the other hand, studied with me at the kitchen table while simultaneously helping my mom decide between regular green beans and green bean casserole.

"Lilith, do you have plans for Thanksgiving? Are you parents going to be in town?" my mother asked as Lilith and I studied for a history exam the following day. It was the last one before the four-day weekend.

Lilith looked over at me. I shrugged. "Um, no. I don't

have plans. Neither of my parents are going to be home, so I was going to just make something for myself and maybe catch up on my reading," she lied. I rolled my eyes.

My mother put her hands on her hips. "You should join us!" she said enthusiastically. "I always make too much, and we would love to have you. No need for you to be alone."

I saw Lilith smile. "I would love to, thank you." I tried to hide a smile.

"Liam will be here too, so that'll be fun," my mother said before turning back to her menu planning. I nearly choked on my water.

"You did what?" I asked, not sure I heard her correctly. I heard Lilith mutter something one should never say in front of parents under her breath.

"I invited Liam. Apparently you neglected to. He's here every year," my mother said.

"I didn't invite him because we still aren't speaking," I said.

"Evie, I'm surprised at you. Regardless of how mad you are at him, you know his home situation. He spends every holiday with us."

I immediately felt guilty. My parents treated him like a son. He'd always been family. But I didn't want him here.

"Mom, I know you mean well, but I'm not comfortable with him being here," I said, trying to be calm about it.

"Are you ever going to tell me what happened?" she asked me.

I looked over at Lilith who was trying her hardest to pretend she wasn't overhearing all of this.

"No, I'm sorry, but it's between me and Liam."

My mother's eyebrows rose. "Oh God, did you two—?"

"Oh my God, Mom, no! Why would you even think that?" I shrieked. Lilith's face turned hard, her jaw clenching.

My mother put her hands up in surrender. "I don't know. You're both practically adults, you spend all your time together. We all figured it would happen sooner or later."

I put my face in my hands. This was humiliating.

"Nothing…like that happened," I said. I couldn't tell her that he certainly tried.

"Well, whatever it is, you'll just have to put it aside. He's family, and he's going to be here," she said sternly. The matter was clearly closed.

Are you okay? Lilith mouthed when my mother turned her back to us. I mouthed back that I was not okay. She carefully reached under the table and rubbed my leg in a comforting gesture. I jumped. With my mother mere feet away, I panicked. Lilith's eyes widened.

I'm sorry, she mouthed. I shook my head. I closed my

government book.

"I think if I read one more thing about government institutions, I'm going to lose my mind," I said, pushing the book away from me. "Wanna go for a walk?" I asked Lilith.

"Yes, please," she said, closing her own book.

We grabbed our things and piled them neatly on the bench in the front hall before grabbing our jackets.

"Be back later," I shouted as I was closing the door. We were halfway down the walkway before I mentioned Liam. "Well, Thanksgiving is going to be weird."

"Isn't that an understatement? Are you going to be okay?" Lilith asked, shoving her hands in the pockets of her brown leather jacket.

I shrugged. "You heard my mom. It's happening. It's only one day. I can be okay for that long, right? Besides, you'll be there," I said, nudging her.

She didn't react. Her face was serious. "I'm sorry about that back there, about touching you like that," she said, staring at her feet walking across the pavement.

"It's okay, I don't mind. I think I just overreacted because we were talking about Liam, I guess. You were just trying to calm me down, and I appreciate it."

Lilith nodded. "It'll be okay. Besides, if he does anything, one of us can always stab him with that turkey carver thing," she said.

"See, other people would think you were joking," I

said.

"And yet…"

We both laughed. As we kept walking, I hoped we wouldn't need that electric turkey carver.

CHAPTER THIRTY EIGHT

EVIE

THANKSGIVING MORNING WAS ITS USUAL nightmare. My mother was snapping at all of us the entire time for a plethora of reasons: I wasn't setting the table correctly, Bea had her dress on too early, my father was stationed in front of the television and not helping. I really wanted to duck upstairs until her head stopped spinning, but I was now peeling five thousand potatoes for six people.

Halfway through my potato peeling, the doorbell rang.

"I'll get it!" Bea yelled, hurling herself toward the door in her yellow dress. I heard her fling the door open and it bounced off the door stopper behind it that had to be installed for this exact reason. "Lilith! You came!"

"I said I'd be here. I couldn't miss spending the day with you," Lilith said cheerfully. I smiled to myself and narrowly missed peeling off a layer of fingernail.

"Hey, everyone. Happy Thanksgiving," Lilith said as she entered the kitchen. I turned my head, looking at her in relief. I was also a little surprised to see that she'd dressed up for the occasion, wearing a short flared black and red polka dot dress under her usual leather jacket. She really was beautiful. I smiled at her.

"You're just in time. Grab a peeler from that drawer next to the fridge. You're helping me," I instructed.

"You got it, boss," she said, taking off her jacket. "Everything smells incredible, Mrs. Franklin."

"Oh, thank you, honey. I'm so glad you could be here," my mother said. In a move no one was expecting, my mother leaned over and kissed her cheek like she did with me and Bea. Lilith and I just stared at each other before I shrugged, pleasantly surprised.

Lilith grabbed a peeler out of the drawer and came to sit next to me at the kitchen island. I shoved half the potatoes in her direction and she enthusiastically dove into the task. I was going to have to reexamine our friendship if this was her idea of a good time.

"Bea, honey, can you tell your father to go to the store? I'm almost out of butter," my mother said. The way she said "your father" was a sure-fire indicator that he was not currently on her good side. I pressed my lips together and tried not to laugh.

Oh, how I loved the holidays.

Dinner was almost ready when Liam walked through the front door.

"Hey, everybody!" he shouted as he stepped into the kitchen. Lilith and I looked at each other as we loaded the table with bowls and platters of side dishes.

"Liam, I'm so glad you could make it," my mother said.

"What can I help with?" he asked, eyeing Lilith.

"Nothing at all," my father said. "Just have a seat. Everything's taken care of."

"Yes, it is," my mother said, sending the biting remark in my father's direction. Dinner would at least be entertaining.

Liam took his usual seat next to Bea. She beamed up at him, and he returned the grin. I wanted to pull her away from him, but I knew he wouldn't hurt her. The only person in the room that wasn't safe from him was me.

I sat next to Lilith across from Bea and Liam, my parents at either end of the table. While I tried to avoid Liam's eyes, I also couldn't help glaring at him from time to time. I tried to keep any conversation between us civil, but it wasn't easy. Luckily, Lilith was a good buffer. She was much better at faking polite conversation than I was. From time to time, she would press her thigh against mine under the table in a reassuring gesture. I might've been afraid a few days ago, but today I welcomed it. I needed to know someone was on my side.

"So, Liam, how did exams go for you this week?" my father asked.

Liam put his hand to his mouth and swallowed what he'd been chewing. "They went pretty okay, I think. I might've barely eeked by on a couple of them, but I think I passed," he said.

"What about you two?" my father asked me and Lilith.

"I did okay," Lilith said. "But I'm sure Evie aced every single one of them. She's really smart."

I looked over at her. She was laying it on a little thick. "I did fine, about as well as usual," I said.

"Lilith, I don't know if you know this, but Evie has had a four-point GPA since she started high school. We're very proud of her," my mother said.

I blushed and Lilith looked over at me, a weirdly proud look on her face.

"Oh, I know. I hear the teachers talk about her. She's an impressive girl," Lilith said, still looking at me. I suddenly felt like everyone was staring and looked down at my plate.

"Um, Bea, how's rehearsal going?" I asked, changing

the subject.

Bea went on a ten-minute tangent about how hard it was to memorize lines.

"But hardly anyone knows what they're supposed to say, so no one's real mad about it," she explained. "Miss Evans says we got time."

"We *have* time," my mother corrected her. Bea rolled her eyes once Mom wasn't looking.

"So, how have you guys been?" Liam asked, looking back and forth between me and Lilith. "Haven't seen you since that Halloween party at Max's. Any new developments?"

I narrowed my eyes at him. What in the hell was he doing?

"Developments?" Lilith asked, lifting a fork of sweet potatoes to her mouth.

Liam propped his elbow on the table, waving his fork a little as he stared at Lilith. "Yeah, you know, new friendships. New relationships," he said, sending a pointed glance at me.

I felt like I couldn't breathe. I couldn't believe he was going to do this here. He was going to tell my parents, or force me to. I wanted to throw up, and I knew the tears would be coming any minute. Was it too late to consider Lilith's turkey carver plan?

"Nope, not for me. The boys around here seem rather possessive," Lilith answered, smirking at him. He chewed his lower lip. "Evie, what about you? I mean, you've been really focused on school, so I'm assuming you haven't had time."

Lilith was giving me an out. I wanted to hug her right here, to thank her for helping me. Regardless of the status of our relationship, she had my back.

"Yeah, just trying to get through senior year," I said, my voice a little shaky. "Gotta keep those grades up for college."

"You really should make time for dating, Evie," my mother started. "It's an important part of growing up."

"Bad timing, I guess," I said. "Maybe one day." I hated this conversation.

The rest of dinner was about as awkward as I thought it would be. There was very little conversation between me, Liam, and Lilith for the rest of it. I felt so uncomfortable in my own home. I just wanted to get up and leave. I almost hated my mother for inviting Liam. If he thought there was any chance of forgiveness after this, he was very, very wrong.

CHAPTER
THIRTY NINE

EVIE

I WOKE UP TO THE SOUND OF MY BEDROOM door being flung open and slamming against the wall behind it.

"Evie! Evie, come look!" Bea excitedly jumped on my bed, and directly onto my stomach. A loud guttural gasp escaped my mouth as I curled in on myself and tried to push Bea away. She giggled and rolled off of me, sitting up next to me on the bed.

"You have to come and see!"

"What's going on?" I asked, sleepily rubbing my face and glancing over at the clock. It was just after seven in the morning.

"It snowed," Bea whispered, her eyes big, round, and

glistening. Bea lived for the first snow every year. She'd always wake me up early, we'd bundle up, and then we'd spent most of the day outside, building snow people and making snow angels. I smiled at the bundle of energy next to me. It was nearly impossible to ever deny her this. And to think that I could have missed it.

"Okay, okay, I'll get dressed and be down in a minute."

Bea squealed and bounced on the mattress, causing me to laugh. She hurried out of the room, closing the door behind her. I sighed. I kicked off my blankets and stretched, feeling the muscles in my arms, legs, and abdomen lengthen. I laid there a second, enjoying the normalcy today would bring. After the last few months, I needed it.

I moved to get out of bed and as soon as my bare feet hit the cold floor, I regretted saying that I'd be right down. It was ice cold. I made a mental note to move my rug from the foot of the bed to the side so that I wouldn't have to touch the cold floor again right away. I got dressed in so many layers that I wasn't sure I'd be able to walk. I pulled my gray snow boots out of my closet, pulled them on, and headed down to the kitchen.

Bea was waiting at the kitchen table, guzzling orange juice and staring out of the large kitchen window with wide eyes. I could see the thick blanket of fresh snow sparkling in the light of the rising sun. It looked like the inside of a snow globe.

"Let's go, let's go, let's go!" Bea yelled, jumping up from the table.

"Honey, let's have some breakfast first," my mother tried to negotiate. It was a no-go; Bea was already putting on her coat.

"It's okay," I said, laughing. "We'll eat in a little while."

My mother shook her head. "One hour," she said, putting up a single finger as if to illustrate her point. "Then I want you back in here for breakfast."

Bea and I agreed before heading for the front door. As Bea opened it and we stepped out onto the porch. The early morning sun bouncing off the snow was almost blinding. I squinted and flinched as I pulled on my gloves. It was significantly colder than it had been the day before, or for the previous week.

Bea was already packing piles of snow between her small hands, forming a ball. Before I could duck, the snowball flew straight for me, hitting me square in the chest.

"Oh, you're going down," I said, playfully threatening her. I bent down to start making snowballs of my own.

For the next half hour, we launched snowballs of all sizes at each other while our mother watched from the kitchen window, laughing. Bea squealed when one of my snowballs hit her between the shoulder blades. We chased each other around the front yard, thick clouds emanating from our mouths and filling the air with each laugh. We were probably driving the neighbors out of their minds.

As we lobbed snowballs at one another, screaming, I heard a car engine start up down the street. Someone seemed to be up. I briefly looked in the direction of the sound, but couldn't tell which neighbor it was. Bea's snowball hit me in the hip and I heard the roar of the car trying to back out of their driveway. This kind of snow, the huge piles of wet snow, made it almost impossible to make a clean pass out of a parking spot. I didn't know who would want to bother with it on a day like today, but that wasn't any of my business. I was content just chasing Bea in the yard. Still, I watched for a second to make sure the car wouldn't need my dad's help.

"Hey, do you wanna build a snowman?" she yelled.

As I opened my mouth to answer, I saw the car lurch over the pile of snow it was stuck on. It narrowly missed a car parked on the street.

"Yeah, let's build one," I said, turning my attention back to Bea. We each began gathering huge piles of snow from all over the yard. I spotted a particularly large drift of snow near the garage and went to grab the red plastic bucket from inside to fill it up as I heard the car's tires squealing a little against the snow on the street.

That was when the screaming started.

CHAPTER FORTY

EVIE

EVERYTHING FELT LIKE IT WAS HAPPENING IN slow motion. I turned from where I was standing near the garage just in time to see the driver of the small blue car lose control. I had a full view of the yard as I watched the car skid across the beautiful white powder and aimed straight for Bea. She looked up just in time to see the car heading in her direction. Her scream pierced the cold air. I barely felt the bucket's handle slip from my gloved hand as I watched as the car collided with Bea's small body.

My mother's muffled scream from inside the house was gut-wrenching. I heard her as she yanked open the front door, and I could somehow hear my father's footsteps on the stairs just inside. Maybe I imagined the sound, I'm not really sure. I couldn't take my eyes off of Bea. I heard the muffled sounds of neighbors screaming as they ran out of their houses.

My legs felt so heavy as I tried to run towards Bea. She'd been thrown near the porch from across the lawn where she'd been standing. The blue car was now idling in my front yard, the driver slumped over the steering wheel. I couldn't see their face…

I felt a neighbor's arms around me, but I didn't respond. I was too busy watching my father reach Bea, my mother stumbling behind him. How did he get to her before my mother? The neighbor's arms kept me from running over too. I watched the snow beneath Bea slowly turn crimson. It looked so offensive against all of the white powder surrounding her.

"Evie!"

The sound of my father's voice seemed so far away that it might as well have been coming from a different planet. My eyes eventually flitted in his direction.

"Evie! Call 911!"

I nodded slowly, mechanically, and pulled out of the neighbor's arms to go inside. My mother was still screaming, and neighbors were now venturing out into the cold to see what was happening.

Suddenly, my entire body woke up, like someone lit me on fire. My legs carried through me through the thick snow like it was nothing but air. Before I knew it, I was standing in front of the telephone in the kitchen. I almost pulled the entire thing off of the wall. I quickly stabbed in the three numbers and listened for the operator.

"911, where is your emergency?"

I rattled off the address and told the operator what happened. As I was telling her, I heard sirens in the distance. The operator confirmed that they were already dispatched when a neighbor called, but that I should stay on the phone until they arrived.

"I can't do that, she needs me," I said, unceremoniously hanging up the phone and running back outside.

A crowd was gathered in my yard when I went back outside. Two men were checking on the driver while our neighbor, Mrs. Wallace, was holding onto my mother tightly. My mother was hysterical. My dad was holding Bea's gloved hand, leaning in and whispering to her, but Bea's eyes were closed and she wasn't moving.

Two police cars pulled up in front of the house, sirens blaring, followed by a fire truck. One officer headed toward the circle around Bea while another ran to pop the hood of the car. The flurry of first responders became dizzying once two ambulances pulled right into the yard.

Everyone was talking at once. A police officer approached my mother, pulling her over toward me. He herded us back toward the garage, away from what was happening. My father hurried over and joined us.

"Did any of you see what happened?" the officer asked quickly. I knew his face but I blanked on his name.

"Please, I need to know what's happening to my daughter," my mother screamed through her sobs.

"Ma'am, we're still assessing that, and we'll let you know as soon as we have an answer." The officer tried to be reassuring, but he wasn't.

I could see the paramedics surrounding her. I watched as they strapped her to a board and loaded her onto a stretcher. A brace had been put around her neck. It looked like everything was swallowing her up. She was so small...

"We were building a snowman," I muttered as I watched the paramedics load Bea onto an ambulance. My parents and the officer turned to look at me.

A paramedic jogged over to us just then. "Mrs. Franklin, Mr. Franklin, we're going to transport your daughter to the hospital. If one of you wants to ride along, we need to go now."

My mother nodded, her face ashen. She shuffled along behind the paramedic as best she could in the snow. My father yelled that we would be right behind them. My heart began to pound like it would burst from my chest.

"Is she...awake?" My voice didn't sound familiar.

The officer took a deep breath and looked at me. His green eyes were warm. I don't think I could ever forget those eyes.

"She's in real good hands," he said.

It felt like someone knocked the wind out of me. I couldn't breathe. I felt my legs give out. My father's arms caught me mid-collapse and pulled me close.

"She's gonna be fine, baby. She'll be fine."

"You said you were building a snowman," the officer said. "What happened next?"

"I think that they maybe lost control...the snow... it hit her, the car...she was screaming...and then it stopped," I said mechanically.

After writing everything down on a tiny notepad, the officer told us the report would be available in two days. I didn't understand why that mattered. Before I could ask, my father was ushering me to his truck inside the garage, parked next to the Cadillac that he'd probably never get up and running, so that we could make our way to the hospital. Once inside, something in me broke open. The sob escaped my throat like the sound from a wild animal. I gasped for air.

I felt my father grab me and clutch me to his chest. I felt his own tears hitting the top of my head in a steady stream of drips. I wrapped my arms around my father, and felt the sobs that shook the strongest man I'd ever known. There, in the dark of the garage, in the front seat of his old pickup truck, we held on to each other.

CHAPTER
FORTY ONE

EVIE

THE EMERGENCY ROOM WAITING AREA WAS a flurry of activity. I sat in a hard black plastic chair next to my parents. The entire place smelled like stale air and disinfectant. People were coughing, crying, complaining about the wait. I knew all of these people. Shouldn't they know that Bea was broken in a room somewhere?

I bounced my right leg uncontrollably and chewed my nails while a fluorescent light flickered above our heads. My father paced back and forth and my mother rocked herself. As I looked over at my mother's fragile frame, I remembered the story she'd told me about my own trip to the emergency room as a baby. If Bea didn't make it, what would happen to my mother?

I pushed the thought from my mind as I heard someone calling my name. I looked up to see Liam rushing toward us. I mechanically stood to meet him. He tried to hug me and my body stiffened, a combination of trying to keep calm and being uncomfortable with the feel of him against me.

"Is she okay? Have you heard anything?" There was genuine concern in his voice.

I shook my head. "They're still working on her," I muttered. "Her head…"

"She has severe head trauma," my mother said, sounding more like a robot than her normal self.

"Shit," Liam muttered under his breath. I knew how much he loved Bea. She was like a little sister to him too.

"How did you even know?" I asked. I hadn't sent him a text or anything. I didn't even have my phone.

"Nothing happens in this town without everyone knowing," he said, a halfhearted attempt at a joke. I didn't bother trying to force a smile.

He took a seat next to me, reaching for my hand. The gesture was meant to be comforting, but it only made bile rise in my throat. I tucked my hands under my thighs, not caring that it was an obvious gesture. He returned his hand to his own lap.

We remained silent, and it felt like it was taking an eternity for anyone to tell us anything. Eventually, a blonde nurse in light blue scrubs, a tall woman named Nancy that I remembered from my parents' church, walked through a door. She called for my parents, startling all four of us. My parents jumped up and followed the nurse.

I rubbed my hands over my face. I needed to know what was happening. I needed to know if Bea was awake yet, if she would be okay. I needed someone who knew something.

I needed Lilith. I wished that she was next to me instead of Liam. I needed to be with someone who made me feel safe, who made me feel like everything was going to be fine. I closed my eyes, wondering if I should call her.

I looked up at that moment to see a blur of red hair move with urgency through the emergency room doors.

"Shit, Evie! I'm so sorry I wasn't here sooner. Are you okay?" Lilith asked, rushing over toward me.

I shook my head, tears spilling down my face. I found myself automatically moving toward her, falling against her. The relief I felt as Lilith wrapped her arms around me was almost overwhelming, like I was finally able to breath a little. I didn't care how she knew, I was just relieved that she did, and that she was here. I wrapped my arms around her, finally taking a deep breath. We pulled apart a few moments later.

"I'm so sorry," she whispered, touching my face.

I could feel Liam watching us, but hoped he would

at least be polite under the circumstances. Lilith and I pulled apart, turning to find him rising slowly from his seat.

"Lilith," he muttered.

"How are you, Liam?" Lilith asked him. She knew how he felt about Bea as well. She kept a hand on my hip, keeping me close to her. An involuntary shiver rose through my spine and I tried to ignore it. Now wasn't the time.

"As fine as any of us can be right now," he muttered, shoving his hands into his pockets.

"I'm sure," Lilith responded, her voice almost sympathetic.

"I'm gonna get a soda or something. Do you want anything?" he asked. I declined and watched him disappear through a set of double doors where the vending machines must have been.

"What do you need?" Lilith asked me.

I didn't know how to answer her question. I didn't know what I needed, aside from needing Bea to be okay. I needed to know if she was going to stay with me here.

I needed her.

CHAPTER FORTY TWO

LILITH

I HEARD EVIE SIGH DEEPLY IN RESPONSE TO MY
question. I couldn't tell if it was relief or
contemplation, but at least she seemed glad to see me.

"I need to know if Bea is going to be okay," she
finally said.

I knew the answer. I knew that in just under an
hour, Evie would again hear the pained wailing of her
mother. Someone would come out to take Evie back to
her sister's room. Her father would tell her that her little
sister wouldn't make it, but that they were keeping her on
life support until Evie could say goodbye. I knew that it
would kill Evie.

I also knew who was likely responsible for all of this,

though I didn't know how this was going to help.

"I'm sorry. She says she needs more time," I told Jax, *pacing back and forth, holding my cell phone to my ear.*

"You're sorry? I don't care if you're sorry. I care that this has been dragging on for far too long," Jax said, his voice laced with frustration.

I stopped pacing and straightened my back. "She has some things to sort out," *I said. I couldn't tell him that I was the thing she needed to sort. That was not part of his plan.* "This will get back on track."

Jax was silent for several beats. When he finally did speak, it chilled me.

"Oh, I know what she needs to sort out," he responded. *"I'm going to make it easier for her, and you're going to help me. When she asks for your help, and she will, you better be ready. No more dragging this out. If you screw this up for me, you will fix it." And then the line went dead.*

"Lilith?"

The sound of Evie's voice brought me back to the busy waiting area. I blinked rapidly, trying to clear the fog from my head.

I used the hand on Evie's hip to steer her in the direction of the chairs in the corner. When we sat down, I placed a hand on her knee, using my body as a shield so no one in the room could see us. I knew that would make her uncomfortable. I felt her body minutely relax when I put my hand on her knee. Evie's watery chestnut eyes locked onto my own.

"Is she going to be okay?" she asked again, searching my face for an answer.

"Do you really want to know?" I asked, leaning toward her.

"Yes," she whispered, her voice sounding a little uncertain.

I leaned in closer to her. There was barely any space between our faces. I reached up to brush a tear off of her cheek. Evie closed her eyes and leaned into it. I wanted to eliminate the space completely, to somehow apologize for what I was about to say to her, but this hardly seemed like an appropriate time.

Instead, I took a deep breath and tried to swallow my sadness at the look on her face.

"In the next few minutes, a nurse is going to come and get you. She's going to pull you into a hallway where your father will tell you that Bea isn't going to make it." With each word I said, I wanted to vomit.

Evie visibly deflated, like a balloon stabbed with a pen. She seemed to stop breathing. What she was feeling, the pain, the fear, the anger and sadness, I felt it deep in the pit of my stomach. I didn't want to finish telling her, but I had to. She needed to know everything.

"They'll take you back to say goodbye to her, tell you all of the medical things that went wrong, but none of that will matter."

I watched the color drain from Evie's face all at once, tears steadily rolling down her cheeks, leaving a trail across her porcelain skin. I could feel her breath in my face. It was ragged. She was barely keeping herself together.

Then it hit me. I could fix this. I could fix this. I had the capability of changing this, but there was a price for it.

"I can fix this, Evie," I whispered to her. "I can fix this so that Bea wakes up. She'll go on to live the life that she was always supposed to live. She'll be happy and healthy and give your parents gorgeous grandchildren."

"How?" she asked, furrowing her brow.

I took a deep breath, my eyes focused on the broken girl in front of me. "You have to do it now."

She stared at me. I searched her face for some idea of what she was thinking, but I couldn't tell. Evie's mouth opened, then closed, then opened again.

"I don't understand. Do what?"

"Do the ritual. It's the only way that I can fix this. It's the only way that I am able to save Bea."

Confusion washed over her face. "I don't understand what one has to do with the other. If you can save her, just do it. Please! I'll give you whatever you want," she begged.

I grabbed her face with both of my hands, as if that would force her to understand.

"It doesn't work like that, honey. I can't do it just because I'm able. A trade has to be made, Evie. If you don't come back with me, if you don't complete the ritual, I can't save her. If you don't do it within the next twenty-four hours, she won't survive. If you back out again at the last minute, she will die. That's the only way this can work. Do you understand me?"

She remained silent. It was making me anxious. I turned and saw the ER doors in the distance slide open and a nurse walk through. My head went back and forth between Evie and the nurse walking toward us. I let go of Evie's face. The nurse was coming for Evie, just like I said she would. The nurse's face was aimed downward, solemn, full of dread. I turned back and focused my eyes on Evie who was still watching the nurse. She snapped her head toward me.

"Yes," she blurted out. "I'll do it. I'll do whatever it takes to save her, whatever you need to fix this. I'll do it tonight. Just fix it, please," she pleaded, the desperation saturating her voice.

I let out a shaky breath. I was both relieved and sad. I didn't want her this way, like this.

"It's done," I told her, reaching up and wiping the tears from her cheeks.

CHAPTER
FORTY THREE

EVIE

MY BREATHING WAS QUICK AND shallow. I saw her amber eyes glow for just a moment before returning to normal. What did she mean that it was done? Before I could ask, the nurse interrupted.

"Evie Franklin?"

I nodded, the knot in my stomach getting tighter.

"Can you please come with me? I'll take you to your parents."

I glanced back at Lilith, who was faintly smiling, her face trying to be reassuring. I shuffled behind the nurse, terrified about what I was about to hear. I couldn't get the image of my sister on the ground, her blood spilling out across the snow out of my mind. Was I about to hear that she was dead, or that she was going to be fine? I wanted to throw up. I clenched my jaw tight.

I stayed behind the nurse as we rounded a tight corner. I saw my parents up ahead, huddled together in the hallway. My mother's head was buried in my father's chest as he kissed the top of her hair. He whispered something to her as he saw me walking up behind the nurse. My mother looked up and took a step toward me, crying but smiling.

"She's going to be okay," she exclaimed, wrapping her arms around me. "They didn't think that she was going to, but she'll be fine. It's a miracle, Evie. We were standing here, the doctor telling us that she wasn't breathing on her own, that she wasn't going to make it, and then she opened her eyes!"

"She...what?" I was stunned. Everything Lilith said was true. I didn't know whether she overheard something, or whether she really did have something to do with it, but the idea that she might have...

"Evie? Did you hear what I said?"

"Yeah. Yeah, I'm sorry. That's just unbelievable. When can we see her?"

"She's getting some tests right now just to make sure they didn't miss something. She made such a sudden change, they want to make sure everything's okay, that nothing was missed or misinterpreted, whatever that means," my father said, smiling and putting his arm around me.

It suddenly occurred to me that no one was mentioning the driver.

"What happened to the driver? Who was it?" I asked, looking up at my dad.

My parents looked at each other.

"What? What happened?" I asked again.

"He's in pretty bad shape," my mother said softly. "He hit his head pretty hard on the steering wheel." For some reason, I thought the driver was fine. Truthfully, I didn't give the driver much thought at all.

"Who was it?" I asked again, my voice cracking. "Who was the driver?"

My mother took a deep breath. "It was a boy from your school, Max Brady."

I looked at my mother, stunned. I remembered recognizing the car right before the accident, but it never clicked. I'd never seen his car in that driveway before.

"Excuse me, Beatrice is back in her room. She's asleep, but you can go in and see her if you'd like," a nurse said, interrupting my train of thought.

The three of us rushed toward the nurse, following her down a hall toward a room near the end. As my parents entered the room, I stayed in the doorway. We were greeted by a chorus of beeping sounds. There were machines everywhere. I followed the tubes and wires from the machines to my sister's body laying in the bed. They were attached to her arms and chest. Her head was wrapped in bandages. She had several stitches above her left eye and scratches all over her face and arms. Both eyes were so swollen. A lump rose up in my throat. Bea was so small and looked so broken.

I watched as my parents approached the bed, one on either side of it. Bea appeared to be asleep, but it was difficult to tell. Just as I was about to step forward, I felt my phone vibrate in the front pocket of my jeans. I didn't even remember grabbing it, but I hurriedly pulled it out and checked the screen.

Friday 10:26 AM

Tonight at 8.

Anxiety flooded my body. The text was from Lilith. Now more than ever, I was reluctant to leave my little sister behind. But I'd made a deal; Bea's life for my own, or something like that. And if it saved Bea's life, I would do whatever I had to.

"Mommy?"

Bea's voice was barely audible over the relentless beeping of the machines. I took a shaky breath and watched my mother lean in, covering Bea's hand in kisses.

"I'm here, baby," she said softly. "Daddy's here too.

So is Evie."

"Evie," I heard Bea's small voice say. My feet moved from their spot on the green hospital linoleum, inching slowly toward Bea's bed.

"Hey, I'm here," I whispered. My father made room for me on his side of her bed so that I could get closer. I looked down and saw Bea's little fingers wiggling slightly and I wrapped them in my own. Bea slowly moved her head in my direction.

"I saw an angel," Bea whispered to me, her throat scratchy. I furrowed my brow. Out of the corner of my eye, I saw my mother clasp her hand over her mouth and look at my father.

"An angel, huh?" I asked, trying to ignore my own skepticism for her sake. I mean, I'd been spending time with a demon, so how far off could that really be?

"Yeah, when I died," Bea said in a matter-of-fact tone. I heard my mother gasp. My father turned away for a minute.

"Bea, you didn't die—" I started, but she interrupted.

"I did. But then the angel came. She said that you asked someone to let me come back."

I opened my mouth to say something, but no words came out. Did Lilith do this? Was Lilith the angel that Bea saw?

"She said you made a deal," Bea finished.

All eyes were suddenly on me. I can't blame them. I'd

have stared at me too. I kept my eyes on Bea, not really sure how much I should, or could, say. Instead, I gave her a non-committal shrug.

"We all wanted you to be okay," I whispered.

"What deal, Evie? What is she talking about?" my mother asked, a distinct edge of seriousness to her voice.

"I…I prayed. I said I'd do anything if she could be okay, that I'd be a nicer sister," I lied. It was the best lie I could come up with at the moment, and it was terrible.

"You're already the best sister," Bea said.

"Yeah, well, you don't have much basis for comparison," I said, feeling a single tear spill down my cheek. I wished that were true. But in just a few hours, I was going to walk away from my family, from my sister. Tonight, I would follow through on my end of the deal because Bea's life was the most important thing. It was more important than getting out of Benson, more important than seeing the world. I'd promised Lilith, and I was going to honor it.

None of us did much talking for the next few hours. When Bea slept, the room stayed fairly silent save for the barely audible sound of daytime programming on the room's television. My mother kept watching me, her eyebrows knitted together. I tried not to look back at her. At one point, mostly to avoid eye contact, I sent a hurried text to Liam to let him know that Bea was okay. I also asked him to meet me at the diner later. I wanted to say goodbye to him. I needed to make a clean break, for me more than him.

At a little after four that afternoon, I told my parents that I was going to go meet Liam at the diner. My father offered to drive me, but I lied and said that Lilith was picking me up. When I hugged my parents, I held on a little longer than normal, squeezed a little harder. I told them that I loved them.

Saying goodbye to Bea was harder. I leaned in close to her ear. She'd been asleep for about an hour, which I was thankful for. If she'd been awake, I couldn't have done it.

"Hey, Bumble Bea," I choked out. "I love you so much. I'm so proud of you. I'm sorry I won't get to see your play opening night. You'll be amazing. No matter what, I want you to know that I did this for you, okay? I did this for you, and for me too. Whatever happens, whatever you hear, I did this because I love you."

As I leaned closer to kiss her cheek, she stirred a little bit. It took everything I had to hold myself together as I walked out of the room.

In the hallway, I pulled out my phone and sent a quick text to Lilith.

Friday 4:13 PM:

I have a few things
to take care of.
I' ll see you
at 8. And thank
you so much.

Seconds later, my phone buzzed in response.

Friday 4:13 PM:

It' s going to be
okay. I' ll see you
soon :)

I shoved my phone into my back pocket. I walked silently through the hospital halls, weaving in and out of nurses, patients, and gurneys lining the hallways. My legs felt like they had sandbags tied to them as I passed through the sliding glass doors, the frigid air blasting against my face. I turned in the direction of the diner.

CHAPTER FORTY FOUR

EVIE

IT WAS GETTING DARK AND STARTING TO snow when I entered the warm glow of Henry's Diner for the last time. It was dinner time when I got there, but the diner was pretty empty. I made a beeline for the booth in the back and positioned myself so that I could watch the door. Liam said he would meet me at five, and I spent the entire walk from the hospital trying to figure out what I was going to say to him. Should I just tell him that I was leaving? Should I just disappear? Just disappearing seemed like a recipe for a Dateline episode.

I decided that telling him I was leaving was a bad idea. I was just going to tell him that while our friendship couldn't survive what happened, I forgave him. I wasn't forgiving him because it was okay. I was forgiving him because I needed it. I couldn't carry this anger and fear around with me forever, and if this would help, I was willing to try it. Honestly, I hoped he would feel guilty for the rest of his life, and I hoped he would never do it to another person again.

I ordered a hot chocolate from the server just as Liam walked through the front door. Nervousness and fear took over my stomach, making me feel nauseated. He looked nervous too, but he gave me an awkward half-smile as he approached the table.

"I was surprised to get your text," he said, sitting down across from me. He sounded almost as nervous as I felt.

"Do you want anything?" I asked him as the server, Patti, set my hot chocolate in front of me.

"Um…a burger with everything, fries, and a soda," he told the server. The blonde gave a curt nod and walked away. "So, how are you? How's Bea?" he asked, turning his attention back to me.

I sighed deeply.

"Well, initially they didn't think that she would make it. They even put her on life support." His eyes were wide, his mouth hanging open. "It was weird. She suddenly woke up. They ran tests, but I don't know if they could figure it out. I spoke to her right before leaving to come here. She said she saw an angel when she died."

He covered his mouth with both hands, his green eyes watering. His hands were covered in splatters of white, blue, and yellow paint. For as long as I'd known him, paint was always covering his hands, or at the very least, caked under his fingernails. It always surprised me that his hands looked so soft. I thought they should look more calloused and rough, but he didn't really do any manual labor.

"I'm so sorry. But she's good now?" he asked, looking for reassurance.

"She will be."

He looked relieved at my words. He really was like family. How was I supposed to say goodbye to someone I'd spent most of my life with? How did everything between us get so screwed up? I'd always been able to rely on him. He knew all of my weird habits, my favorite foods, favorite movies, least favorite books, my secrets.

Most of my secrets. He had suspicions about Lilith. I didn't know how to tell him that he was right. I didn't know if I should tell him.

Patti stopped back at our table and practically threw Liam's order in front of him, per usual. A few small specks of grease splattered the table.

"Liam, I need to talk to you," I finally said.

He looked nervous but resigned. He dropped the fry he was about to eat. "Look, I really am sorry about that night," he started. "I know that I screwed up so bad. I was out of line. It was not okay."

He was right, but that wasn't what I wanted to talk about. "I appreciate that, I do. But that's not what I want to talk about. I don't even know how to say this," I said, mostly to myself. I really wished I'd practiced this out loud.

"You know you can tell me anything."

I took a deep breath. Maybe I should've just disappeared and let Keith Morrison and the Dateline producers try to unravel the mystery. Just as I felt the urge to go to the bathroom and climb out of the window, he leaned back and waited for me to say something.

"I'm really sorry," I started.

He shook his head. "Nope. You do not get to apologize for my fuck up. You get to say whatever you need to say, even if you tell me to get lost."

I pressed my lips together. "Okay. But there are some things that I do have to apologize for, and I need you to listen. I'm sorry that I shut you out. I'm sorry that I chose Lilith over you, because I did. I'm sorry that I don't feel about you the way that you feel about me." Everything came out in a rush that I wasn't expecting. I wasn't even sure why I was saying all of this.

He hung his head. That last part stung and embarrassed him and I knew it.

"I do love you, Liam. I just don't love you like that, and I never will," I whispered. "And after that night…"

He nodded and stayed silent. He knew what I meant. When he finally did speak, I wasn't ready for it.

"I know. Everything's different. We can't go back," he said sadly. "Can I ask you something?" He didn't look up from the table, but I nodded anyway. He took a deep, steadying breath. "Are you in love with her? I don't have any right to ask, but I want to know. Please tell me the truth."

I should've known the question was coming, but I still wasn't prepared. I didn't know what to say. Unfortunately, when I opened my mouth to tell him that I liked her but I didn't know if it was love, a high-pitched nervous laugh bubbled out of me.

"Am I what?"

He wrinkled his brow, clearly unable to believe the sound that was coming out of me. He quickly regained his composure and just stared at me while I struggled to get my nervous laughter under control. I looked around nervously and saw that only Mae Hesser was looking from a nearby table. Great.

My brain began working overtime. I knew that I felt something for Lilith, but I had no context for whether it was love. I thought Lilith was interesting, mysterious, gorgeous, and I felt some draw to her that was beyond my control. I knew that my entire body lit up like a live wire when she was near me. I could barely stand to look away from her, and I wanted to touch her every time she was near me. I knew that Lilith was flirtatious, always finding ways to touch me. She winked at me all the time. There was the way she held me in the emergency room waiting area. And while everyone seemed to want Lilith, I was the only person she paid any real attention to.

My mouth gaped open as I looked at Liam. His eyes widened.

"Oh my god," he muttered. "It's true. You're—"

"Liam—"

"You're in love with her. Wait, you really are gay?"

Again with my nervous laughter, but this time there was an edge of fear, confusion, surprise. I didn't know what I was supposed to say. I'd always felt like such an outsider among people who seemed to fit so perfectly into the fabric of this town. While the girls here were fawning over the boys, I struggled to figure out why I couldn't do the same. I'd never dated anyone. My only real crushes were on girls, and I definitely noticed them. My first real kiss would've been Lilith, until that very elegant collision of our heads in her car. I constantly wanted a redo on it. I was so focused on running away from Benson that I didn't give any real thought to all of the things I was running from, and it wasn't just about looking for opportunities. I wanted the chance to fall in love.

"Evie?" he asked.

"I don't know," I blurted out in a frantic whisper. "I

don't know. I - I like her, but I don't know if I'm in love with her. How does someone even know that? And being gay…I don't know that either. I mean, maybe?"

"I knew that I was in love with you when you were all I could think about," he started, his face looking directly into mine. He somehow looked…different, vulnerable. "You were the first thing I thought about in the mornings, and the last thing at night. I started worrying about which ones were my best t-shirts so that I didn't look like a total slob," he explained, laughing sarcastically. I knew what he was doing. He wasn't telling me this to make me feel bad. It was the only context he had, and he was telling me so that I could figure it out for myself.

I stared down at the table. All of the things he said, they were true for me too, but only about Lilith. I never felt it about anyone else.

"I don't trust her," he said.

"Liam—" I started, finding myself suddenly more annoyed with him.

"I'm serious. Something isn't right about her. I think she might be dangerous. I mean, she just shows up here, no parents, no one knows anything about her."

"Stop," I said, interrupting him. Whatever he was about to say, I didn't want to hear it. I wanted to tell him that he was wrong, but I wasn't so sure that he was. Lilith could definitely be dangerous, but it was too late for me to do anything about it. "I know who Lilith is, and that's all that matters to me. She's taken the time to get to know me in a way that no one in this town has ever bothered to, not even you."

"What's going on?" he asked, his voice laced with caution.

I took a deep breath. "I wanted to tell you that I forgive you."

He stared at me, and then he looked down at the table. "You shouldn't," he muttered. "I don't deserve it."

I shook my head. "It isn't about whether you deserve it. I have to be able to move on. I'm leaving Benson soon, and I don't want to carry this with me. I need to be able to leave knowing that I'm free to move on and away from that one moment…so it doesn't destroy the memories of all the years that came before. I don't want them to poison the friendship we had before it happened. I need to be able to hold on to that, for me, and the longer I hold onto this anger and hurt and sadness, the more likely it is that I have to let all of the good stuff go," I explained. I didn't know if this made sense to him, but I had to say it either way.

We didn't say anything for a few minutes. We just stayed on our respective sides of the booth, each of us in mourning for what we'd lost and couldn't get back. Each of us on different sides of the same rope, me letting go and him desperately trying to hang on.

"I understand," he whispered. "Maybe someday…"

"Maybe," I said. "But…make space for the possibility that it might not happen."

He nodded, defeated.

I slowly let out a breath I didn't know I'd been holding. "I need to go. I have some things to take care of," I told him, grabbing my coat and pulling out my wallet.

"I've got it," he said, waving me away. "It's the least I can do, right?"

"You'll be okay," I said. I carefully slid out of the booth and walked away. As I passed Mae Hesser's table, wiping a tear from my cheek, she grabbed my wrist. I spun around to face her, startled.

"Choose wisely, Evie. Not every right choice has good consequences. You won't get another chance," she warned. I stared at her, not knowing what to say. Instead, I slowly, carefully, pulled my wrist out of her grip and backed away from her, making my way to the door and leaving.

CHAPTER FORTY FIVE

EVIE

6:43 PM

ITRIED NOT TO SPEND TOO MUCH TIME LOOKING around on my walk home. I didn't want to risk getting caught up in what I was leaving behind - the predictable comfort of small-town existence, my family, my best friend – and running the risk of changing my mind. I tried to remind myself that I was giving myself a shot at a life where I could be myself without having to hide, or lie, or stay nervous all the time that someone might be watching and judging.

I was giving Bea a shot at a life.

I listened to the sound of my boots crunching

over the snow, watched the shadows thrown across my path by the glow of the street lamps. I tried to steady my breathing. If I could focus on my breathing, maybe I wouldn't focus on the sadness threatening to come to the surface. My heart was pounding so hard, and my stomach was in knots. I was biting the end of my tongue to keep from crying. Was I doing the right thing? Would Lilith abandon me once the ritual was finished? Did it guarantee that Bea would be okay, or was it just a tactic to get me to agree to all of this? I shook the thoughts from my head. I knew none of that was true.

Before I realized it, I found myself standing on the sidewalk in front of the house I'd lived in my entire life. It was all I knew. Benson was all I knew. I took a deep breath and walked the path to the front door. When I stepped inside, the house was so dark. I was greeted by the familiar scent of lavender and French vanilla. I reached for the light switch to the entryway. I didn't have a lot of time, but I didn't want to forget any of this either.

I walked into the dark kitchen and turned that light on as well. A warm yellow glow spilled out across the cabinets, the counters, the island, and the kitchen table. I almost expected to see my family at the table, but it remained empty. Overwhelming sadness hit me all at once, knocking the breath out of me. All of the dishes from that morning were still scattered all over the table, the counters, the stove. It was the very picture of a morning that had been brutally interrupted. A sound that I didn't recognize escaped my throat, but I choked it back.

I looked at the clock on my cell phone. I had to be at Lilith's house in less than thirty minutes. I quickly opened a ride share app on my phone and scheduled a ride to pick me up in fifteen minutes. I always found it interesting that in a town this size, we had a ride share. I laughed to myself. Of all the things to be thinking about...

On the way home I'd decided against leaving a note for my family. Instead, I scrawled a single sentence on the refrigerator whiteboard: I love you.

I left the kitchen and walked across the hall into the living room. I flipped the light switch. There was my dad's oversize recliner and my mother's cream and floral sofa. My sister's backpack was sitting next to the fireplace. The television was dark, a rarity in this house. I smiled to myself. I didn't feel quite as nostalgic about this room as I did the kitchen, but it was close. I turned off the light and left the room.

My legs felt like lead as I walked up the carpeted stairs to my bedroom. The hinges on my door squeaked as I gingerly pushed it open, echoing in the darkness. My bedroom suddenly didn't feel like mine anymore, but I couldn't put my finger on why. Maybe it was because it never really would be again. As I looked around at the three shelves full of books and DVDs, my desk with my Lisa Frank pencil collection, and my unmade bed, I felt sad all over again. I'd spent eighteen years in this bedroom. I read, watched movies with Liam, danced to music I'd never admit to liking, and played Monopoly with Bea.

As my eyes passed my closet, I realized that I hadn't thought about clothes or phone chargers or photographs that I wanted to take with me. I darted toward my bed and grabbed my backpack from the floor next to it. I emptied out my notebooks and textbooks and began replacing them with a few clothing items, the rolled up cash from the back of my sock drawer that I'd been saving from two years' worth of babysitting jobs and allowance, a couple of family photographs, and the cell phone charger from my nightstand.

I heard a soft meow behind me and turned to see Agnes staring up at me.

"Hey, Aggie," I said softly, reaching down to scratch her ears. Agnes purred loudly, circling my legs.

"Aggie, you have to take care of Bea for me, okay?" Agnes mewed in response, flopping over and showing me her belly. I smiled and picked her up. I'd had Agnes since she was three months old. She was twelve now. The parts of her fur that had once been black were now graying a little, especially around her face. Her green eyes were as bright as ever though. I nuzzled my face into her fur and kissed her head. When I set her back down, she sauntered out of the room. And then there was a ping on my phone. My ride was outside.

I took one last look around, turned off my bedroom light, and closed the door behind me.

CHAPTER FORTY SIX

LILITH

JAX, IT'S FINE. I DON'T KNOW HOW MANY times I have to tell you. She will be here," I said into my phone.

"It is imperative that this happens, especially after today. How do you know she will go through with it?"

I hesitated to tell him. I wasn't supposed to interfere with the decision-making process, not supposed to force anyone's hand. It was my personal code. But I also wasn't sure this entire thing wasn't orchestrated by him in the first place.

"Lilith?"

I took a deep breath. "I need to know: did you fix things so the accident would happen?" I asked him. He didn't say anything for a moment.

"So what if I did? You were taking a ridiculous amount of time to get this done. Did you think I was going to wait around for the two of you to stop mooning over each other long enough to get to work?"

"Because of this, I had to get her to trade herself for her sister's life. I pretty much had to manipulate her into doing this. Is that what you wanted, for someone to basically be forced into it?"

There was silence on the other end of the phone. I immediately regretted saying anything. I was also regretting forcing Evie into an impossible corner at the hospital. I wasn't afraid of what he'd do to me, not in the slightest. But it felt like I'd betrayed Evie.

"Your entire thing is built upon her making the choice without any input from you. I knew you would go this route," he laughed. "You used her sister to get what you wanted. How does it feel to get your hands truly dirty for once?"

His question knocked the breath out of me. "No, I had to use her sister to get what you want. It isn't like you gave me much of a choice, Jax. Was I just supposed to let her sister die and hope she'd do the ritual anyway? You don't know this girl."

The quiet and menacing chuckle coming from Jax was disturbing. I opened my mouth to say something, but a banging on the front door interrupted. Annoyed, I stood up and went to answer it. When I swung the door open, I was a little surprised to see who was standing in front of me.

"Jax, I'm going to have to call you back."

I hung up while Jax was in the middle of saying something I didn't care about anymore. Liam's tall frame was standing in my doorway, towering over me. The very sight of him annoyed me.

"What do you want?" I asked, resting my hand on my hip.

He didn't even wait for an invitation. He pushed right past me and into the house.

"Please, do come right in," I said sarcastically. I closed the door. As I turned around to follow him, he stopped abruptly in his path and rounded on me.

"What do you want from her?" he growled, his teeth gritted together. "Why can't you leave her alone?"

I let out a dry laugh. "Because she didn't say that she wanted me to. She never said that she wanted me to go away, that she didn't want to see me. I think the better question is, why can't you leave her alone?"

"I need to know how you feel about her. She's my best friend."

I tilted my head. "Best friend, huh? One best friend doesn't follow the other around like a lost puppy, batting their big eyes, hoping they'll fall in love and live happily ever after. And they certainly don't sexually assault one another."

I saw him clench his fists.

"Did I hit a nerve?" I asked.

"You don't know what you're talking about."

"Are you saying I'm wrong?" I asked, taking a step toward him. "Because who do you think she turned to?"

He didn't say anything for a moment. He just stood there, fuming, his eyes boring holes into me. His lips parted a little, like there was something he wanted to say but didn't know if he should. And then he seemed to make a decision.

"Are you in love with her?"

I stared at him. In love with her? I knew that I wanted to be with her, but what in the hell was love? All it did was cause problems and get people into, well, situations like this. So, I changed the subject.

"She's never going to love you, Liam. Not the way you love her. Between you and me, I don't think you're her type, and I think that you know it. I think you've known it for a while. I also think that you know she'll never find anyone here, that she'll never be happy here. Do you want that for her?"

Just as he took a step forward, the door opened behind me.

"Liam? What are you doing here?" Evie's voice was low, measured, cautious. I raised my eyebrows and looked back at him.

"I was just asking the same thing," I said, positioning myself next to her.

"Yeah, I heard. We'll get back to that later. Liam?" she asked again.

"Evie, you can't do this. She's not good for you." Liam started to sound like he was begging.

She sighed, stepping past him and into the living room. "We both know that you won't understand," she said, dropping her backpack on the floor next to the sofa.

"You never gave me the chance! You just sprang all of this on me like I'm supposed to know what to do with any of it. You never explained," he said.

She covered her face with her hands for a second and then dropped them at her sides. "I don't have to. I don't owe you any explanation. Do you not remember the conversation we had, like, an hour ago? This," she said, gesturing between them, "isn't happening anymore. We are not friends. We will not be discussing my love life. Period."

I was surprised to hear her use the phrase "love life." But that wasn't the most important thing happening. Something in her changed. Despite her red, puffy eyes, despite all that she was walking away from, she seemed resolute in her decision.

"Okay, so you're gay. Fine, I can accept that, but this thing with her, it's never going to work! And if it does, it'll be temporary. It won't last. She's never going to know you like I do," Liam shouted.

The entire room went silent. I watched Evie's eyes widen and her face begin to redden. I could see her clench and unclench her jaw, ball up her fists at her side. I watched her chest rise and fall in slow, deep, calculated breaths as she stared Liam down, trying to decide what to say.

"First of all," she started through gritted teeth, "her not knowing me like you do is the point. Second, I am so glad my sexuality is okay with you because I didn't know how I was going to live the rest of my life without your permission to be who I am!" Her voice boomed through the living room. "And how do you know I'm gay? Did I specifically tell you that, or was that one of a million assumptions you and everyone else have been making about me and Lilith? And believe me, I know what they're saying. I am very aware. Do you have any idea how hurt, how terrified I've always been? Do you have any idea what it's like to feel like you have to hide this big part of who you are? And it all got so much worse when Lilith got here, but she never once made me feel like I had to be someone else, something I didn't even feel safe enough to do with my best friend." I watched Liam's face go pale as he took the brute force of Evie's hurt and anger.

"Evie, I didn't—" Liam started to say, but she immediately put up a hand and stopped him.

"You need to leave. I need you to leave. Go home," she said, her voice calm and even.

The corner of Liam's mouth turned up as he chuckled to himself and I thought he might finally be losing his mind. "Have you even told her?" he asked Evie, who didn't say anything in response. Liam took a step toward her. "You haven't, have you?" he challenged before turning toward me. "You know she's in love with you, right? I mean, you have to know. And she thinks you're capable of loving her back. We both know that isn't going to happen, don't we?"

I didn't say anything. I wasn't even sure what was happening anymore. While I've never had feelings for anyone before this, it wasn't the first time someone else thought they were in love with me. This time was different though. This was a big deal, for Evie and for me. But since Evie wasn't saying a word, and I didn't know what in the hell I was feeling, I didn't know what to say. It felt like a boulder sitting in my stomach.

"Evie," I whispered involuntarily. I wanted to go to her. I wanted to throw Liam out. But I was rooted to my spot. I was oddly terrified to do or say the wrong thing. I was scared that she would leave.

Evie remained silent, avoiding eye contact, staring down at the floor. The tension between the three of us was palpable. The only sound came from the crackling fireplace and the wind picking up outside. The shadows from the fireplace licked at the ceiling, the walls, across Evie's pale face. The pain and embarrassment on her face were enough to push me to act.

"Okay, this is really none of your business, Liam," I said, finally able to step up next to Evie. "Whatever is going on between me and Evie—"

"Lilith, please. I need to deal with this," she finally said. I watched her take a shaky breath. "She's right though, it really isn't any of your business. I know that maybe you mean well, but I don't have to explain a fucking thing to you, and I'm tired of you making me feel like I do. Whatever might or might not be happening between me and Lilith, or me and anyone else, has zero to do with you."

The idea of her with anyone else felt like a punch to the gut.

"I'm sorry you're not getting what you want and that your feelings are hurt, but it doesn't give you the right to think you have any control over my life. If you can't handle any of this, it isn't my problem – it's yours. So figure it out someplace else," she finished.

Liam stumbled backwards a few steps as the words flew from her mouth so quickly and with such force that even I felt compelled to take a step back. It felt like it did at the Halloween party.

"You don't understand what I'm dealing with, so just…back off," she said, her voice a little quieter.

I watched them stare at one another. I wasn't sure why, but it was making me nauseated.

Liam threw his arms up. "That is such bullshit and you know it. I thought I was coming here to help you, but I see that was a serious mistake."

"I don't want your help. You need to go. I want you to go," she told him. She was done with this conversation. He looked shocked, like she hadn't said it twice already.

"Evie—" he started.

"Just go. Please."

After a moment of staring at her, he eventually looked defeated.

"Is this really what you want?" he asked, taking a step toward her. The way he kept attempting to manipulate her made my skin crawl. I wanted to intervene, but I also knew that she wanted to do this for herself.

"This is what I want, and what I choose."

Without asking if it was okay, as usual, he put his arms around Evie, pulling her against him. Evie stood stiffly, not responding. He ignored her body language and kissed the top of her head. A level of fury I'd never experienced washed over me. I fought the urge to rip them apart, to rip him apart. I watched him close his eyes and squeeze Evie's thin body before walking away.

CHAPTER
FORTY SEVEN

EVIE

AFTER LIAM WALKED AWAY I JUST STOOD
there, tears spilling down my face. I didn't
bother trying to stop them. There was too much to cry
about that no one person could've possibly stopped the
flood. The hardest part was Liam. No matter what our
past consisted of, I would never feel safe near him again,
not even with Lilith standing next to me.

"Are you okay?" Lilith asked cautiously. I didn't look
up. I couldn't look at her, not yet, not after everything
that was said. I wasn't ready to have that conversation yet.
So, I closed my eyes, wiped my face, and I took a deep
breath.

"So now what?" I asked, finally looking up at her,

determined to ignore everything until later. Lilith looked uncharacteristically uncomfortable, and her eyes were downcast. The loaded silence between us did nothing for my anxiety.

"I'm sorry he showed up here like that," I tried, my voice cracking.

Lilith looked up at me, her eyes warm and soft, her expression solemn. "He had to try, didn't he? I would."

We stared at each other. I didn't know how to respond to that, and she didn't offer anything further. To say I felt exposed would be an understatement if ever there was one. I felt like I'd arrived naked to school without my homework, having grown a beak, and it was all on national television. Everything between us was different now. So much was said, so much forced out into the open by someone who had no business doing it. None of it could be put back.

It couldn't be ignored either. Liam told her that I was in love with her, and she didn't say anything. All she said was that, in his position, she would try. Try, to what? Keep me here? Ruin things for me? Humiliate me?

"You would try?" I blurted out. I immediately wanted to take it back.

"I would. I mean, if I was in Liam's shoes, I would do whatever it took."

I nodded, more than a little disappointed. That wasn't the answer I expected, and it wasn't the answer I hoped for. I thought that maybe she might feel something for me too. Maybe I just thought that after the hand-holding, the almost-kiss, the way she held me in the waiting room, I just assumed that –

"No, that's not what I meant," Lilith said, interrupting my thoughts. "I meant that if I was – if you were going to – I don't know what I'm trying to say. This is all really new."

"Um…what's new? Haven't you –"

Lilith shook her head. "No, I haven't."

"Wow. Honestly, that surprises me," I told her, making my way to the sofa. "I just kind of assumed you had a lot of…experience."

She smiled. "Not with this part. Oh, people have tried. In the beginning, I may have taken advantage of a situation or two, but that stopped a long time ago. It wasn't fair to them."

I felt myself deflate. I wish I hadn't asked. My lack of experience felt glaringly obvious now. I thought maybe I was the only one, which really wasn't realistic. She'd been around a long time. While I might be embarrassed about my romantic deficiencies, she didn't seem to be bothered by them. She was here, standing across from me, looking at me like maybe I wasn't the only one who didn't know what they were doing.

CHAPTER FORTY EIGHT

LILITH

S O WHAT DO WE DO NOW?" EVIE ASKED.

Her question caught me a little off-guard. With the entire evening being one surprise after another, I wasn't sure which part she was referring to.

"About what?" I asked her.

"About the ritual…? I mean, this is kind of your show, right?" she asked, laughing with a tinge of nervousness in her voice. Truthfully, she sounded more relaxed than she'd been since she walked in the door, and I was glad for that. I didn't know what changed over the last few minutes, but I felt relieved. The tension was still there, but it was different. Our eyes locked for just a second before Evie smiled and flushed and looked away.

"Okay," I said, trying to get down to business. "I should talk you through some of the steps for tonight." Evie was listening intently. "First, there's the ritual bath," I told her.

"This requires a bath?" she asked, laughing. I stared at her. "Okay, but serious question: will there be bubbles?"

I gave her a small laugh. "Focus. I'll set it all up for you. While you're doing that, I'll get everything else ready. Please, take your time. Don't rush. It might not sound like much to you, but it's an important step."

"Serious and important bath. Got it." I watched as Evie pressed her lips together in an attempt not to laugh. I rolled my eyes and continued.

"After the ritual bath, there will be a black robe in the bathroom. You'll dress in only that, understand?" Evie nodded slowly. "Then we'll make our way outside," I finished.

"Outside. In nothing but a robe. Are you serious?"

"Yes. Trust me, you'll be fine. There's a crossroads in the woods. The ritual will need to be done there."

"Lilith, I don't know about this…" Evie started.

"Don't know about what?" I asked hesitantly.

"Don't get me wrong, the bath sounds great after today, but running around naked, outside, in the pitch black and snow? Do you know how many weirdos are out there? I mean, aside from us? Also, there are animals that will definitely try to eat us."

A boisterous laugh bubbled from me. It was my turn to catch Evie by surprise. It took a minute, but once I got myself under control, I apologized for the outburst. Unfortunately, I continued laughing a little, so she didn't look at all amused by me.

"I'm serious, Lilith."

"I know you are," I said. "That's why it's so funny."

She crossed her arms over her chest as I tried to pull myself together.

"Okay, I'm sorry. Look, sit down, try to relax. I'll go upstairs and get the bath ready." I turned to leave the room and made it to the bottom of the stairs before I heard her call my name. I walked back into the living room to find her sitting anxiously on the edge of the sofa.

"What happens next?" she asked.

"I told you, we'll go outside –"

"No," she said, shaking her head. "I mean, after the ritual. What happens next?"

I took a deep breath. I'd thought about it a hundred times. I planned for every possible scenario: we leave together and travel, she freaks out and refuses to leave Benson and we're stuck here, and so many other possibilities. The one I didn't want to plan for, the one I hated thinking about, was the hardest: what if, after the ritual, she changed so much that she didn't want me anymore? What if everything Liam said was true now, but afterward, it wouldn't be?

What if Evie discovered she'd rather try life without Lilith after all?

I bit my lower lip and stood in the entryway. "What happens after the ritual is whatever you want to happen. That's the deal. The deal we made was that you'd be helping people in the same way that I do, but at the end of the day, you do what you want to do. You may be called on from time to time –"

"I can still stay with you?"

My heart was pounding. "If that's what you want, yes. Absolutely."

She nodded. She seemed relaxed by that, so I walked away without saying anything else. I ascended the staircase in the hall. At the top, I stopped in front of a thick, ornate bathroom door with vines and flowers carved into the wood. I grabbed the equally ornate brass doorknob, hoping she'd still want to stay with me in a few hours.

CHAPTER
FORTY NINE

EVIE

I STARTED WHEN I HEARD LILITH CALL FOR ME from the top of the stairs. I anxiously stood up and went to meet her. I looked up at her from the bottom of the staircase, half-cloaked in darkness, and told myself to walk. It was a weird night, and now I was supposed to take a bath. This did not feel like a time to relax. Or maybe it was the perfect time. It was hard to tell. My night was not making sense to any degree. I hoped it would later.

I climbed the stairs, my right hand on the banister, my eyes locked with Lilith's. At the top, she gestured to the door on my left.

"Take your time," she whispered. I nodded and

reached for the doorknob.

Inside, the bathroom was huge. The white tile floor led to an old cast iron claw foot tub surrounded on three sides by floor-to-ceiling windows. The windows faced the woods, which looked foreboding from this vantage point, but somehow still beautiful. The room smelled of jasmine. Candles adorned every surface. They were positioned on the counter of the vanity, on the floor surrounding the tub. I'd never seen anything this beautiful, no matter how many photographs I'd thumbed through or how many movies I'd watched. It almost took my breath away. It was magical. It was…romantic.

I relaxed in spite of myself. I carefully undressed, folding my clothes and placing them in a neat stack on a nearby chair. I stepped toward the tub. Steam was rising from the water, making it look so inviting. I dipped my fingers into the water and found the temperature to be perfect. I climbed inside and let the warm water envelope me.

As I sank down into the water, my thoughts wandered through the day. I woke up to my sister begging me to play in the snow, then I sat in a waiting room to see if she would survive a freak car accident in our front yard. I'd listened to my best friend announce that I was in love with another woman in front of that woman. Now I was naked in that same woman's bathtub while she waited downstairs to take me into the woods – still naked – and what? Feed me to wolves? Sacrifice me to some deity I'd never heard of?

I groaned in frustration and sank deeper into the tub. The only thing I knew for sure was that Liam was right about me, I was in love with Lilith. Did Lilith even feel the same way about me? There was really only one way to know, but the idea of asking her…it was terrifying. The entire situation made me feel like my head would explode and like I might throw up. I felt like I was obsessing.

In the last twenty-four hours, my life had become so complicated. I'd agreed to this ritual in exchange for my sister's life. Did this happen to regular people? Still, I didn't exactly feel forced into it. And did Lilith even have that much power? Did she have any at all? I mean, my sister did survive that accident…

Would I have that kind of power?

I had so many questions, questions I probably should've asked before the ball started rolling on any of this. Would the ritual hurt? Would it work? What if we tried and it didn't? Would my sister die if it wasn't my fault the ritual didn't work? What would I be like after? Would I remember my life from before? When I made the decision to do this, none of it seemed as important as saving Bea. Besides, I trusted Lilith. I didn't always know if I should, but I did.

I wasn't sure how long I'd been in the bathtub, only that the water was starting to cool and my fingers looked like very old raisins. The thought of getting out and putting on the robe made my stomach flop. If I was going to do this, I needed to get my nerves under control. No matter what the ritual entailed, I needed to be mindful of what was happening. I took one last dunk under the water, my eyes shut tight. I let my hair soak up the water and then sat back up. It was now or never.

I pulled the plug from the drain, staying in until all of the water drained. I imagined all of my worries, fear, and insecurities going down the drain with the water, through the pipes, and out into the sewers under the sleepy, boring town of Benson. As the water drained inch by inch, I felt my body becoming increasingly heavy. I also felt myself becoming increasingly sure that I was making the right choice for myself. Once the tub was empty, I stood up, took a deep breath, and got out.

I saw the robe I was supposed to wear hanging on an old coat rack in the corner. Who kept an old coat rack in their bathroom? I half-expected to see a cane and a top hat with it. Little else would surprise me. I walked across the floor, careful not to slip on the tile. The robe was made of heavy black velvet. I pulled it around my shoulders, putting my slender arms inside the sleeves. It fit perfectly, better than anything I'd ever worn before, like it was made for me. The material had a scent to it that I couldn't place, something warm and comforting. As soon as I tied it around my waist I felt warm, no longer chilled by the tile floor.

I walked around the room blowing out all of the candles. I wasn't sure if I was supposed to, but the day had been traumatic enough. There was no need to start a house fire. When I was finished, the room was black as coal. I hurried to the door.

The stairs made no sound as I walked down them. Before going into the living room, I stood in the entryway and watched Lilith sitting silently on the sofa, her expression serious. Then, as if she could feel me watching, she turned her head. She looked up at me and smiled.

"All clean," I said awkwardly.

"Then I guess we should get going." Lilith stood and picked up an old carpet bag that was sitting just outside the entryway. I caught the familiar scent of plum and fig as she passed and led me to the front door.

"It's going to be cold out there. Where are my shoes?" I asked, looking around.

"You won't need them," Lilith replied, reaching for the doorknob.

My jaw dropped. "There's at least a foot of snow out there! I'll freeze to death!"

She reached out and took my hand. A jolt went through my arm.

"I promise, you'll be completely fine."

Without another word, Lilith pulled open the front door and I reluctantly followed her out onto the porch.

I braced myself for the biting cold of the snow on my feet...but it never came. I was naked, outside, wearing nothing but a robe. I should be freezing, but instead it felt like I'd stepped outside in the spring, my foot stepping onto a blanket of clouds.

"How are you doing?" Lilith asked, the corner of her mouth turned up. I looked at her, my mouth hanging open.

"I'm fine. I'm not cold at all. How is that even possible?"

"Magic," Lilith joked.

Lilith led me off of the porch. The sky looked like thick tar dotted with flecks of silver. The moon, however, seemed to be non-existent. When I commented about it out loud, Lilith said it was the dark moon, the new moon, a time for rebirth and starting new paths. No wonder the sky was so dark. With no light to guide us, Lilith moved forward with me trailing close behind. Before tonight, this would've made me feel isolated, uncertain, and full of fear. Tonight, I felt like I was floating. The uncertainty that accompanied the darkness wasn't fearful - it was exciting.

As we entered the woods, the wind began to pick up. I could hear it whistling through the trees. Somewhere in the distance, an owl hooted. I heard something scamper past us across the snow, something large.

"Don't worry about that," Lilith said, seemingly

reading my mind. "Nothing is going to bother us tonight."

"Easy for you to say. You're wearing shoes. Besides, I'm more worried about tripping on this underbrush and losing an eye."

I heard Lilith laugh. The sound of it seemed to wrap through the trees and finally spread out through the forest. Despite the lack of light, shadows followed beside us, all different shapes and sizes. Some moved with the grace and agility of a cat. Others appeared to be twitchy and jerky in their movements. Some of the shadows were short and compact, while others were long, stretched tall and thin, the span of their arms something I'd never seen before. I waited to feel afraid of them, for my nerves to roar back to the surface but, like the cold, they never came.

As yet another shadow danced, spinning past me and Lilith, I felt something that caused my feet to stop for a moment. But it wasn't out of hesitation. I wasn't second-guessing this path I was walking, literally or metaphorically. I wasn't just doing this for my sister. I wanted this. I wanted it for me. I wanted to dance with these shadows, to taste freedom so sweet, like melting cotton candy on my tongue. I wanted to know what it felt like to say no and not feel guilty about it. Better yet, I wanted to know the feeling of saying yes to someone or something without it feeling like an obligation. I wanted to never feel like I was hiding myself for the comfort of someone else. I wanted to always feel as safe in the darkness as I felt right now. Here, now, I didn't worry who these shadows belonged to. I instinctively knew that they were here for me, that they wouldn't hurt me. I knew that each of them was somehow welcoming me to this new life, this existence that I never knew I would be part of someday.

For the first time in my entire life, as I looked up at Lilith looking back at me with an expression of curiosity, I knew that this was fate. This was exactly where I was supposed to be. I'd always had a feeling that there was some place I was supposed to be, some place I needed to get back to. Maybe this was it.

Tonight, in this moment, it was beginning to make sense. I felt like I was finally coming home. Lilith, the darkness, all of it was my home.

"Evie?" Lilith broke through my thoughts like a baseball through a pane of glass. I snapped to attention. She looked so nervous, so uncertain.

"I'm okay," I said, smiling. "Let's keep going."

Without another word, Lilith turned around and continued leading me through the woods. After a little while longer, we entered into the crossroads clearing that Lilith mentioned earlier. It was so different from the forest that surrounded it. There were the tall snow-capped trees and blankets of white covering the ground, but it was so eerily silent here. I spun in a slow circle, trying to take it all in. In this clearing, there were three separate paths, each leading in a different direction. Each of them looked the same, but they each felt so different. Maybe because it was a choice, each path providing something different. It felt a lot like a metaphor for my life right now.

"We'll be ready in a minute. I just need to set a few things up," Lilith said, again interrupting my thoughts. I turned back to her as she was pulling things out of her carpet bag.

"Do you need any help?"

Lilith shook her head. "No, you just hang out. I'll only be a minute."

I watched as Lilith poured a single glass of red wine and lit two candles, one red and one black, and set them on a large tree stump sitting in the very center of the clearing. Lilith pulled a full red rose out of the bag. She began pulling at the petals one by one, sprinkling them around the stump and across the ground. Lilith then lit a stick that emitted plumes of resinous and musky smoke. I watched Lilith close her eyes and inhale deeply, smiling as the smoke filled the space around us. Finally, Lilith placed an old leather-bound book on the stump. It looked like a television marriage proposal.

I couldn't help but allow my eyes to linger on Lilith as she moved around setting everything up. Her every movement was fluid. She was so confident, and sometimes that made me envious. She always seemed to fill up any space she was in, no matter how big. But she never once made me feel small, like she didn't see me the same way I saw myself. A warm feeling spread through my belly. Lilith was filling up this space too. I felt my fingers twitch, wanting to reach out and touch her. I wanted to breathe in the scent of plums and figs that always seemed to be wafting off of Lilith's skin.

For the first time in my life, I began to feel weightless, like all of my fears, doubts, disappointments, and sadness were slowly lifting off of me, one by one, until all that was left was me. I felt...different. I couldn't describe the feeling if I had to. In my stomach, a pressure began to slowly grow bigger and bigger as each moment passed, a building of anticipation. I imagined that this was how a first kiss was supposed to feel, the first time a person fell in love, the first time a person—

"Are you ready?"

I didn't notice that Lilith was now standing right in front of me, though I don't know how I missed that mane of red hair. I smiled, nodding.

"I'm ready. Let's do this."

CHAPTER FIFTY

EVIE

I STARED AT LILITH STARING AT ME IN THE candlelight, the only light in the forest, danced across her face. Her eyes locked on mine, and I took a deep breath.

For the first time in my entire life, it felt like someone finally saw me. Not the person that I carried out into the world, but the one I was when I was alone. The one that danced around my room, that imagined what it would be like to stand at the top of the Chichén Itzá pyramid. Lilith raised her hands to my face, sweeping my hair back and running her fingers through it. Her hands slowly traveled down my robed arms, leaving a trail of fire and electricity in their wake, even through the thick velvet. She took my hand, tangling our fingers, and led me to the tree stump and the book and the rose petals and the candles. I now knew that I would follow Lilith wherever she led. I was absolutely in love with her. My stomach filled with butterflies whenever I saw her, and that warmth spread through my entire body whenever she touched me.

I knew that the only place I wanted to be was with her.

Lilith picked up the leather book, opened it, and handed it to me. It was heavy and thick. The leather was so old and worn, the edges of the pages yellow and frayed. On the front cover of the book, there was no title. There was only a large symbol the size of my palm that looked like two large overlapping snakes or something with a double-headed arrow through the length of it. I ran my fingers over it. It was familiar to me, like I'd seen the symbol somewhere before. It was beautiful and strange. The book buzzed in my hands as I opened it. I looked at Lilith for instruction.

"You need to read from the book," she said, her voice low and raspy but still authoritative. Lilith cleared her throat and pointed to a spot near the center of the page. I stared at the place she was pointing to, trying to read the words in the candlelight. They didn't appear to be in any language I'd ever seen before, not that this was saying much. There were a lot of languages I hadn't seen before. Slowly, as I continued trying to figure out how to pronounce each word, they began to change, to glow a little. Almost instantly, I knew exactly what I was reading without recognizing a single word.

"Oh, Ancient One, I hear your call," I said hesitantly, not sure what this was going to do.

As the words spilled from my mouth, I looked up and saw the shadows around us change. They began to morph, become three-dimensional. There were more of them than before and they felt like they were getting closer. I looked at Lilith to find her staring back at me. Her amber eyes looked different somehow. They almost had the same faint luminescence as the lettering in the book. I stared into them, not realizing that I'd stopped reading until Lilith's hand touched mine, raising the book slightly to get me back on track.

"You, Creator and Destroyer, who speaks Truth and offers Wisdom and Knowledge. May the night winds carry my voice to your ear, and may it strike true as thunder," I continued, a little more confident.

The wind began to change, sweeping around us. The flames of the candles danced wildly but they never went out. The smoke of the incense became stronger.

"I offer up myself to you, seeking Truth, Wisdom, Freedom, and Knowledge." As I recited this line from the book, I could hear what sounded like a distant choir of voices but I couldn't make out what they were saying.

I watched the shapes of the shadows grow so close that I could reach out and touch them. They were stretching out above our heads. It made the candlelight grow brighter as the shadows darkened the sky overhead.

"W-what now?" I stuttered. I could hear the blood rushing in my ears.

"You have to sign."

I blinked at her. "I don't have a pen," I said dumbly.

"You have to use the knife," Lilith answered.

"Oh," I said, surprised. "I don't have one of those either."

I watched as Lilith reached down and pulled a knife from her carpet bag. She turned my hand over, my palm facing upward. Using the sharp tip of the blade, Lilith pushed into the tip of my index finger. She watched my face, but I didn't flinch. I was still staring into her face. Lilith turned the pages of the book in my hand until she came to a blank page.

"You only need to press your finger to the page," Lilith instructed.

I felt lightheaded, but I didn't feel any hesitation. Any trace of nervousness I'd felt before the ritual was completely forgotten.

Maybe I should be nervous, but I wasn't.

So much fire and electricity flowed through every cell in my body that I was sure I would bounce away at any second. But I didn't. Something in the way that her hands felt on mine made me feel still, strong. Was this what Lilith was talking about when she said I would be different?

I didn't even feel the slightest bit self-conscious when the next words came out of my mouth.

"I am yours," I whispered to Lilith without any hesitation. I saw Lilith's breath hitch. I pressed my finger to the page, leaving a thick wet drop of my blood behind. Lilith moved to take the book from my hand, and I noticed that she seemed to be trembling. Our hands brushed against one another. The touch was so slight, but it felt like flames licking at my skin. The look on Lilith's face said that she felt it too. The build-up of anticipation in my stomach was almost too much. What was happening?

Maybe Liam was right, maybe she was dangerous, but it wasn't in the way that he implied.

"What happens now?" I finally asked, my voice soft.

Lilith looked over at me, her eyes warm. "Anything you want."

"Anything?" I was beginning to feel a boldness in me that I'd never felt before. I felt like I could do anything and survive, like hike the Dyatlov Pass or face down a lion. I didn't know where it was coming from, but I liked it.

Lilith nodded. I bit my lower lip, smiling. I stepped forward, closing the distance between us. For some reason, she flinched a little when I reached up and brushed my fingers over her hair. I then let my fingers trace the shape of her jawline. I saw her body tense up, her jaw clench. She seemed as unsure as I did about what was happening. I smiled warmly at her before stepping away and slowly walking around the clearing, watching the shadows move around me in response. They seemed to be dancing, so I slowly spun in a circle with them. The shadows moved around me with such fluidity, like a dance partner. I closed my eyes, moving rhythmically to a song I couldn't hear but somehow knew anyway. I just felt it in my body. I didn't fight against it when it felt like hands slipping the black robe off of me as I danced.

CHAPTER FIFTY ONE

LILITH

I WATCHED WITH SURPRISE AS EVIE STARTED dancing with the shadows around the clearing. They all seemed to be moving as one organism. Evie was beautiful and I wondered if she knew that. It felt good to see her feel free for once, and the fact that she was naked didn't escape my notice. While I certainly didn't hate it by any stretch of the imagination, I also didn't know what to expect next from her. Goosebumps rose all over my skin.

I'd only done this ritual with someone once before, so I didn't know if each time was different, but this time was drastically different from the time in Germany. I wanted to believe that it was because Evie meant more to me, meant everything to me. And she did. Liam said she was in love with me, and at the time, I didn't know how to respond. But I did now. I didn't know how to tell her, but since that day at the cove, I knew it. I knew that my heart would always be hers, whether she knew it or not.

I watched the shadows undulate around her. Ordinarily, the shadows were observers, standing around, watching, not moving much. That's how it was every time I'd attended someone's ritual. This time, with Evie, they danced, sang, howled, and caressed her skin in the candlelight that somehow seemed like a roaring fire now. They seemed to worship her.

I didn't understand what was happening anymore. I found my entire world changed by a girl who seemed to start out as just an assignment. I'd spent every moment since the ER terrified that Evie would change her mind about wanting to be with me. I didn't think that I could spend the rest of my existence without her.

I also knew that I'd laughed more in these last few months than I ever remembered doing before I came here. I found myself craving ways to physically connect with Evie whenever we were together. I wanted to keep her close, a feeling I definitely hadn't felt before. I felt parts of me waking up, parts of me that I didn't know existed. I never let myself feel anything like this. I didn't let myself feel much of anything.

I couldn't risk losing this. The idea of it was so

painful…

"Lilith!" I heard Evie call out to me. "Come and dance with me!"

I laughed and shook my head, but she didn't seem to be taking no for an answer on this. She laughed as she walked over, dragging the shadows with her, and grabbed my hands. I suddenly felt shy and exposed, but I let her pull me into the center of the clearing, trying not to stare at her too much, and not even sure of where to touch her. I was very aware of her nakedness, but I wanted to enjoy this. I didn't want to overthink it. I wanted to lose myself in the feeling of Evie's joy, in her excitement, her softness, but something continued to gnaw at my insides. Regardless, here I was, dancing in the woods with this person who was somehow both so familiar and a total mystery, and she was changing more and more by the minute.

Before I knew it, we were no longer dancing. We were mere inches from one another, as close as we'd been in the waiting room, as close as we'd been that night in my car. I felt myself holding my breath, not sure if either of us would go through with a kiss this time. I could smell the jasmine oil on her skin mixing with the patchouli and lavender that she always smelled like. And then Evie's lips were on mine. My head spun. If this feeling was a river, I would happily drown in it. My stomach was fluttering like nothing I'd ever felt before.

My body was an explosion of sensation. The soft fullness of Evie's lips against mine, the warmth of her skin. This was worth every agonizing moment of waiting. After a few moments, Evie pulled her lips away from mine but kept our foreheads pressed together, her eyes closed. I felt lightheaded. The entire world was silent.

Before either of us pulled away, a piercing shriek filled the air, causing both of us to startle and hurry to cover our ears. The shadows, which had been so methodical and welcoming before, were now spinning wildly, everything moving around us at a dizzying speed.

"What's happening?" Evie asked loudly, trying to project her voice over the sound of the screeching.

"I have no idea!" I yelled back, frantically looking around for the source of the noise.

Then, as quickly as it came, the sound was gone. The wind settled and the shadows began to still. Evie hesitantly uncovered her ears.

"What was that?" she asked again, more to herself than to me.

"That's never happened before," I said, still looking around carefully.

It took a moment for my breathing to slow and for my body to relax. The candles on the tree stump were somehow still lit. The shadows were wrapping around the clearing, creating what looked like a circle of people.

"Are you okay? How do you feel?" I asked her.

"Well, aside from the screaming, pretty good. It's weird, I feel more…well, everything. I feel like I could conquer the world," she said, a grin spreading across her face. "I wish I could tell my family that I was definitely okay. I wish I could tell my mother that I was okay."

I was confused. "Why would you want to go back?"

"Why wouldn't I want to at least tell them that I'm okay, that they don't need to worry? They're my family."

"You asked for freedom. You asked for autonomy. You said you wanted to do this and leave with me. You said you wanted to save Bea. Not going to them is part of the deal." This was it. This was her changing her mind.

Confusion washed over Evie's face this time. "What is happening with you right now? I'm not going back. I just care enough to make sure they don't worry that something is wrong with me, that something bad happened. Don't you care that people know you're safe?"

"There isn't anyone to tell. You agree to give up your old life when you accept this new one."

She laughed. "I never said any of that. I said I wanted the chance to leave, to live my own life, but I never said I'd never speak to them again. What made you think I had to give them up that way?"

"Because that's the way it is," I told her. "That's the way it is for everyone. No one has ever gone back to their old life after the ritual." She looked stunned. "It's okay, you probably won't remember them after a while. Most of them don't."

"And what about you?"

"Like I said, there's no one to remember, no one to tell that I'm okay." The idea that I had no one never really occurred to me before. I was fine on my own. I didn't miss anyone and I assumed there was no one out there missing me. But what if there was? What if I had an entire life before this and didn't remember it?

"Hey, are you okay?" Evie asked. I looked up to find her staring at me intently. I wasn't really sure how to respond to her question. I didn't feel okay. I felt confused.

"He never told me if I had a life before this," I said, my thoughts trailing off. I was speaking more to myself than to Evie. "He never told me if I had a family."

I felt Evie grab me by the shoulders and look me directly in the face. "Lilith, you need to take a deep breath. Who is 'he?'"

"Jax. He said—"

"Did you ask him?"

I laughed, but there was no amusement in it. "You don't ask Jax for things. He asks you. I think I'm going to throw up," I said, continuing to laugh. It was probably bordering on hysteria. I tried to take a deep breath.

I watched Evie dive to the right, grabbing the black robe off of the ground and wrap it around herself.

"Okay, why don't we head back to the house? You can tell me what's going on. You can maybe tell me more about this Jax guy," Evie suggested. I nodded absently, staring off into the distance. I watched the shadows begin to retreat a little, whispering words to one another that I couldn't make out. A chill began to creep through my insides that had nothing to do with the cold air. Evie blew out the candles, threw everything in the bag I'd brought, and then grabbed my arm, leading us back in the direction of my house.

CHAPTER
FIFTY TWO

EVIE

NEITHER OF US SPOKE ON THE WALK BACK to her house. I wanted to ask questions. I wanted to ask if this was actually about the kiss, but I knew that wasn't it. And at the rate Lilith's black boots obliterated the snow in her path, I figured it might be best to keep a safe distance back. I didn't know why this Jax guy thought he could keep the existence of Lilith's family from her, but it was a special kind of sick. This guy sounded like a sociopath.

This was just another item on a long list of strange things surrounding the ritual. One would be my sudden lack of modesty. Before the ritual, I wouldn't have had the courage to be publicly naked. But there I was, frolicking in the woods without a stitch on. I'd kissed Lilith without any hesitation. I smiled at the thought of it, and touched my fingers to my lips, remembering the feel of her lips on mine. I didn't feel any shame or embarrassment or fear. For the first time, I felt like the person that I was supposed to be.

I wanted to ask her about the shadows. I'd never encountered anything like them. Before the ritual, I would've been terrified, and I might've run as far as I could get. But, they felt like extensions of my body. They felt like beings from another world, set loose to welcome me home.

Home. There was that word again. Did the ritual feel like a homecoming for everyone? Did it feel like that for Lilith? Did it feel like this because of Lilith? It was like I was away for so many years that I forgot what my old life felt like. Except this wasn't my old life. It was my new one. It was full of things I'd never done before, feelings I'd never felt, all with a person that I felt like I knew but didn't.

Since our first meeting in the diner, something about Lilith, about the buzz in my body and the pull in my chest, was so familiar, and I knew she had to feel the same way.

When we were finally back at the house, Lilith stomped onto the porch and flung the unlocked door open. I slowed my steps a little bit, not quite sure if I was ready to come down off of my high and deal with Lilith's fury toward whoever she was angry with. Also, I was trying really hard not to trip on this robe and break my face. I could hear her pacing when I finally did walk inside.

"I can't believe that he would keep this from me!" Lilith yelled as soon as I stepped into the living room. I pressed my lips together and stood there silently. "All of these years together, and he just kept lying to me, and maybe I was lying to everyone else when I told them they'd forget! I could kill him, Eve. I could kill him."

"Evie," I replied, still standing in the entryway.

She spun around to face me. "What?" she asked, exasperated.

"You called me Eve. My name is Evie."

"I know what your name is," she said, rolling her eyes.

"Then why did you call me Eve? And are we going to talk about what happened out there?"

Lilith stood there, her mouth open but no words coming out. Maybe it was just a slip of the tongue. But as soon as it happened, as soon as I corrected her, the air between us was charged with something I couldn't name. It wasn't that I was upset. On the contrary, I was just... confused? Curious? I had no idea, but I wanted some kind of reason, an explanation, from Lilith. But it became clear that I wasn't going to get one right now.

"I can't deal with this right now," she said, pointing her index finger back and forth between us. I was a little annoyed. Okay, more than a little.

"I'm going to call Jax. He has to explain," she said "Are you going to ever explain who this guy is?" I asked, still confused, forcing myself to ignore that she didn't want to talk about us.

She ignored me completely. Instead, she began punching numbers on her cell phone before putting it up to her ear. I threw my arms up and sat down on the sofa to wait.

CHAPTER FIFTY THREE

LILITH

JAX PICKED UP AFTER THE FIRST RING.

"You are angry," he said in lieu of a greeting. He didn't sound worried or surprised. He seemed more frustrated and annoyed than anything else. "That makes two of us."

"What do you have to be angry about? You lied to me," I told him through gritted teeth.

His laugh was deep, husky. I hated it. It made him sound like some made-for-TV movie villain.

"I never lied to you, Lilith, not once."

I gripped the phone so tightly that I thought I might crush it in my hand. "You never told me if I left a family behind, that I left a life behind."

I wasn't sure if I was angry with him about lying, or angry that I had feelings for someone that could be so easily taken away.

"Maybe I said it because it was true. Maybe I said what you wanted to hear. You do it all time, Lilith. It is how we get things done. We extract the desires that our target has, and we reflect those desires back at them with a road map to get there."

"That's not what I do, and you know it," I spat back. He didn't respond. "She isn't just any target, is she?" I asked.

"Do not worry about that now. You did your job."

I scoffed. "My job? How can you even—"

"Lilith, you and I have been doing this since Man first wandered into the desert. Well, since you did anyway."

His humor didn't translate, not today. I was far too angry with him.

"Why did you give me this assignment? Tell me the truth, for once."

I heard him sigh, bored. "It has always been the same. You do what I tell you to do when I tell you to do it, no questions asked," he said.

"That's not it. There's more to it than that."

"And if it was your business, I would tell you. But I see now that I should have sent someone else. You have forgotten your place and gotten too attached. From the beginning, you agreed to doing the job, no questions."

"I was young and naive when I agreed to that bullshit," I told him, my voice a little more even.

"You may have been young, but you were never naive, Lilith. Peddle that nonsense someplace else. You need to remember who you are."

"And who is that?" I asked, starting to feel pretty deflated by that point.

"You are Lilith. You walked out of that garden and into the desert, refusing to bow to anyone. You refused to grovel at anyone's feet. You were created out of the very dirt, and look at what you have made of yourself. You have been the most powerful of any that I have created. Act like it. Have some pride."

"Garden? What are you talking about?" He didn't answer me. I saw Evie sitting on the sofa, pretending not to be listening. The bare leg sticking out from underneath her robe all the way up her thigh was distracting, and I didn't need that right now. I turned and went out into the hall. I couldn't have the rest of this conversation in front of her anyway.

"I called her Eve," I whispered. "Who is Eve?"

The laughter on the other end of the phone was immediate and robust. I was embarrassed and confused, and all he could manage to do was laugh at me, again.

"Now there is a name I haven't heard in a very long time. Well, not from your mouth."

"Yeah, well, I don't understand why I would call her

that. Sure, the names are extremely similar, any idiot can see that, but until tonight, I'd never done that. And I let her kiss me."

He was silent for a minute before he spoke. "Well, that is disappointing."

"What?" He wasn't making any sense.

"You truly do not remember, do you? I guess it worked a little better than I thought."

I didn't know what he was talking about.

"What? What worked?"

"Lilith, when I found you in the desert, it was not the first time you left that garden," Jax started. "It was not the first time you and I met. It was the second. The first time, you were angry. I did not offer you anything at that time. You had your own agenda, and it was not yet the same as mine. In the garden, you were replaced by another woman. She was beautiful, with dark hair and chestnut eyes. She was meek, subservient. She was no match for you, but it didn't matter then. Once you saw her, that was the end of the Lilith that first left that garden. Once you saw her, you were no longer angry. You were lost. You wanted her. You fell for her in a way that I had never seen before that day, or since. You spent day after day teaching her to cultivate the garden, a garden you started from the very ground from which you were created. As each day passed, you loved her more and more, and you wanted her to love you.

"The problem was not that she could not love you back. She did love you, instantly, and without hesitation. At night, you stayed just outside the garden, but during the day, you went in and sought her out because it was the only time that she could get away from Adam and tend to the flowers." I wanted to vomit. A garden? Adam? Eve? Before I had a chance to ask, he continued.

"You begged her to leave with you. So many times you pleaded with her. You told her that the garden was no longer a place for women like you, that the two of you were meant for better, meant for more, and meant for each other. And she believed you. She believed you right up until you offered her the fruit from the tree, giving her the knowledge of the world the two of you could build together. It is funny, people have believed for centuries that it was some devil that tricked her into disobeying. It was not her love for you that cursed her, but it was her fear of it. It was what they convinced her would happen if she chose you."

I listened to all of this, my heart pounding. I could remember only snippets of what he was telling me, and none of it made any sense.

"The girl in the garden was Eve. Normally, I think that the idea of soulmates is a ridiculous one, some concept created by human beings to make themselves feel better about being alone, but the two of you...that was different. It was not the way their god intended, but you were soulmates, Lilith. Perhaps your Eve has come back to you," he said, laughing robustly.

I stayed silent. This was so much to process at once. Soulmates were not real. I told woman after woman this, explaining exactly what Jax said, that it was a way of dealing with being lonely and alone. But now Jax, the most unromantic person I'd ever met, was joking about Evie being Eve's reincarnation, and that we were soulmates.

"Why don't I remember any of this?" I asked him.

"Look, I'm going to be frank with you. Being involved with her could prove disastrous. There are many things in play that you have no knowledge of, that you cannot fathom. Once Eve chose fear over her love for you, a choice had to be made, and not to sound dramatic, but the fate of the world rested on it. I took precautions to make sure you could not remember because if you did, I knew that you would never stop searching for her. It was imperative that you did not find her. So, I gave you that ring."

I looked down at my hand at the silver ring I'd been wearing for as long as I could remember. This kept me from remembering my old life?

"Then I'm asking you again, why did you give me this assignment?"

"It was a test. I needed to see if the ring would work if you were with her because she was going to be one of us no matter who I sent. Unfortunately, it is a test that you seem to be failing."

"And if I take the ring off?"

"If you take it off, you will experience that heartbreak for the second time, just as intensely. You will refuse to leave the girl there with you now, and it will prove to be to the detriment of, well, everyone and everything. As I said, there are things in play that you cannot understand, and that you cannot know. You were made to forget for a reason."

I felt completely overwhelmed. I didn't know what to think. "Jax, I don't know what to do with all of this."

"There is really only one thing you should do, and that is to treat this as business as usual and get out of there. Leave her to choose her own path. You move on, continue to forget she exists," he instructed.

I took a deep breath. "And if I choose to stay with her?"

"You will assume the consequences, and believe me when I say that they will be great."

"I can't leave her, Jax," I said, on the verge of tears, my heart feeling like it was being painfully squeezed.

"Then you must be prepared to accept the consequences."

"Why didn't you tell me any of this before?"

I heard him sigh on the other end of the line. I could tell that he was bored with this conversation. He rarely humored anyone for this long. Regardless, I wanted an answer and I was going to get it.

"I needed you to be useful to me, and a sad girl with a broken heart was not useful to me. A powerful goddess was what I needed, and so a powerful goddess is what I created. I'm going now. I hope that you know what you are doing, Lilith."

With that, Jax hung up the phone and I was left standing in the hallway, trying to figure out what to do next.

As I walked back into the living room, Evie wasn't there. I felt tremendous dread in the pit of my stomach.

"Evie?" I asked frantically. She couldn't have left. She wouldn't do that without telling me. She wasn't like that.

"I'm in the kitchen," she shouted back. I felt my entire body relax and made my way there. When I walked in, Evie looked up at me, worry and anticipation all over her face. We stared at one another, and fear took me over. Do I tell her? Do I walk away? Do we deal with this together?

"Did you get the answers you were looking for?" I heard her ask softly, hesitantly.

That was the understatement of the century.

CHAPTER
FIFTY FOUR
LILITH

H E THINKS I'M WHAT?!" EVIE EXCLAIMED. IT took me so long to get the story out, and now that I had, I needed it to go right back in so that I didn't feel so stupid.

"Not what, who, though I guess both are accurate in this scenario," I mumbled, finally sitting down at the kitchen table.

"What are we supposed to do with all of this? What are the consequences he was talking about?" she asked.

"I have no idea. He wouldn't tell me. But we don't have to do anything, not if you don't want to. It's a lot of weird information, and honestly, Jax might be lying. I don't know—"

"I'm in love with you," Evie blurted out. I knew this was a huge deal for her. I was probably the first person she'd ever said it to, and our relationship was complicated on its best day.

"So Liam was right," I said, more of a statement than a question. "And that's why you kissed me. How long have you felt like this?" I asked, looking her in the eye for the first time since I'd gotten off the phone.

"I don't know. Since you came to me in the emergency room. Since the night you tried to kiss me in your car. Since the day I met you. I don't know, but here it is," she said.

I felt my eyes watering. I nodded but didn't say anything. I didn't know how to say it back yet, not after everything I'd just thrown at her.

"Look, Lilith," she said. "We can just…put this on the back burner for a bit. At least until you have time to process everything Jax just told you, and I process what all of this means for me, for us."

I felt relieved, which bothered me a little. "Yes, please. This is all—"

"—so frigging much," she said, finishing my sentence. We both chuckled sadly.

"Yeah, I mean, you may realize that you absolutely hate me. Who knows?" I shrugged.

The corner of her mouth turned up, but she didn't look amused. "Lilith, I don't think that would ever be possible."

For some reason, I felt unbelievably guilty.

"Give it time," I said.

"What is that supposed to mean?" she asked me.

"It means that this is liable to become a disaster. I'm willing to accept the consequences, but I'm not going to let you get caught in the crossfire."

When I looked up at her, she was fuming, the black robe slipping from her shoulder a little. "You're not going to let me? I'm in this. I'm in this just as deep as you are. If you don't want to be with me anymore, fine, but have the guts to fucking say it instead of making up some lame excuse."

This was coming out all wrong. "I do want to be with you. I just don't want this to end badly. And when Jax is involved, things usually end up bad...and bloody."

"Well, that's his problem."

"It might become ours."

"Fine. Then it becomes our problem. Together."

Neither of us said anything else for a while. We sat at opposite ends for nearly two hours. I knew that we needed to move on, to get out of Benson, if we were going together. I also knew that Evie was going to have a hard time with it, so I didn't say anything just yet. Instead, I watched Evie drink three cups of hot tea and stare out at the snow in the backyard. I was still nursing my first cup, which was far too cold to enjoy at this point.

"This has been one hell of a day," Evie said, still gazing out of the window. I nodded in agreement though Evie wasn't looking at me. "Like, if someone wrote a book about this day, they'd have to label it as fiction. I just…it's just a weird day."

"Your life has definitely taken a turn."

For the first time in two hours, Evie looked at me. "My life? What about yours? Just a few hours ago, you thought you were a demon without a past. Now, you have been given this information about your old life that you'd forgotten, found out that the person you just turned into a demon or whatever might be your soulmate, if that's a real thing. You learned that I'm in love with you, but if we're together, we might destroy the world, so there's that. I have no idea what I am now, and we still don't know what to do next!"

"Immortal," I said, staring down at the teacup I held in both hands.

"I'm sorry, what?"

"You're immortal now. Well, sort of. You can be destroyed, but it's really difficult and almost never happens." I watched as Evie's eyebrows reached new heights on her forehead. "Guess I should've said something earlier?"

"That might've been good information to have. I mean, I don't know what I was expecting. This seems to fit with the collective weirdness of today. We're going to come back to this later though, because I am definitely going to have some questions about it. So, what do we do next?"

I sat back in my seat and gave a long exhale. "Well, if we're staying together, we need to get out of Benson sooner rather than later. If we stay in one place for too long, it gets harder and harder to keep our identities a secret. Plus, your parents, your sister, and your best friend live here, so that will not work out well for you, or for them, if what Jax says is true."

Evie stared at me, a confused look on her face. "If I stay with you? I told you out there in the woods, in your living room, in here a little while ago…I intend to stay with you, Lilith. I don't want to leave. I didn't just do this to save my sister. I did this to be with you."

I didn't know what to say. I just stared at her. I wanted her to stay, I needed her to stay, but all I could hear was Jax telling me that my relationship with her could be disastrous.

"I feel so weird about leaving all of them here without them knowing what's happening," Evie said, continuing on like there was no debate. "I'd love to say goodbye, but I know that's a terrible idea now."

"I'm sorry. I really should have been more upfront with you. I feel horrible, if that matters at all."

She shrugged. "It sucks, but I guess I get it."

I didn't know what else to say about that, so I just

asked what she wanted to do next.

"Honestly, I think that I just want to sleep," Evie replied through a yawn.

If I was being honest, I was a little disappointed that she wanted to go to sleep. I could have stayed up all night talking to her, and now I could. She could drive me up a wall, but she was smart, funny, and more interesting than she knew. She was never boring, and I appreciated that fact. Considering the hundreds of thousands of people I'd met over the years, Evie was the only one that made me feel both restless and at ease, amused and annoyed. I wanted to stay with me, but I couldn't blame her if she ever decided to leave.

"Hey, are you okay?" Evie asked. "You look so sad all of a sudden."

"Yeah, I'm okay. Just being morose again. It's my default tonight."

"Well, knock it off. It's going to be okay. So, where should I sleep tonight anyway?"

I stood up and took both of our mugs, putting them in the sink. "You can have my bedroom. I'll take the sofa. I didn't think we'd be here tonight, so I never got the guest room ready, and it hasn't been cleaned or dusted since I've been here."

Evie scrunched her nose. "That's gross. I'm happy to take the sofa. Or we can both just sleep in your room, if that's cool. I promise I don't steal the covers, I don't kick, and I'm pretty sure I don't snore."

I wanted to slam my head into a wall. Was she trying to make this more difficult than it was already going to be? Was this some kind of weird punishment from the universe for something?

Apparently I was taking too long to answer because a panicked expression slid across Evie's face. "Okay, that was weird. I'm really sorry. I shouldn't have asked. You sleep in your room, I'll take the sofa. It's totally fine, I do it at home all the time. I'm really sorry for assuming…"

I shook my head. "No, it's fine. It's a huge bed."

"Are you sure?" she asked, searching my face.

I plastered my most reassuring - and probably most frightening – smile. "It is absolutely not a problem." And it wasn't. It was definitely not a problem.

This was going to be the longest night in the history of man.

CHAPTER FIFTY FIVE

EVIE

I STARED AT THE CEILING IN THE DARK FOR what felt like hours. I wasn't sure what was supposed to happen now. I tried so hard to not look at Lilith asleep next to me, but when I finally got up the nerve, I found her staring back at me.

"Hey," I said quietly.

"Hey."

"Not sleeping either?"

"No, I'm totally asleep. You're having this conversation by yourself," Lilith said, joking. I smiled at her.

"You're ridiculous."

"That's what I hear," Lilith said. "So why can't you sleep?"

I wanted to tell Lilith what was keeping me up - the fight with Liam, the ritual, the kiss – but I wasn't sure how to say anything about any of it. I wanted to tell Lilith that all I wanted to do was reach across the bed and touch her hair, to kiss her again, but it felt like bad timing. Instead, I opted for a simple question.

"What do we do now?" I whispered in the dark.

I heard Lilith take a breath. "I don't know. I have no idea how this works."

"You know, I don't really know what to do either. I've never done any of this before at all." I stayed silent for a moment. The room was too dark to read Lilith's face.

"Well, what do you want to do right now?" Lilith asked me.

I hesitated before answering. I wanted to tell her that I wanted to feel the softness of her skin, that I wanted to feel her breath in my ear, that I wanted to hear her breathe my name. I wanted to say all of these things. I wanted to just lean across the bed and press my mouth against hers, but I said nothing. My heart raced inside my chest and my mouth went dry. The idea of telling Lilith any of this filled me with a completely suffocating feeling of fear, fear of being rejected, fear of having no experience with this. It all felt dangerous. So I took a deep and shaky breath, and told her the only thing I could manage in this moment.

"Right now, I just really want to hold your hand," I

whispered. Lilith didn't respond. Instead, she reached across and entwined her fingers with mine.

The following morning, I was up before the sun. I tiptoed toward the bathroom, hoping to find a spare toothbrush, but how often did that really happen? It didn't happen this time either. I used my finger, an old trick I saw in a movie once. I quickly learned another lesson: a finger is a terrible substitute for a toothbrush. I took off the large nightshirt I borrowed from Lilith and put on the clothes I'd worn the day before.

The windows in the kitchen faced east, so I watched the sun come up over the horizon as the scent of freshly brewing coffee filled the kitchen. I poured a cup and then stood in front of the window watching as the red-orange light of the sun reflected off of the falling snow. Benson may have been the most boring place on Earth, but I was also fairly certain it had to be one of the most beautiful, especially this time of year. I closed my eyes and held the coffee cup under my nose, inhaling the scent of it, thankful for a quiet minute alone.

Well, it was almost quiet. I finally heard a soft buzzing sound. It took me a minute to realize the steady buzzing was coming from the living room. Not sure what was making the sound, I decided to investigate. When I entered the living room, I saw my cell phone lit up on a side table, buzzing horribly. I dove for it and looked at the screen.

Thirty-seven missed calls, all of them from the same number. My parents were trying to reach me. I swiped up to unlock the screen. There were thirty-six voicemail messages and more missed text messages than I wanted to acknowledge. I took a deep breath and pressed the play button on my voicemail. I only made it halfway through the messages before I just stopped listening and started hitting delete. My mother was frantic, my father angry.

I held my phone in my hand, staring at it, not knowing what to do when it started vibrating again. This time, it was Liam's number. I let it ring three times and then very cautiously hit the answer button with my thumb.

"Hello?" I asked meekly.

"Good. You're not dead. Call your mother. Now." His voice was rough, angry.

"I'm sorry if she has been calling you a lot. I just can't talk to her right now."

"You know what? This is cruel. What is wrong with you?"

"I have a lot going on right now. Once I get it figured out —"

"They're going to call the cops, Evie. Is that really what you want, cops showing up on Lilith's doorstep? They have no idea what happened to you, and they're scared. For fuck's sake, your sister almost died yesterday, and then you disappeared. They're terrified! They aren't even angry anymore. They're worried that you're dead in a ditch somewhere."

I felt terrible, but what was I supposed to say to them? How was I supposed to explain all of this?

"Okay, but why exactly would the police investigate this? I'm eighteen, and unless things got really crazy after I left, there's no blood anywhere. If they call you again, please tell them you spoke to me and I'm fine, and I will call as soon as I can. And I promise that I'll call them. I just have something that I have to do first."

"You always have something else to do first. You know, you're my best friend. I thought that I knew you. Obviously I don't know you at all."

With that, the line went dead.

"Who was that?"

Startled, I dropped my phone. I spun around, relieved that it was Lilith and not a serial killer.

"That was Liam. My parents are freaking out."

Lilith ran both hands through her hair and then let them flop down at her side.

"Well, you have to call them, I guess. You'll just have to do it from the road."

We spent the next hour upstairs in the bedroom, Lilith on the phone while grabbing things and throwing them into suitcases while I sat on the bed watching her.

She was also pointing at things for me to grab for her from time to time, and that was pretty annoying. I could only hear Lilith's end of the conversation, but it sounded like she was making arrangements for traveling. I heard her say something about Australia and then London before finally putting the person on hold to ask if I had a passport. When I laughed at her, she rolled her eyes and booked two First-Class airline tickets to Hawaii.

I was excited about the mere idea of traveling to Hawaii, let alone actually doing it. And traveling in First-Class was something I only saw people do in movies.

"Are you about ready?" Lilith asked me as she hung up the phone. "It's going to take forty-five minutes to get to the airport and then we still have to make it through security."

"I only came with my backpack, so…yeah, I'm pretty much good to go."

"Good. I have one thing left to do, so I need you to call a cab or whatever you have out here."

"Oh, give me a break, Lilith," I said, rolling my eyes and laughing. "We might be a little old-fashioned here, but we're not living in the Stone Age." I got on my phone, pulled up my ride share app, and announced that our ride would be here in twenty minutes.

I followed Lilith downstairs and watched as she dropped the two suitcases in the hall and then walked toward Samael's habitat. Somehow, I managed to forget about the snake for awhile. Lilith opened the habitat and carefully removed the boa from it. Samael's tongue darted out as Lilith kissed him on the nose.

"I have to go now, Samael. Don't worry, Jax will send someone for you tomorrow. You should be okay until then. I will see you again soon. Until then, behave," Lilith said to him. I was a little disturbed at how she spoke to the snake as though it were a real person, as though it understood what she was saying. She planted one last kiss on its nose and then held it out toward me.

"Yeah, I'm not doing that," I said. Lilith rolled her eyes and put him back inside his habitat.

A knock at the door interrupted us.

"That must be our ride," she said.

"That would be weird. They never come to the door."

Lilith closed the habitat and went to get the door.

Liam stormed into the living room. He looked furious. I had no desire to deal with him right now.

"Your mother has called me seven more times, Evie. Seven. You have to call her now."

I opened my mouth to answer, but Lilith interrupted.

"She can't do that right now."

Liam turned on her. "I'm not talking to you," he hissed.

"Hey! Can you both just take a breath?" I interrupted. "Lilith, I can handle this myself, but thank you. Liam, I am so sorry that they keep calling you, I really am. But I can't call them right now. A lot has happened, and it just isn't a good time to call them. I can't explain what's going on, and you definitely wouldn't understand. Just…block their number or something."

"Block their number? Is that a serious suggestion?" Liam was incredulous. "Sorry, I'm just not as cold and heartless as you are."

Something in me clicked, like the flipping of a switch. The feeling of guilt I had for worrying everyone was suddenly replaced with a bright white anger. Lilith tried to say something, but I raised my palm to stop her, not taking my eyes off of Liam.

"You know what? How about, for once, you maybe mind your own business. Maybe you can stop being so fucking judgmental all the time. I thought that we'd gotten somewhere when you were here yesterday, but I see that I was wrong. Maybe, just maybe, you could stop acting like you run my life." I was furious. It was like all these years of listening to him make plans for us, decide what we were going to do every night but pretending it was my idea, what kind of person I should be were banging together inside me, sparking something… strong, forceful, controlled.

I watched him narrow his eyes at me. He stared at me as I walked around the room and then stopped to lean against Lilith's antique desk.

"Who are you? I don't even know you anymore!

Ever since you started hanging out with her," he shouted, gesturing angrily at Lilith who was standing off to the side, arms folded, watching the imploding of a years-long friendship with concern.

Just as I opened my mouth to defend Lilith, to say it had nothing to do with her, something strange happened. Three spindly shadows began to creep up around the room, coming from the floor and clawing their way slowly up the walls and across the ceiling. The shadows were similar to the shadows from the night before, like witnesses to what was unfolding. They seemed to be blacking out the light and making a strange hissing sound that only I seemed to hear. I glanced over at Lilith. She seemed to notice them as well.

The only person who didn't seem to notice them was Liam.

"You know what? Just stop," I said to him. "I am so sick of you feeling like you are so much better than me."

Liam laughed, but there was no amusement in it. "I act like I'm better than you?" he asked, stepping toward me. "Is that supposed to be some kind of joke? For the last ten years, all I've heard from you is how you can't wait to get out of this town, how everyone here is boring and stupid and useless. You've looked down on your parents, your grandparents, on me. And I'm the one who needs to stop acting like they're better than you. You really are something."

By the time his rant was over, he was standing directly over me. I didn't remember ever hating him, but I sure felt something akin to that now. Neither of us was the same person anymore, and I didn't know how Liam felt about that, but I felt just fine about it at this point. And the fact that he was blaming Lilith…well, that compounded my anger, the implication that I couldn't make a decision for myself. It was insulting.

"Well? Are you going to call them, or am I?" Liam threatened.

A warmth spread through my insides like fire as I looked up at him. I began to feel like I did at the Halloween party, how I felt the night before this one when he confronted Lilith and I again. Warmth and electricity and a surge of unbridled power rose up in me. As I braced myself on the desk, I felt something cold and hard bump against my hand. I glanced down quickly and saw that it was one of those ornate silver letter openers. I stepped to the side, screaming internally for Liam to shut up. I wanted him to just stop talking and go away. The feeling was strong, overwhelming.

Suddenly, his eyes widened. Without blinking, he leaned down to pick up the letter opener. For a moment, I panicked, worried he was going to use it to threaten me, or worse. But he didn't. Instead, while looking me right in the eye, he brought the letter opener up and stabbed it directly into his own neck, right next to his Adam's apple. He must have severed his carotid artery because the blood rushed out of him and sprayed right across my face. I stumbled back a little as he fell against me and his warm, sticky blood covered my hands and arms. I pushed him to the ground, my eyes wide. Panic flooded all of me. The blood continued to spill out of him as I watched something in his eyes change. It was like the flickering of a damaged light bulb.

The letter opener was still in his hand, the garnet-colored blood coating the blade. He gurgled as blood continued to spill out of him. His eyes were looking in my direction, his face blank. I continued to stand over him as the shadows slithered around, washing over him. Finally, after a minute or two, the flickering light in his eyes went out.

CHAPTER FIFTY SIX

EVIE

I STARED DOWN AT THE BOY LAYING AT MY FEET, my eyes wide. It took a moment for me to notice that my hands were shaking, that I was shaking.

"What in the hell just happened?" Lilith asked. I looked up to see her eyes wide, staring at Liam's body on the floor in front of me.

"I don't know," I said. "I just wanted him to shut up. I just wanted his mouth to stop making words." My eyes stung and the boy at my feet became blurry as the tears filled my eyes. I'd been so angry with him, so hurt by him, but this wasn't what I wanted. Bile rose up in my throat as I fought to keep standing.

"Well, that was definitely accomplished."

I jumped at the sound of Lilith's voice in my ear, the feel of her hands on my shoulders as she turned my body to face her own.

"This was not your fault, Evie. Whatever you think you did, you didn't. He did this to himself. I don't know why, but he did." Lilith's voice was low, husky, and wrapped around my nerves like a blanket. I nodded, my mind blank. I wanted to do a million things at once. I wanted to run away, I wanted to curl up in Lilith's arms, I wanted to scream.

"I want to take it back," I said out loud. "I can do that, right? I can give him his life back?"

I felt Lilith's hand caress the back of my neck and I closed my eyes, letting the gesture comfort me the way it was intended to.

"I'm so sorry, Evie, not this one. He's already dead. Neither of us has that kind of power."

Before I could respond, I heard my cell phone ping.

"Shit," I muttered, looking down at the front of me covered in Liam's blood. "Can you get that out of my back pocket?" Under normal circumstances, this might be kind of sexy. Right now, this was the least sexy thing that could be happening to me.

"It's our ride," Lilith said, looking at my phone.

"Oh, good. I'm sure they won't notice the immense amount of blood covering the front of my body," I said, panic rising up in my voice.

"Wow, okay. Well, you'll have to change and wash up, obviously. Then we'll get out of here."

I was kind of surprised by Lilith's response. I wasn't sure what I expected, but it was not an instruction to wash my hands and board a plane.

"That's it? We just wash up, get on a plane, and forget this?" I asked, gesturing to Liam's bloody body on the floor.

"Well, like I said, change your clothes, but yeah, that's what we do. It's all we can do."

"This is not good, is it?" I asked, knowing the very obvious answer.

"No, it isn't. But I just want to know one thing: how did you not get any blood in your hair?" Lilith asked.

I glared at her, the joke not welcome at all, and Lilith nodded in understanding. I looked down at the lifeless body of my best friend staring up at me and I suddenly felt a new feeling wash over me: relief. As bad as I felt only seconds before, I was startled to find that it was fading. The montage of all the good times we shared were suddenly replaced with his distrust of Lilith, his perceived claim on me, the way he forced himself on me in my bedroom.

"Why don't I feel bad anymore, Lilith? What's wrong with me?" I looked over at Lilith. A tear that pooled in my eye let go and slithered down my cheek. I felt worse about not feeling bad that Liam was dead.

Lilith shrugged. "Okay, so it isn't exactly socially acceptable for you to not feel bad that someone you care about is dead, especially since his blood is all over you. But you didn't do it, Evie. Besides, you aren't the same person anymore. Yes, you love your family, you loved him, and you might…love me," she said, stuttering through that last bit. "But you are very different from who you used to be, Evie. You really have to start accepting this."

I nodded absentmindedly.

"What happens now?" I asked, feeling absolute panic.

"We already covered that."

"Oh. Yeah. I guess I need to find my backpack," I muttered.

"I'll take the suitcases outside and tell the driver you'll be out in a minute. Head into the kitchen and start getting cleaned up. I'll bring your backpack in a minute."

Lilith strode out of the room, leaving me alone with Liam's body. How long would it be before anyone found him? Did anyone know he was here?

I shook the thoughts from my head and made my way to the kitchen, careful not to get blood on anything. I carefully kicked off my shoes, took off my jeans, and managed to get my t-shirt off without getting blood all in my hair. Another good reason for the messy bun. It wasn't just for lazy girls anymore, I guess. Miraculously, my bra and my underwear seemed more or less okay.

"Evie?" Lilith shouted from the hallway.

"I'm in the kitchen," I yelled back, pouring dish soap into my hands.

Lilith was explaining that the car said he'd wait five more minutes, when I heard her sharply inhale as she stopped mid-sentence when she walked in on me standing at the sink in my underwear, scrubbing unsuccessfully at the blood on my arms.

"I keep getting blood on my hands," I explained dumbly.

"Well...hurry up, Lady Macbeth," Lilith said, putting my backpack on the table and digging out my clothes. She came over and helped me get the blood off. I dressed quickly and grabbed my backpack. I threw the bloody clothes in the trash. Probably not my best move, but we would be long gone by the time that anyone found the body in the living room.

I didn't look in the direction of that living room as I hurried out of the house and into the waiting car, but that didn't stop the feeling of dread and nervousness.

CHAPTER
FIFTY SEVEN

EVIE

AFTER LILITH AND I ARRIVED IN HAWAII, I waited a week before calling my parents. Things were so hectic from the moment our plane landed that I just kept putting it off. Lilith's friend, Joanna, had a very large home on a private beach, and she threw a huge party that night to welcome us. There were so many people to meet. It wasn't until a week later that I finally had a moment to myself.

I sat on a quiet section of the beach one morning, phone in hand, and tried to think of what to say when they answered. Should I bother apologizing? Was I even sorry anymore? How was Bea doing? Did anyone ever find Liam's body?

I took a deep breath and scrolled through my contacts until I found my parents' home number. My thumb hovered over the call button for about thirty seconds before I finally pressed down on it. After three rings, a tiny voice answered.

"Hello?" It was Bea. My chest tightened at the sound of her voice.

"Bea? Is that you?"

"Yes…who's this?" Bea asked, caution in her voice.

"Bea, it's me. It's Evie."

Bea screamed excitedly and I laughed, pulling the phone away from my ear.

"Evie, is it really you? Where are you?" Bea asked loudly.

I could hear my mother in the background saying my name and then demanding that Bea hand her the telephone. Bea just kept asking questions until she was finally cut off.

"Evie?" My mother's fragile-sounding voice came over the line. Panicked, I had to fight the urge to hang up.

"Um..hi, Mom," I stammered. Suddenly my mother was crying into the phone. I couldn't understand anything she was saying.

"Mom, Mom, calm down. I'm fine. I promise, I'm okay," I interjected.

"Where are you? What happened? You were just gone, we didn't know if you were dead…"

"I'm really sorry that I didn't tell you I was going to leave. I'm sorry I did it on the day of Bea's accident, and I'm really sorry that I didn't answer any of your calls. I don't have any excuse for any of that," I told her.

"Your father and I have been worried sick. Did you know that Liam is missing too? He told his father he was going to go looking for you, and now no one can find him. He isn't answering his phone or anything. Have you heard from him?"

I took a deep breath to try and settle myself. "Um, he called a couple of times, but we kept missing each other," I lied. "I left that night, so I haven't seen him. Have you tried his cell phone?" I felt like an episode of a murder podcast waiting to happen.

"When are you coming home?" she asked, clearly indicating that she may not be ready to accept an apology just yet. "Where are you?"

"I don't know when I'm going to be able to come back home," I said, ignoring the inquiry about my location. My mother was silent on the other end of the phone. "I'm probably not coming home. Not any time soon, at least."

I could hear her mother trying to muffle her crying. Neither of us said anything for several minutes. Finally, my mother's voice broke the silence. "You'll miss your sister's play."

"I know. Please tell her I'm so sorry. I'll call her as

soon as I can."

"I will." There was a long pause, as if my mother was building up to something. " I feel silly, but I have to ask. Evie…is this the deal you made?"

It felt like being punched in the gut. "What do you mean?" I choked out, trying to pretend I didn't think about that all the time.

"The one your sister said you made. Was this the deal? If it was, I'll understand."

I took a deep breath and tried hard to hold back the sob that threatened to escape. "Mom. I told you. I made a deal to be a better sister. Now I'm trying to do that."

"Evie, we both know that doesn't make any sense," my mother said. "Besides, you're gone. How does that make you a better sister?"

"I'm trying to show her that sometimes you have to follow your heart."

The only sound for a minute was her crying. It broke my heart. The only way to fix this was to go home, and I couldn't do that.

"Well, I hope your heart is full. Knowing that your sister is okay, knowing that you're okay, my heart is full. Sad, but full. I love you, baby girl. The world is a big place, but don't forget that, okay?

"I won't," I said, finally crying. "I love you too. All of you."

We said goodbye and hung up. I began wiping the

tears from my face when I heard someone calling my name.

"Evie!"

I turned to see Lilith standing on the porch of the beach house, her flaming hair blowing wildly in the wind. Lilith's skin looked golden from her time in the sun since we'd arrived. I smiled at the sight of her and wished we could just hang out alone, but there was a party that night, and we needed to get ready. It seemed like Joanna was always having a party. It had only been a week here, but she had people coming in and out all the time. When I asked Lilith how they knew each other, Lilith explained that she and Joanna were part of a large network of others that worked with Jax, a network of which I was now a part of.

I stood up and trudged through the sand back toward Joanna's house. Lilith waited for me on the porch.

"How did it go?" Lilith asked, brushing her hair out of her face. She looked at my red, puffy face and bit her lip. "That well, huh?"

"She's sad, but she's not angry. I think she understands more than I thought she would. Bea seemed excited to hear from me. Her play's getting ready to open," I told her.

"That's great," Lilith said.

"They think Liam is missing. They thought he was with me."

"Well, I'm sure his body has been disposed of and the house cleaned," Lilith informed me. I nodded, my eyes downcast.

"It'll be fine," Lilith reminded me. She reached out and took my hand, squeezing it.

Later that night, the house was buzzing with activity. There were probably sixty or so people wandering around the house. Beautiful people were grouped in every corner of the bottom floor of the house, each of them holding glasses of wine or champagne. All of them were very welcoming, telling me that they were thrilled to finally meet me, welcoming me to the family, whatever that meant. Men and women alike fawned over me, and it made me feel a little awkward, especially in the dress Joanna gave me to wear. It was a beautiful yellow slip dress that cut deeply in the back and hung loosely from me, the fabric spilling onto the floor around my feet. The heels Joanna gave me pinched my toes, so for the last hour, I was walking around barefoot, dragging the hem of the dress behind me.

Lilith, on the other hand, was dressed in a tailored black suit that made me wish no one else was here. Seriously, it was difficult to remain at all chill around her. She stuck fairly close to me all night, always with one hand resting on my lower back, lightly tickling my skin.

She seemed extremely proud to be walking around with me.

As welcoming as everyone was, every once in a while, someone would say something strange that would throw me off.

"We've got high hopes for you, Evie," an older man in a white tuxedo said to me. He handed me what would be my third glass of champagne that evening.

"Why?" I asked, finally feeling bold enough to ask.

The man in the white tuxedo pulled a young woman just barely older than me against him. He creeped me out.

"We've all just been hearing such splendid things about you. We're all very excited to see how you progress once you're more comfortable in your new role."

"Yeah, a lot of people have said that tonight. What exactly have you been hearing?" I asked.

"Don't you know?" the man asked, taken aback.

"If I did, I wouldn't be asking," I said sarcastically, smiling tightly. At my side, Lilith laughed, trying to play the statement off as a joke. The man and his companion also laughed awkwardly.

"Well, rumor has it that you have already made quite a name for yourself," he started, gesturing around the room. "It isn't every day that a new recruit, if you will, ends up with a body at their feet in the first twenty-four hours and just walks away."

They were talking about Liam. Everyone was congratulating me on killing Liam. The man smiled, but I couldn't return it. I looked to Lilith for some kind of guidance, but Lilith looked just as perplexed.

"He did that to himself," I told the man.

He laughed. "Sure he did."

This was definitely not something I wanted to celebrate. I started to insist that he was wrong, but Joanna was clinking the side of her glass, calling everyone's attention to the front of the room. Everyone in the house congregated to the main room, eager to hear her speak.

"Thank you so much for coming, everyone. As many of you know, we have come together to celebrate our newest member, Evie Franklin. Evie, darling, come up here, please," Joanna said, her voice carrying over the crowd.

Joanna was stunning. She was statuesque with long, flowing hair that looked like white satin. She wore a white button-down shirt tucked into a black pencil skirt. The high-heeled shoes she wore added an easy three inches to her already impressive height.

I smiled uncomfortably and looked over at Lilith, who encouraged me to go. I hated having everyone's attention focused on me. It was uncomfortable. Joanna, on the other hand, was beaming, holding an arm out to greet me. I took the spot next to her.

"If you've not yet had the chance to meet her, I'm

sure you will at some point this evening. That is, if you can get her away from Lilith." The room erupted in laughter. I pressed my lips together uncomfortably. "Anyway, we'd been anticipating Evie's arrival for some time, as I'm sure many of you know. Her ritual was the most highly-attended ritual anyone can remember," she told the crowd.

I was confused. What was Joanna talking about? Who was called to attend? It was just me and Lilith during the ritual. As I looked around the room, the realization hit me that many of these people, their shadows on the walls behind them, looked an awful lot like those that I'd danced with a week before. Is that what Joanna was talking about? I looked over at Lilith, who smiled and winked at me. What was happening? I was suddenly uncomfortable, nauseated. Something didn't feel right. I wanted to ask Lilith about it, but I didn't know how to get her away from everyone.

"Tonight," Joanna continued, "we officially take Evie into our fold as a unified entity. Tonight, we celebrate all that she will become, and all that she will do. Tonight, she will become one of us!"

The room erupted in applause.

CHAPTER FIFTY EIGHT
LILITH

ONIGHT, SHE WILL BE MARKED WITH OUR symbol," Joanna said as I kept my eyes on Evie. More applause. I watched Evie's eyes dart around nervously. She had no idea what was happening, and when she looked over at me, I smiled at her and applauded with everyone else. I hadn't prepared her. I felt horrible. Joanna then called for me to join them.

"Lilith, it has been many, many years since you brought us a woman this powerful," she said. Evie looked at me, confused. "This is the one that will change everything," Joanna said just loud enough for me to hear, leaning in toward me. I gave her an uncomfortable half-smile. She placed a scalpel in my hand, and then I turned to Evie as Joanna stepped away.

"I promise I will try to make this as painless as possible, but it will probably hurt," I said, trying to be apologetic.

Evie's breathing looked shallow. "What's going on? What is everyone talking about? Something isn't right."

"I promise, everything is fine. I wouldn't let anything bad happen to you, I swear it," I told her.

I took Evie's hand and pulled her to the center of the room. As we stopped in front of a chair that almost looked like a rudimentary throne, the crowd parted, circling around us. They looked like starving animals. It was one of the things that I hated about this group. Everyone always looked ready to devour anything beautiful. In an effort to suppress the panic that seemed to be creeping into Evie's face, I leaned forward and placed a light kiss on her shoulder. I pulled away and motioned for Evie to take a seat in front of me.

"Evie," I said softly. "Tonight, I give you our mark. This cements your place among us. In receiving it, you promise to answer when you are called, to never deny your own power, never bend to the power of anyone else, and do whatever is necessary to protect the legion. Do you so promise?"

"Lilith?" Evie asked.

I leaned in. "You have to say yes. I swear, nothing

weird is going to happen," I whispered.

"Are you sure? Something feels…off."

I wasn't sure what she meant, but to the best of my recollection, it all seemed pretty normal for one of these things.

"I know, it's a lot of rules. But nothing scary is going to happen," I said, trying to reassure her.

"Do you promise?"

"I swear it."

Evie took a deep breath, staring into my eyes. I swallowed hard and licked my lips.

"I promise myself to you," Evie said, loud enough for only me to hear. Upon saying it though, something in the room changed. The atmosphere felt like a live wire snapped through it. Everyone was whispering to one another and looking back and forth between us and each other. That seemed to happen a lot to us.

"I have to lift your dress," I told her.

Evie's eyes widened. "Excuse me?"

"Just to do the mark. Everyone else will just be watching," I told her. Reluctantly, Evie slowly pulled her dress up, exposing her thigh, never breaking eye contact with me. My breath faltered at the intimacy in the moment.

Just as I raised the sharp instrument in my hand and positioned it at Evie's right thigh, up near her hip, I saw something move out of the corner of my eye, a flash of red through the crowd beside them. I shook my head, hoping that it wasn't who I thought it was, and brought the scalpel down to Evie's skin. I felt Evie wince and heard her hiss as the blade pierced her skin. She held on to my shoulders and squeezed as I carefully began to carve a symbol. It was the symbol for Jaxarus, or Jax, as he was most commonly known.

I grabbed a napkin nearby and dabbed at the incisions with it, attempting to soak up the blood that was beginning to ooze from it.

"Hold that on there for a minute," I instructed Evie. "Are you okay?"

Evie nodded, her eyes locked onto mine. After a moment, I took her hand to help her stand.

"Everyone, I present to you our newest member," I announced.

Evie smiled at me.

"To power, and to freedom," everyone shouted in unison. I looked around the room as everyone in attendance began raising their glasses in Evie's direction. And that's when I noticed the flash of red from before, in the form of a dress on a lanky woman with long, inky black hair. It was a face that I hadn't seen in decades, maybe much longer. It was exactly who I hoped I hadn't seen a moment before. I suddenly felt nauseated as the woman raised a glass toward me and Evie, a smirk across her lips. It made me uneasy. Nothing good came from a look like that.

I looked over at Evie who seemed to notice the change in my demeanor. I quickly shook it off, smiled at Evie, and then raised Evie's hand to my lips, kissing the inside of her wrist.

"To power and freedom," Evie said, smiling back at me and then bit her lower lip, as if she were going to laugh.

I suddenly felt overwhelmed with something I didn't immediately recognize as desire. I turned to Evie, leaned in, and pressed my lips to Evie's for several moments while people around us continued cheering and clinking their glasses. I then took Evie's hand and raised it high above our heads.

"This is just the beginning of a wonderful and exciting life, Evie," Joanna said, moving in and handing her another glass of champagne.

I watched Evie put the glass to her lips and hoped that Joanna was right.

MELISSA MEYER (she/her) is an author of one novel, several short stories, and many poems that probably won't see the light of day. Her work is often dark (and sometimes violent), challenges societal norms, and has scared a few people. She's not particularly apologetic about that last part. She also focuses on writing LGBTQ characters.

Melissa is also a Sagittarius sun, Gemini moon, Sagittarius rising, and tarot card slinger. She collects coffee mugs, true crime stuff, cross stitch patterns and supplies, books, and recipes. She's an avid watcher of *Schitt's Creek*, *The X-Files*, *Game of Thrones*, and *Hell's Kitchen*. Most of the trivia she knows is about serial killers.

When she's not writing about demons and human monsters, she can be found making candles, being the Mother of Cats, and being married to her butter half, Aaron (they/them).

Melissa currently resides in Cincinnati, Ohio. NIGHT MONSTER, the first in a series, is her debut novel.

Social Media
www.melissameyer.com
www.facebook.com/authormelissameyer
www.twitter.com/shadwlandswitch
www.instagram.com/authormelissameyer